Praise for *The Dachshund Wears Prada*

"London's characters leap off the page... It's a delightful start to a series that promises to be good fun."   –*Publishers Weekly*

"Funny and sweet, with great characters and a diva dog who completely stole my heart. I devoured this book in one sitting!"
—*New York Times* bestselling author Jennifer Probst

"Don't sleep on this heartfelt romance."   –*Kirkus Reviews*

"This is the romcom Carrie Bradshaw would have written if she were a dog person, and I'm obsessed!"
—Teri Wilson, *USA TODAY* bestselling author
of *A Spot of Trouble*

"One of the year's most delightful rom-coms. Ms. London pens a sparkling confection of all the feels and I devoured it."
—*New York Times* bestselling author Julia London

"Heartwarming, charming, and adorably sexy, *The Dachshund Wears Prada* made my dog-loving heart smile."
—*USA TODAY* bestselling author Tawna Fenske

"At turns both witty and tender, *The Dachshund Wears Prada* is a delightful treat of a novel, guaranteed to give you the warm fuzzies."
—*USA TODAY* bestselling author Melonie Johnson

Also by Stefanie London

Paws in the City

The Dachshund Wears Prada

For additional books by Stefanie London,
visit her website, stefanie-london.com.

Pets *of* Park Avenue

STEFANIE LONDON

HQN

HQN®

Recycling programs for this product may not exist in your area.

ISBN-13: 978-1-335-49819-9

Pets of Park Avenue

For questions and comments about the quality of this book, please contact us at CustomerService@Harlequin.com.

HQN
22 Adelaide St. West, 41st Floor
Toronto, Ontario M5H 4E3, Canada
www.Harlequin.com

Printed in U.S.A.

To Justin, my always and forever.

Pets *of* Park Avenue

1

Scout Myers could think of several good reasons to be on all fours with her ass in the air, but pandering to the world's most disagreeable cat was not one of them. Isaac Mewton—and yes, that was his real name—was a Scottish fold with the sweetest face you'd ever see. Unfortunately, despite the adorable camera-ready mug, the cat had the same disposition as those grumpy old Muppets who liked to sit on a balcony and heckle people for sport.

And Scout *loved* animals. One of the best things about her job at Paws in the City, New York's premiere pet social media and talent agency, was getting to be around furry critters all day long.

Isaac Mewton, however, was officially on her shit list.

"I can see something shiny back there." His owner pointed. "We can't carry on without his favorite toy. He won't sit still."

Scout gritted her teeth and wedged her hand between the wall and a white IKEA bookcase. Cringing, she prayed none of New York's finest creepy crawlies were hiding back there and wriggled her fingers.

"Come on," she muttered. "Where are you?"

Eventually her fingertips brushed something hard and plastic. That had to be it. How the cat had managed to bat his toy so hard it lodged itself into such a small space was incomprehensible. Almost as incomprehensible as this client's expectations. Seriously, how were they supposed to turn her precious kitty into a star if it wouldn't even sit still for a headshot?

"Got it!" Her hand—and the toy—popped mercifully free.

"Great, now can we get on with it?" The client looked at Scout like this was all her fault. "I have an appointment to get to."

Paws in the City wasn't only Scout's workplace; it was the brainchild of her best friend *and* the lifeline Scout had needed when her life couldn't sink any lower. She came into work every day striving to do the best job possible, both for herself and her boss.

That meant pasting on a can-do smile, even when she wanted to launch a cat toy at someone's head.

"Why don't you get him to play with it?" Scout said, handing over the hard plastic ring, which was clear and suspended with glitter. "He might be more receptive if it comes from you."

The woman crouched in front of the cat and attempted to engage him with the toy. But he immediately batted it across the room, where it slammed into the wall and bounced onto the floor.

The photographer, who had shown a level of patience that

should make her a shoo-in for sainthood, raised an eyebrow. This was going nowhere. Isaac Mewton sat on a velvet pouf with an artfully arranged bookshelf behind him that Scout and the photographer had prepared for his portrait, staring down everyone in the room like an angry king.

It was time to try something new. Scout retrieved a feather toy from their stash in the office. She needed to get these photos done *now*. Isla was due back in less than five minutes and they hadn't gotten a single decent shot of the cat.

Let's be real, what client would want to work with such a demanding, fussy model anyway?

Still, Scout didn't want it to look like she didn't have things under control.

"He doesn't like those." The cat's owner shook her head and pointed at the feather toy. "It won't work."

"Well, we've tried all the toys you brought with you, so maybe a Hail Mary is exactly what we need," Scout replied tightly, her smile turning brittle. Lord give her strength to deal with this woman! The cat was a pain, sure, but animals were animals. They couldn't be blamed for their behavior. Their human counterparts on the other hand...

Click!

Isaac Mewton had gone still, his eyes on the new toy, and the photographer seized the moment to start snapping. Scout moved the feather in gentle sweeping motions, and the cat's eyes followed with intense focus. He raised one paw and batted at it, ignoring the steady *click, click, click* of the camera.

So much for him not liking it.

Scout shoved the snarky inner comment to one side and focused on getting the cat to engage so they could wrap up the meeting as quickly as possible. Next to her, the owner huffed in annoyance as though she couldn't believe her darling Isaac had proven her wrong.

When they were done and the woman and her cat had left the Paws in the City office, Scout's shoulders sagged in relief. She was a people—and an animal—person at heart, but she had a pet peeve, no pun intended, about entitlement. Call it a leftover from her childhood. Her mother's legacy was little more than a collection of emotional scars and personal quirks, but she *had* taught Scout one very important lesson.

Nobody owed her anything. Whatever she wanted in life, she would have to earn it.

"Are all your clients like that?" the photographer asked as she packed up her equipment. "The woman seemed to think her cat was royalty."

Scout shook her head. "Most clients are lovely and happy to have our assistance. But there's always the rare few who think they're superstar material, without being willing to put in the work."

"How long have you been open now? Only a few months, right?"

"Six months." Scout couldn't help her beaming smile. It might not be *her* business, but she was damn proud to be part of it. "And we've already signed over twenty clients."

"Including Miss Pain in the Rear and her angry feline overlord?"

"We've had several requests for cats lately, and he was by *far* the cutest we've seen." Scout sighed. "Let's hope he's in a better mood when it comes time to front up for a paying job."

Paws in the City represented clients with four (and six) legs. They provided social media coaching to the humans running the accounts, worked on brand strategy and generally acted as a go-between in brokering sponsorship deals and other types of opportunities. They also booked animal talent for commercial shoots, both of the print and television variety. Every day was different. Scout managed the operational parts of the job, like booking appointments, supervising headshots, fielding media enquiries and consulting with the freelancers, such as photographers and grooming specialists. Plus any other random bits and bobs, like making sure they hadn't run out of dog treats or pods for their coffee machine.

Isla always said their mission was to make the internet a happier, furrier place, and Scout loved that sentiment.

A few minutes after Scout bid the photographer farewell, the front door swung open. Though cute, their office wasn't much bigger than a postage stamp, so Scout's desk was situated in the waiting area and therefore doubled as their reception desk.

Isla breezed in, a wool coat slung over one arm and her long dark hair bouncing around her shoulders in soft curls. She was dressed in a pale blue blouse, fitted black pants and a killer pair of silver stilettos—a much fancier outfit than what she usually wore in the office. Black, though it was one of Scout's favorite colors, was *not* the best when working with their furry clients.

But Isla had been at an important networking event today, so there was no need to worry about dog fur.

"Those shoes," Scout gasped. "Wow!"

"They're gorgeous, but they've been killing me all day." She dropped onto one of the pink velvet seats lining the far wall and kicked off the shoes, groaning in relief.

"That's a rookie move," Scout replied. "Now your feet are going to puff up and you won't be able to get them back on."

"I don't care if I have to meet Theo barefoot tonight, there's no way I was keeping them on a second longer than necessary."

"Hmm, barefoot to a white-tablecloth restaurant. Classy."

Isla grinned. "Theo loves me as I am, blisters and all."

It was true. Scout wasn't sure she'd ever seen a man so in love. *Not even on your own wedding day?*

Scout shoved the unpleasant reminder to one side. The last thing she needed right now was for her mood to take a dive, thinking about inconvenient things like the fact that she was *still* married.

Or that she hadn't seen her husband in five years.

"I was thinking," Isla said, as she leaned down to rub at one of her heels, "I know we haven't been at this long, but maybe it's time to think about bringing someone else on."

Scout's heart plummeted.

And you thought it might be time to talk about a promotion. Delusional.

It didn't matter how many times an employer initiated "the talk," it never hurt any less. And she'd been fired more than the average person by a lot…like, triple-digits a lot. She was, as her grandmother had once said, an "acquired taste." At first she'd thought it meant she was unique.

Over time she realized it wasn't a compliment.

Being fired by Isla would hit especially hard because they were best friends. They'd been inseparable since day one of high school, when Scout was the new kid on the block. She'd gotten bullied for her young mother's questionable hairdressing skills and their family's thrift-store wardrobe. Isla had stood up for her and they'd been thick as thieves ever since.

Getting fired by the one person she'd thought believed in her would suck *hard*.

"Someone else?" she croaked.

"Yeah." Isla seemed oblivious to her inner turmoil. "Things are going even better than I could have hoped. If we get someone junior to help you with the admin side of things, then you can focus more on client management."

She blinked. "Oh."

Her shock must have registered loud and clear because

Isla looked up from her battered foot and raised an eyebrow. "What did you think I meant?"

"I wasn't sure, exactly." Scout's face grew warm.

Doubting herself came as naturally as breathing. But it was hard to put on a front when you were working with someone who knew you inside and out. Isla knew all her good bits, like her friendly disposition and ability to make people feel welcome and included, *and* all her bad bits, like that despite trying her hardest, she could be a little…scatterbrained. And tardy. And maybe it took her being told something a few times before it stuck.

"I'm not going to fire you," Isla said, looking her dead in the eye. "And that's not just because we're friends, either. I'm happy with your work and I think we make a great team."

Scout let out a breath, relief filtering through her. "Me too."

"But we need a client to break out, whether it's a new client or an existing one." Isla's gaze was fixed on something Scout couldn't see, like some imaginary mountain she wanted to climb. She'd always had that look in her eye, as long as they'd known one another. "If we do that, then I'll feel confident that we're establishing a track record of success, which means we can work with bigger advertisers and negotiate better-paying contracts. Then we can move you into client management full-time and get someone else to do the admin."

Instead of thinking about firing her, Isla wanted to plan for a promotion!

A warm and fuzzy feeling filled Scout. "Really?"

"Yes." Isla nodded. "I know you can do it."

For the first time in Scout's life, she had a job she liked, working with people she respected and the possibility for progression laid out in front of her. A sense of hope budded in her chest. It had been *so* long since anyone believed in her capabilities. So long since *she* believed in them, even.

Now Isla had given her a challenge, Scout was determined to hit that goal and earn her promotion with hard work. Back to that whole hating-entitlement thing? Yeah, she'd put hand-outs in that category, too. So *not* interested. She was going to bust her ass for this opportunity.

"We'll find the next viral sensation," Scout said with a confident nod. "I know it."

Isla beamed. "Good. Now, I need to head off and meet Theo. You seeing Lizzie tonight?"

"I am." She couldn't even think about stopping the big grin that took over her face.

"Take some of the promo cookies from my office." Isla winced as she shoved her feet back into her stilettos. "The ones shaped like cats and dogs."

"You sure? She'd love those."

"Please. I've been snacking on them when I'm too busy to get a proper lunch. I need them away from me." She slung her purse over one shoulder and headed to the door. "See you tomorrow."

"Have fun at dinner."

Isla grinned and waved as she headed out. Scout locked the front door from the inside so she could complete the end-of-day routine, which involved vacuuming the floors to keep them free of fur, answering any last-minute emails, wiping down all the surfaces and spraying some air freshener.

They may work with animals all day, but they certainly didn't want to *smell* like it.

And business might be going well, but they couldn't afford to pay for excess services like a cleaner. So Scout and Isla took turns sharing the duties. When everything was sparkling, she stashed the cleaning tools away, flicked the lights off and grabbed her coat and purse before heading out. Another successful day at Paws in the City!

Outside, Manhattan was crisply cool. Winter was hanging on, with dirty half-melted snowbanks lining the streets, but nothing could dull her mood. Not even the early nightfall, sidewalk slush and biting wind.

A possible promotion into client management… Wow. When Isla had agreed to hire her, Scout had secretly worried it might ruin their friendship. But she'd desperately needed something good and solid in her life—not to mention a steady paycheck—and Isla had always been there for her.

Besides, she wanted to see her friend's business soar and if she could have a hand in making that happen, even better.

For years her life had felt like a procession of failures—failure to win her mother's attention, failure to do well in school, failure to please her strict grandparents, failure to make her marriage work.

This time you won't fail.

Maybe things were finally going her way.

Forty minutes later, Scout walked along her grandparents' street, clutching a small box filled with the adorable animal-shaped cookies from the Paws in the City office. As usual, her stomach churned and anxiety crawled up the back of her throat.

Despite having been kicked out of their house shortly before her eighteenth birthday—which felt like a lifetime ago—she still experienced a strange sense of regression whenever she came here. It was like stepping into a time machine and being transported back to her teenage years. Maybe it was because they still viewed her as that person—rebellious, careless, selfish.

Things she tried so hard not to be.

Things she hadn't *really* been back then, either. Not underneath the surface.

But after years of emotional and physical neglect from her mother, high walls had encircled her heart. Growing up, her mother had been estranged from Scout's grandparents. They hadn't even been aware of her existence for the first twelve years of her life.

When they returned from a stint in the UK, they'd found their daughter not only with one child but pregnant with a second. At thirteen, Scout had gone from living in a semi-squalid one-bedroom apartment, which smelled like damp towels and had cockroaches scuttling across the floor in the middle of the night, to having a proper bed. No more sleeping on a pullout!

At first it had made her feel like a princess.

A real bed. A wardrobe she didn't have to share with her mother and household cleaning supplies. Snacks whenever she was hungry. Dinner steaming on the table at the same time each night.

Back then she thought her grandparents were stinking rich. Now she knew they were average Joes—they had a nice house, but it was far from the biggest on the block. They had a sleek car, but it was double digits in age. They went on regular vacations but always looked to get their flights at a discount.

At the time, however, Scout hadn't experienced such luxury.

Too bad the gilt castle turned out to be a cage.

Nerves jangled in her belly as she approached the house, walking up to the short set of steps that led to the entrance. For a house that looked so cozy and ordinary, she knew to expect an arctic blast as her greeting. Lizzie was never allowed to answer the front door—stranger danger and all that. Her grandmother usually took that opportunity to make sure Scout was aware of the "house rules," like she hadn't been hearing the same damn speech for years.

What she wouldn't give to have Lizzie come and visit her, rather than having to come here. Or, even better, *live* with her.

But that was out of the question. She'd been so close once before but, like usual, her impulsive nature had ruined it all.

She raised her hand and jabbed the doorbell, preparing to cringe at the obnoxious melodic chime, but no sound came. Just as she was about to try again, footsteps sounded inside and Scout raised an eyebrow. Her grandfather didn't usually answer the door, but since he walked with a slight limp from an old car accident, his gait was unmistakable. A second later the door swung open.

"Scout," he said with a stiff nod. He was a tall man with thick silver hair and small rimless glasses permanently perched on his nose. Even relaxing at home, he wore a collared shirt and neatly pressed slacks, and strongly exuded a professor vibe. "Come inside."

"Norman," she replied with a nod. The day she'd packed her bags, tears gathering in her eyes and something irrevocably broken inside her, she'd vowed to only ever call them by their first names. They no longer deserved to be addressed as Grandma and Grandpa out loud, even if that's still how she thought of them in her head. "Good to see you."

He let out a hoarse laugh as he held the door. "No, it's not. But I appreciate you attempting the pleasantries."

Scout walked through the front door, memories assaulting her as they always did whenever she returned to this place. It still smelled the same—like a mixture of lavender and wood polish and something cooking in the oven.

"We're all adults here. I think we can be civil for a few hours for Lizzie's sake." She white-knuckled the container of cookies, trying to hold on to her inner strength. "So you don't need to give me the 'house rules' rundown. I know what you expect."

Her grandfather cocked his head and looked at her as though he was studying an animal at the zoo. An academic through and through, there'd always been something aloof about the man. Like he viewed the world through a microscope and nothing meant more to him than data. She wondered if he'd ever seen her as an individual, or if she'd always be a failed experiment to him.

"I'm glad you understand the rules, but I do need to have a talk with you before we have dinner. Come into my office for a minute." He motioned for Scout to follow him.

Her grandfather's office was exactly what you'd expect of a man who'd dedicated his life to knowledge and education. His multiple degrees and qualifications were framed and hanging on the wall alongside various photos of him in graduation-ceremony garb. Two huge bookcases dominated the wall behind his desk, the shelves sagging under the weight of textbooks, encyclopedias, academic journals and binders of research. His desk was large, meant to accommodate a man of his stature—both physical and academic—and a vintage leather chair sat behind it. Papers were scattered across the desk, dusted with chicken-scratch handwriting from his favorite pen.

He looked out into the hallway, as though checking to make sure nobody was there, before closing the door. "I'm coming out of retirement."

"Oh." Scout blinked. She wasn't sure what to expect, given his clear attempt at discretion. "Congratulations?"

"Is that a question or a statement?" He shook his head. "It doesn't matter. In any case, I wanted to let you know because the position is at Berkeley."

For a moment Scout thought her heart had stopped. "Berkeley...in California?"

"That's correct."

"And is...?" Her head swam for a minute, the reality of this news crashing down on her like a tidal wave. "Lizzie..."

"We're *all* planning to move," her grandfather replied with his usual stone-faced, difficult-to-read delivery. "Including Lizzie."

"No." She shook her head, the word coming out as a whisper.

As it was, her visits with her sister were monitored and brief. Never frequent enough, because she wanted her little sister by her side at all times. But her grandparents kept strict control over how much influence and involvement Scout had in Lizzie's life, claiming they only wanted the best for the youngest Myers grandchild.

Her sister's life had been vastly different than Scout's, because when Lizzie was born she came home from the hospital to this house. She'd lived in one place her entire life, didn't know what it meant to go hungry or wonder when an adult would come home to put her to bed. She missed the *idea* of who their mother was, rather than the reality.

But those things had kept her delicate, like a kid should be.

"I know this is not good news for you," Norman said, his features softening in an uncharacteristic way. "But we feel it will be best for Lizzie to stay with us, even if it means moving."

Scout's knees wobbled, but before she could fully process what was going on, there was a noise from upstairs. "Is that Scout? I heard the door!"

Norman shot Scout a look. "Please don't say anything yet. We want to break the news to her as gently as possible."

Numbly, Scout nodded, her brain swirling. She'd lost every single family member she'd ever known—her mother when she overdosed, her grandparents when they kicked her out of

their home, her husband when he'd shown his true colors...
and now her darling baby sister.

Everybody abandons you.

Norman opened the office door and Scout followed him
on shaking legs into the hall. A second later, her grandfather
hollered out, "Scout's here."

A pounding of footsteps ensued, and a gangly figure came
flying down the stairs, long blond hair fluttering like ribbons
behind her. "Scout!"

"Lizzie."

The thirteen-year-old careened around the corner of the
staircase, almost sliding right into the wall on sock-covered
feet, and launched herself straight into Scout's arms. Their
grandfather rescued the cookies just in time, and that left
Scout free to wrap her arms around her sister's slender frame
and bury her face into her hair. She smelled like watermelon
shampoo and that sickly sweet perfume teenage girls loved.

It was the best smell in the world.

"I've missed you," Scout whispered, fighting tears. "So
much."

"I've missed you, too. You shouldn't be so busy at work,
okay?" Lizzie pulled back and looked at her, big green eyes—
their mother's eyes—filled with sincerity. "Tell your boss you
need more sister time."

Something hot and angry unfurled in Scout's gut. It *killed*
her to let Lizzie believe Scout chose work over seeing her,
when it was simply her grandparents trying to control things
with an iron fist.

*Because they think you're a bad influence. A bad person. Exactly
like your mother.*

"I'll try. I promise," she said, tucking a strand of hair behind her sister's ear. "You're the most important person in the
world to me."

Lizzie's face sparkled. Despite officially being a teen as of the previous month, there was still something so young about her. Still something so sweet and open and frighteningly naive. She didn't have a single brick around her heart and it scared the hell out of Scout. What if someone hurt her one day? What if someone saw that sweetness and took advantage of her?

What if they took her away and she forgot all about Scout?

You can't let that happen.

2

The following Monday Scout was pottering around the Paws in the City office when her cell phone rang. It was Isla. Which was odd, because she'd left only thirty minutes ago to head to a photoshoot for one of their clients.

"Hey, what's up? Did you forget something?"

"No, it's Dani. She's got a stomach bug." Isla sighed. "She got sent home from school and now she's puking her guts up. I don't want to leave her alone, especially since she's still getting used to the new place."

Isla and her younger sister, Dani, had moved into Theo's a few weeks back, and the teen was taking time to adjust. "What can I do to help?"

"Is there any chance you can head to the shoot in my place?

It's that one for the fancy pet shampoo, where they've hired like *ten* animal influencers. It's a big deal and a good chance to get our name out there."

Scout's ears perked up. This was an opportunity to prove herself. She could help Isla out of a jam and get some experience doing the kind of work she would do if she got her promotion.

Not if…when! Think positive.

"Absolutely."

"Thank you. That would be a *huge* help," Isla said. "I really don't want to miss out on such a good chance to network."

"It's no problem. The only person we had scheduled this afternoon called earlier to ask if she could come in tomorrow instead, so I was going to catch up on emails and Instagram comments. But that can wait."

"You're the best. I owe you." Isla told her where to find the details of the shoot in her inbox. "I'll be back in tomorrow, for sure. But please call if you get stuck on anything."

"I will. I hope Dani feels better soon."

Scout ended the call, even more excited than usual about her day. Was this how people felt when they liked their jobs? Wow. If only she'd known sooner that it was possible to find work that wasn't a complete drainer. Although it was probably because she'd always taken whatever jobs she could get rather than hunting for something that fueled her passions.

Really, Scout wasn't passionate about too many things. She loved clothes but lacked the verbal filter to do well in retail, and she really enjoyed video games but didn't have anything remotely close to the qualifications required to work in that field. Hell, it was a miracle she'd finished high school. And she'd always loved animals, but her one ill-fated job working at a pet store had seen her fired for refusing to sell a guinea pig to a man who'd been aggressively tapping on the glass, because she was worried that he wouldn't care for the animal properly.

But that had all changed now.

Gathering her things, she headed outside and navigated her way into the subway. Isla was always reminding her that she could take a cab and charge it to the company credit card, but Scout was used to the subway, and often it was quicker if you were only going within Manhattan.

On the ride, Scout brushed up on their client's details.

Sasha Frise was a Bichon Frise with a rising-star status at the agency, which meant their social presence was between zero and two years old and had a minimum combined follower count of one hundred thousand. Sasha's owner, a woman by the name of Gina Caravella, had made a name for her fluffy pooch by dressing her up in colorful outfits and snapping pictures around Brooklyn. What had launched the account into a recent surge of success were the TikTok videos of Sasha wearing loads of leopard print and acting out scenes to sound bites from Fran Drescher in *The Nanny.*

Scout didn't really *get* TikTok. Just as she was becoming interested in something, the video was over. *And* she was concerned about some of the bad information on the platform, like the icky diet-culture crap that Lizzie had shown her one time. "Detox" drinks, her ass.

But that was precisely why Isla chose to stick to the pet space online—animals made everything better.

Scout alighted at the required subway stop and hustled through the station and up to ground level. Excitement bubbled in her veins along with a healthy dose of nerves. She hadn't been on any of the client outings before.

"You can do this," she said to herself. "Channel Isla."

The shoot was taking place in a small warehouse event space in Chelsea. Scout knew the address because she'd been there a few times when it was a pop-up restaurant with a rotating schedule of up-and-coming chefs, and one time when it had been turned into a garden-themed nightclub.

Glancing at her phone, she checked the time as she walked quickly up the street toward the warehouse. The shoot would already be underway, but she could still make a good impression on any potential clients.

Immediately inside the entrance of the warehouse, there was a young bored-looking man sitting at a trestle table. Scout wrote her name on a small card with the word *guest* printed on it and then the man slipped it into a plastic pocket dangling from a bright yellow lanyard.

"In case of a fire, the exits are here and here," he spoke in monotone as he pointed to two doors with glowing signs above them. "Restrooms are through there. Craft service will start at twelve. If you need anything else, I'll be here all day."

"You've said that a few times, huh?" Scout smiled as she slipped the lanyard over her head and fluffed her hair out the back.

"Just a few." The guy nodded, his attention already back on his cell phone.

Scout headed toward where the shoot was set up. There were big lights and lighting umbrellas—which probably had a technical name that she wasn't aware of—and other bits of photographic paraphernalia.

It looked as though they were preparing to get all the animals onto the set at once.

Scout immediately spotted Sasha Frise with her owner, Gina. She spent a few minutes saying hello and admiring Sasha's adorable outfit—which consisted of leopard-print booties on her front two paws, a bling-y leopard-print collar and a little black wig in the style of Fran Drescher's signature curls.

The photoshoot had been staged to look like a fancy salon—

complete with those big silver dryers that sat over your head, pink chairs, a chandelier and even a bedazzled handheld blower. One of the dogs was wearing a puffy pink hat like the kind that was popular to set and dry hair rollers in the 50s and 60s.

As Gina was called to bring Sasha onto the set, Scout stepped back to watch the action. She recognized a few of the influencers, including an incredibly gorgeous Afghan hound with fur the color of champagne and a French bulldog with a red bowtie, whose name was Pierre. From the research Scout had done on the way over, Sasha Frise was actually one of the smaller influencers here, which was probably why Isla had been so excited about the shoot.

But before she could get around to introduce herself to anyone, a familiar voice caught her attention. "Scout!"

She turned to find a familiar person waving at her, so she headed right over to the grooming station. "August, so great to see you."

August Merriweather had bright red hair, freckles and big eyes that made her seem younger than she was. But considering she was one of the most sought-after dog groomers in Manhattan, her baby face hadn't held her back at all.

"I don't normally see you at the shoots," August said. She was currently in the process of affixing some silver bows to a very large, very *pink* poodle and fluffing up the dog's fur. "What a nice surprise."

Scout was mesmerized by the poodle. It was shaved in that strange way that they sometimes were, with a big bauble of fur around its upper body, two smaller tufts on its back, and one on the end of the tail and around each of the ankles, which made it look like it was wearing fabulous legwarmers.

"She's gorgeous, isn't she?" August said. "This is Peony Parker."

"Oh yes, I'm familiar." Peony was one of the biggest pet influencers in the game. "I've always wondered, why *are* poodles shaved like that?"

"Well, poodles can be shaved in lots of different ways. This is called a Continental Trim," August said, as she continued to brush out the fur on the dog's chest. Peony stood patiently, looking relaxed and happy. "But plenty of poodles have much more easily maintainable cuts than this."

"I bet it takes a lot of work."

August nodded. "If the poodle is being presented at a dog show, they often require six to seven hours of grooming the day before the event. If the show runs for a full weekend, it's probably about twenty hours of grooming, total."

Scout gasped. "Seriously?"

"Uh-huh. My godmother had standard poodles most of my life and she was super into the show scene. It's actually where I first developed my love of grooming." August stepped back and appraised her work before frowning and going back in to perfect one area of the dog's fur. "This cut looks strange, but poodles were originally bred for water retrieving, and so this cut was designed to minimize resistance when they were in the water but also to keep the dogs warm where they needed it. You can see the fur is clustered around the joints and where their vital organs are. The ball on the tip of the tail was to prevent frostbite."

"I had no idea. That's fascinating."

"You learn something new every day." August grinned. "And you, Miss Peony, are done."

August and another woman helped the dog down from the grooming table so Peony could be led to the photography area. Scout watched as the dog trotted over without a leash, impeccably behaved, while some of the other animals on the shoot appeared to be getting rowdy.

"She's a real pro, huh?" Scout said.

"Peony? Oh yeah. She's an ex–show dog, *super* well trained and has a great temperament." August began to reset her grooming station. "I've groomed her quite a few times for events. Her owner is lovely but has terrible arthritis these days and can't manage the show-level grooming on her own anymore. I've been trying to convince her to let Peony grow her coat out so she can go for a more low-maintenance cut."

"No dice?"

"Uh, no. Perfectionistic tendencies are basically required to be part of the dog showing community." August laughed. "So I'd be a hypocrite if I complained too much about it."

Scout had no idea what that would be like. She was as far from being a perfectionist as was humanly possible. "Done is good enough" was her motto most days. In fact, Scout's MO was setting the bar so low she could trip over it. Why set yourself up for disappointment by aiming higher?

She supposed people like August probably didn't set themselves up for disappointment. They were wired to succeed. Scout, however, had to be realistic about things. Right now, perfection was a fairy tale. A myth. She'd happily settle for getting a single promotion in her career and figuring out how to keep her sister from being dragged away to California.

"August." A woman wearing a sleek pair of pants, a pinstripe shirt and sharp pair of oxblood loafers and holding a clipboard called out. "Can I get your help here?"

One of the smaller dogs was getting a bit snippy with Pierre, who had so much energy he was struggling to sit still. Sasha Frise started barking at the commotion and Peony simply stared into space as if to say *ugh, amateurs.*

"I told them this was too many dogs for one shoot," August said, unclipping the leather tool belt, which housed all kinds of brushes and other grooming implements, from around her

waist. "Just because they sit still long enough for their parent
to snap a pic on their iPhone at home doesn't mean they're
well trained enough to participate in something like this. And
I got out of dog-training work for a reason."

August went over to help the woman, muttering angrily
under her breath. Gina headed toward Scout, her nose wrinkled.

"No offense, but this whole thing seems like a shit show,"
she said. She had a head full of frizzy curls and two extra-
chunky gold earrings in her ears. Her outfit looked like a
throwback to the 90s and it was clear where Sasha Frise acquired her TikTok wardrobe. "I've seen more organization at
a Black Friday stampede."

Scout bit down on her lip. Gina had a point. It seemed
that both the photographer and the woman who appeared to
be directing the shoot were having trouble wrangling all the
animals. August was trying her best, but she looked overwhelmed and was being pulled in three directions at once as
they tried to calm down both the little black dog and Pierre,
as well as stopping an inquisitive terrier mix from terrorizing
a poor Chihuahua by repeatedly and enthusiastically sniffing
its nether regions.

"You're not wrong," Scout replied, cringing.

"Look, seeing as you're here," Gina said. "I've been desperate for a smoke. Can you keep an eye on Sasha while I'm
outside?"

Scout gulped. Given how things were currently going, that
seemed like a lot of responsibility, especially since she had only
met Sasha a handful of times. But she could hardly upset the
client when she was standing in for Isla.

"Of course," she replied with a confident nod. "Take your
time."

Gina disappeared outside, seemingly having no hesitation

in leaving her dog in a stranger's hands, even during something she'd described as a "shit show." Scout frowned. That
didn't exactly strike her as good pet ownership.

Says the woman who can't even keep a cactus alive.

That was an unfair statement from the critical voice in her
head. Plants were fickle, and trying to grow anything in an
apartment with one window was a losing game. She could
hardly be called irresponsible for killing off a plant or two.
Or five.

Shut up, brain.

It looked for a moment like everything was about to calm
down. August had Pierre sitting in front of her, his tongue
flopping happily out of his mouth, one paw raised in the air
in hopes of a treat, which August supplied from her pocket.
The Chihuahua had been rescued from the inappropriate sniffing, and Peony was still in exactly the same position as before.

"That's what a truly capable woman looks like," Scout said
with a sigh. She liked August a lot, and the three of them—
including Isla—had become good friends as they spent more
time together working in the same industry.

Isla often booked August for grooming jobs and passed a
lot of freelance work her way, and August always gave Paws
in the City a mention if she came across a potential client.
They'd started a bi-monthly dinner out, to talk shop and personal things, and Scout always looked forward to it.

But was it tough to sometimes feel like the dud of the
group? Of course. Isla and August were badass businesswomen
with big ideas and plans to make their mark on the world.
They had a lot in common—drive, smarts and ambition in
spades—and Scout was the odd one out, an employee rather
than an entrepreneur.

Someone who'd never had dreams of her own.

"Stop! No!"

The peace of a moment ago shattered like crystal against concrete and Scout watched in horror as chaos erupted. The Chihuahua suddenly threw a fit, baring its teeth at the dog who had been sniffing its crotch and making a lunge for its tail. The other dog yelped and skittered backward into one of the standing hair dryer units, which swayed back and forth before toppling over and landing on the tail of the Afghan hound, who let out a startled yelp.

The dogs all seemed to go wild at once, except for Peony, who simply walked away from it all like she couldn't believe she was being forced to work in such conditions. Pierre raced around in circles, dodging August's grabbing hands, until he ran smack into a table that was holding a vessel filled with some kind of thick blue liquid.

It was supposed to look like a giant, fancy shampoo bottle. But when it toppled over the edge of the table and hit the ground, the lid flew off and blue liquid splattered in a wide arc that would have had Dexter peeing his pants with excitement. Unfortunately, it splattered all over the poor dog who was standing closest: Sasha.

"Uh-oh!" Scout rushed into the fray to grab the small white dog and rescue her from the blue sludge before she could get too dirty, but her muzzle was already covered in gunk.

There were people everywhere, trying to snatch up all the dogs and separate them. The Chihuahua was having a full meltdown, and the high-pitched sound bounced off the walls of the warehouse.

Scout grabbed Sasha and held her up, blue dripping from her paws and her fluffy tail. Thank goodness she had two little booties on her front feet. Her back feet however, looked like she'd stepped in Smurf vomit. Not to mention the fact that the liquid was splattered all across her sides and had saturated her muzzle where the dog had bent down to sniff at it.

"August, what do I do?" Scout held the dog away from her, not wanting to drip dye all over herself.

"Put her in the sink. There's some dog shampoo in my kit." August was currently trying to wrangle two of the smaller animals, while the photographer stormed off, apparently having had enough drama for one day. Two other pet owners held on to their dogs and berated the woman with the clipboard.

Scout spotted a deep sink near the grooming station and hurried over with Sasha, leaving a trail of blue dots. Whatever was still going on behind her didn't sound good at all, and she was pretty sure that one of the pet owners was in the throes of quitting the shoot.

"So much for networking," Scout said to Sasha as she put her in the sink. "Okay, bath time for you."

She started the water running, and the dog tried to scramble out of the sink, which was high enough that Sasha would hurt herself if she fell.

"Nope, you stay here." Scout held the dog in place as best as she could, but the little thing wriggled like a worm. As the water ran over the dog's fur, the blue liquid didn't appear to be coming out. She had to act fast. "Sasha, no! Stay still."

Holding the dog with one hand, she stretched out toward where August's kit was sitting on the table. There were dozens of things inside it, bottles of all kinds of doggy-fur products. But before Scout could grab one, Sasha made a break for it, ducking from under her hand and clambering up the side of the sink.

Screeching, Scout managed to catch her before she tumbled over the edge and put her back in the basin, though she'd wetted herself in the process. To make matters worse, Sasha shook her entire small body, spraying Scout thoroughly. Now her white blouse was see-through in patches and bore a few faint blue spots, stained from whatever had temporarily colored the dog's fur.

"Oh my god, will you stop?" She got a better grip on the dog this time, making sure she held the collar so as not to hurt Sasha, and reached back with her free hand to grab a bottle of shampoo.

She caught sight of the words "clean dog-safe formula" on the bottle alongside a picture of a happy pink dog and grabbed it. Flicking the cap open, she realized that trying to "spot clean" Sasha would be pointless. It would probably be better to wash her completely, since the dog was clearly going to soak them both in the process anyway.

"Goddammit, Gina, why did you have to go for a smoke now?"

She squirted the shampoo onto the dog's back and rubbed it vigorously to create a lather. Only it didn't lather. And it was hot-pink.

Gasping, Scout looked at the bottle more closely. The "clean dog-safe formula" did not mean *clean* as in *shampoo*. No, it was *clean* as in no harmful ingredients. And then she noticed "Peony" was written across the bottom of the bottle in marker.

It was dye.

"Shit." Scout looked down to where Sasha now had a thick stripe of pink dye along her back. She looked like a skunk who'd gotten a makeover at Sephora. "Shit, shit, shit!"

She tossed the bottle to one side and cranked the water up higher, hoping the dye might rinse off without doing too much damage. But the stripe refused to budge. The dog's usually snowy white fur was now the approximate color of Barbie's Dreamhouse.

Panicking, Scout looked back again and this time located the shampoo. The bottle was exactly the same size and brand as the dye, but this one had bubbles on it. Squirting a generous handful onto the dog's back, she tried to scrub the dye out.

"Please wash out. Please, please, please."

But the color refused to fade. Tears pricked Scout's eyes as she watched her promotion crumble right in front of her. Once the bubbles all rinsed down the drain, she squeaked the taps off. Sasha glared at her, sopping wet and seemingly half the size she was before, shivering like a lamb in snow.

The pink stripe was unmistakable.

"Did it all come out?" August came up behind her and gasped. "What did you do?"

"I made a mistake. The shampoo…" *How can you be this much of a hot mess?* "I got the bottles mixed up."

August grabbed a towel from the grooming table and wrapped the dog up, drying her off while Sasha looked at Scout like she'd stolen her lunch.

"Tell me it washes out," Scout pleaded. "Like a few good washes and she'll be back to new, right?"

"It's permanent dye," August said, as Gina walked back into the warehouse through the front door. "She'll have to shave her down to get rid of it."

"I'm doomed," Scout said, dropping her head into her hands. "Absolutely freaking doomed."

Scout was in a cab back to the Paws in the City office when Isla called to find out what had gone down.

"I don't quite understand what happened." Isla sighed. She sounded exhausted. "Can you walk me through it?"

"I'm so sorry. I was panicking because Gina left me in charge of the dog and…"

You want custody of your sister and you can't even take care of a dog that's the size of a loaf of bread for three seconds without fucking it up?

"The shampoo bottle and the dye bottle looked exactly

the same. It was an honest mistake." Scout scrubbed a hand over her face.

"Why were you even called to wash the dog in the first place? That's ridiculous. It sounds like the shoot got completely out of hand. I've already heard from one of the owners I've been in talks with and they're furious at how it was handled." Isla let out a tutting sound. "They should never have had so many dogs together in such close proximity."

That sounded promising. Maybe Isla wouldn't lay all the blame on her shoulders.

"How was Gina?" Scout asked, knowing that their client had already called.

Silence stretched on for a few beats before Isla answered. "Pissed. Like, mega pissed."

"Understandable." Scout nodded. "I messed up big-time."

"Sasha is booked for the Lively Paws shoot next week. That's a *huge* booking for us."

Scout's stomach churned, and for a minute, she thought she might have to revisit the latte and croissant she'd had for breakfast.

"Can we get a stand-in?" Scout asked, her mind whirring as she tried to think of a way to salvage things. The photoshoot this morning had fallen apart and now they might lose the Lively Paws campaign as well.

This was the opposite of what Scout needed to secure her promotion. Not to mention that letting Isla down made her feel like complete and utter crap.

"Do you know a well-trained Bichon Frise with nothing better to do?" Isla asked with a humorless laugh.

"Actually, I do."

"Seriously?"

"Uh, yeah."

Lordy. What had she just suggested?

Because the doggy doppelgänger was her husband's furry pride and joy. And to say that he probably didn't want to see Scout ever again was putting it lightly. Hell, she wasn't even sure that *she* wanted to see *him*.

But if she came through for Isla and helped to salvage this important advertiser—not to mention trying to get back in the good books with the client, Gina—then maybe she wouldn't be out of the running for her promotion?

More importantly, she wanted to prove to herself that she could make this all work. Because if she ever had any chance of convincing her grandparents that she could take custody of her sister *and* give Lizzie the happy, stable life she deserved, then she needed to check every item of the be-a-perfect-adult checklist, and cleaning up her messes was a big one.

"Remember Lane's dog…?"

"What?" Isla squeaked. "Lane? As in your should-be-ex-husband, Lane? The guy who married you only to decide he wanted to keep you at home like a goddamn trophy on a shelf instead of letting you be part of his life? *That* Lane?"

Scout sighed. "Do you want to fix this issue or not? If I'm willing to deal with him, that's on me."

"I don't even know if switching the dogs is an option," Isla said. "It's skirting the borders of ethics, if not crossing over them entirely."

But she sounded interested. As a small company, they couldn't afford to lose such an important booking, not to mention the fact that Sasha and Gina were the biggest clients they had. If they walked, that would be a *huge* blow.

A pink dog wasn't ideal. It was far less than ideal, actually. But rather than dwelling on how she'd messed up *yet again*, Scout was going to think outside the box. She had to fix this.

And that meant potentially putting herself on the line.

"Let me talk to Lane," Scout said. "There's a chance he'll

say no anyway. And you talk to Gina. Maybe we get a stand-in for this one shoot and it will be our little secret."

"Okay. We'll talk, but we won't make a decision yet. I need the evening to digest this."

"I'm really sorry, Isla."

"It's okay," Isla replied, ever supportive even though she sounded at her wit's end. "We'll figure it out."

Scout ended the call and stared at the blank screen of her phone, a faint reflection of herself looking back with a wrinkled brow and flattened mouth.

Going to see her husband was the last thing she wanted to do.

Because when she'd walked out of Lane Halliday's apartment five years ago, she might have had tears in her eyes and a lump in her throat, but she'd never had *any* intention of going back. Scout had experienced a lot of failure in her life—at school, in her family, in any of her numerous jobs. But the one failure that had almost broken her completely was her ill-fated marriage to Lane.

You have literally nothing to lose in asking for his help.

Worst-case scenario: she would end up in exactly the same position she was now. Then she would try to track down another dog. But Scout knew Lane's dog—the hilariously named Twinkle Stardust—would be perfect. She was a gem of an animal, well-behaved and sweet natured, friendly with everyone she met.

The perfect solution to this problem.

"Excuse me." Scout leaned forward to catch the cab driver's attention. "We need to change direction."

She gave the address off the top of her head, like the information was permanently branded there. Lane's apartment—the place where she'd lived as his wife for a single blissful month.

Well, three blissful weeks and one total disaster of a week.

She leaned back against the seat and pressed a hand to her chest. Her heart was already beating a little faster, because the thought of seeing Lane Halliday made her feel like... Gosh, she didn't even know. A bomb about to go off? Like a soda can that had been shaken up?

Fireworks and fancy champagne and silky sheets?

Option D. All of the above.

He'd always had that effect on her, ever since she'd caught him staring at her while waiting for a fancy casino elevator. She'd been struck by him. Mesmerized.

And while walking away might have been absolutely and 100 percent necessary, she'd still loved him with all her heart.

3

L ane Halliday leaned back in his office chair, eyes blurring
from too many hours staring at his computer screen. It
wasn't super late—but he'd gotten into work at the crack of
dawn. Most days it felt like it was dark when he came in and
dark when he finally looked up again at the end of the day.

But that was the life of a tech entrepreneur. Work, work
and more work.

It was precisely the reason he brought Twinkle Stardust,
his Bichon Frise, into work with him a few days a week, because he couldn't stand the thought of her being home alone
for thirteen hours a day. Minimum.

And yes, Twinkle Stardust was her real name. That's what
he got for agreeing to let his niece be in charge of naming

her. He should have known better. It was common knowledge that toddlers had terrible taste in names.

As if sensing that Lane was thinking about her, Star lifted
her fluffy white head from her cozy spot in the corner of the
office. He had a doggy bed there, with blankets and toys and
everything. Perks of running your own business—you could
enforce whatever pet policy you wanted. And the building was
dog friendly, since there was some kind of expensive doggy
daycare place on one of the other levels. Lane didn't always get
a chance to take Star outside himself, but his assistant, Julie,
was only too happy for the excuse to get some fresh air, and
she loved walking Star.

"Mate." His business partner, Rav, poked his head around
the corner and into his office. "And mutt."

Lane frowned. "Just because you're not a dog lover doesn't
mean you get to call her names."

"I'm a dog lover," he said, looking affronted. His Australian accent made the word sound more like *love-ah*. "I mean,
I prefer *doggy* rather than dog. But I still like mutts."

"Hardy har." Lane rolled his eyes as Rav winked. "And
now that you've sullied this conversation with your gutter
talk, what can I do for you?"

"I wanted to see if you fancy a pint?" Rav walked into the
office, looking slick as always in a tailored suit and a custom-
fit shirt with no tie. The white cotton contrasted against Rav's
brown skin and dark hair, and an expensive watch glinted on
one wrist. Of the two of them, he was the face of the company. It was a wise business decision. Rav was outgoing and
better suited to the networking and sales aspect of running
a start-up, while Lane was happier behind the scenes getting
stuck in the details. "Sarah and I found a pub that's showing
the cricket."

"Aka the world's most boring sport," Lane teased, knowing his friend and partner would get a little wound up. Rav might not be serious about most things in life, but cricket was one of the few.

"I've watched baseball, mate." He made a derisive sound. "So don't give me that shit."

Lane pushed up from his desk and arched his back. "As much as I'd love to stay up until some ungodly hour watching a game that might end in a tie—"

"They have tiebreakers in Twenty20. Don't you know anything?" Rav scoffed.

"—I can't," Lane finished.

"Oh, come on. Sarah would love to see you. It's been ages since you came out."

Sarah was Rav's girlfriend—and was also Australian, although they'd met in New York nearly two years ago. Great people. They were like family. But Lane didn't have it in him to socialize tonight.

Something had been swirling around in his head all day and he needed peace and quiet. He loved his work and the company he and Rav had created, but some days he wanted nothing more than to seal his door shut with crime scene tape so people would leave him alone.

"It's been so long she wants a proof-of-life check," Rav added.

Lane rolled his eyes. "My mother isn't retiring yet, so I'm not looking for someone *else* to badger me about my personal life, okay? You and Sarah are going to have to find a new pastime."

Rav snorted. "Don't you dare say a bad word about Mama Halliday. That woman is a saint."

He couldn't help but smile. When Rav first moved to New York and they became friends, Lane's mom couldn't stand the thought of anyone spending holidays alone. So every Fourth of

July, Thanksgiving and Christmas, Rav attended the Halliday celebrations and was firmly cemented as an honorary family member. Now Sarah came along, too. His mom still had a soft spot for Rav and always sent him home with extra food.

So Rav wouldn't *ever* hear a single complaint about Lane's mom.

"Is everything okay?" Rav came closer, his dark eyes narrowed. "I know you're a bit of an old man sometimes, but you've been off lately."

"Fuck you," Lane replied with a laugh. "I'm not an old man."

His business partner grinned. "You sure? I swear I thought I saw some slippers under your desk."

"Aren't you happy to have a business partner who's so invested in their work?" Lane replied flippantly. "I would have thought you'd be pleased I'm doing all the heavy lifting."

Rav narrowed his eyes but didn't take the bait. "There's a line between being dedicated to your work and not having a life, you know."

He wasn't sure he agreed with Rav about that one.

The previous year they'd made it onto the *Forbes* "30 Under 30" list—skating in during their last eligible year—and that *hadn't* come from being concerned about work-life balance. It had come from late nights and long hours and the relentless pursuit of what they knew could be a game changer. It was the result of throwing *everything* they had into their plans for Unison—their "dating-style app" for start-ups and venture capital firms.

Unison was changing the way that young entrepreneurs accessed investment funding, and it lowered the barriers for people to bring much-needed innovation to the market. It was also helping to break down obstacles for entrepreneurs from marginalized backgrounds and socioeconomic groups where folks didn't have the Ivy League contacts that their privileged counterparts did.

Being someone who came from humble beginnings himself, it was important to Lane that he helped others find their way in business.

And to be playing at the level that he and Rav were, sacrifices had to be made.

Easy for you to say when you don't have a personal life to give up in the first place.

"Seriously." Rav laid a hand on his shoulder. "What's going on?"

He and Rav had worked side by side on their business for the last seven years, but they didn't really dig into the touchy-feely topics with each other very often. There'd only been a handful of occasions—when Rav's mother had died and he'd needed to miss an important VC meeting to fly home to Perth for the funeral, and once more when he'd broken off an engagement that he'd never wanted, after falling in love with Sarah. Oh, and when Lane woke up to find his wife's wedding ring on his kitchen table along with a Post-it note saying she'd left him.

But beyond that—well, it was more of the my-sport-is-better-than-yours kind of banter. Not so much of the real stuff.

"Oh shit." Rav slapped his forehead. "It's the anniversary soon, isn't it? I totally forgot."

"Is it? I haven't thought about it," he lied.

Rav looked at him as if Lane had as much credibility as a toddler who claimed not to have eaten any cookies while sporting a smear of chocolate on his cheek.

"Okay, maybe I've thought about it a little," he admitted.

Had it really been that long since Scout Myers walked out of his life and left his heart in a billion glittering shards? Five whole years since he'd lost the woman he was convinced was *it.* True love. The one. His soul mate. Five years since he'd trusted the wrong person. Five years since he'd made a promise to himself that, going forward, companions of the four-legged variety were the only kind he would commit to.

"All the more reason to come out for a drink," Rav said, nodding like it had been decided. He was like that, sometimes. Pushy. Insistent. But he had a heart of gold. "It'll make you feel better."

In truth, *nothing* would make him feel better. He had no idea how much time needed to pass for these particular wounds to heal. Logically, he should have moved past the breakup years ago. How the heck could he still be pining after a woman he'd been married to for a month?

Technically, you're still *married to her.*

Oh yeah. That.

"Star has a vet appointment," he said.

"Can't Julie take her?"

"No, she's *my* dog. So I take her to the vet." Rav didn't really get the whole pet thing. "Besides, I don't feel like going out."

"Lane, no ex is worth what you put yourself through every year when this date rolls around. Especially not one who didn't have the balls to say goodbye to your face."

It was easy to say that. Easy to believe in the logic of it. But did that change a damn thing?

Nope. Every year when the anniversary came by, Lane did the same thing. He moped. He cursed the fact that he *still* hadn't dragged himself to see a lawyer about getting divorced. He bemoaned every decision that had led to this point—choosing *that* hotel in Vegas, marrying a woman after knowing her only a week, believing her when she said those three magic words.

Pathetic.

"So, do the vet appointment and then come for a drink," Rav cajoled.

Lane glanced guiltily in Star's direction.

"Tomorrow," he said eventually.

Rav looked like he wanted to argue, but instead, he shook his head. "Tomorrow. I'm holding you to it."

He bid Lane a good night and left him alone in his office. The soft, even breathing coming from the corner of the room soothed him a little. Star kept him going. Seeing her happy, fluffy white face in the morning started his day off with something positive, and passing out on the couch with her at night because he was too tired to crawl into bed made him feel less alone.

Why couldn't people be as good as dogs? Seriously, dogs were loyal and they loved you without question or judgment. They missed you when you were away. And they didn't sneak out while you were sleeping.

Really, they were too pure for this world.

"Come on, girl," he said, crouching and waking her up. "It's time to get going."

Rav was right. He needed to let go of this ridiculous moping every year. In the grand scheme of his life, it was nothing. A whirlwind romance of uncharacteristic proportions, and it was gone as fast as it came. There was no logical reason he should still be tangled up about a woman who'd ghosted him in the worst way possible. Because it wasn't like he'd heard from her at all. She hadn't tried to lay claim to anything he owned, like some had suspected. She hadn't taken him to the cleaners. She'd simply...vanished.

Tomorrow night he *would* go out and have drinks with Rav and Sarah. He would have a good time and he would start doing what he should have done from the beginning—forget all about Scout Myers.

★ ★ ★

It was a rare evening where Lane made it home at a reasonable time to eat dinner. But the vet's latest appointment was at 6:00 p.m. As far as he was concerned, the dog was the closest thing he'd ever get to having a family...so he was damn well going to be the best dog dad he could be. That meant he *always* took her to the vet himself. No exceptions.

This was how he'd came to be sitting on his couch, contemplating whether to head back into the office and how much of a hard time Rav would give him if he got caught in the act. Star had crawled into her dog bed and was happily snoozing away, but Lane was twitchy.

Being at home with nothing to do was a low-key form of torture.

There'd been a point in his life where his home was his sanctuary. Yes, he'd always worked long hours, but coming home at the end of the day and chilling on the couch had never felt like a prison sentence the way it did now. After all, he'd grown up on Staten Island and buying an apartment in Manhattan after selling his first app was a capital *B* big deal.

At the time it had felt like a gold medal.

The place had a great view of the city and he'd loved to watch the lights twinkle. Sometimes he would stand at the glass, staring out after it had gotten dark, wondering how he'd ended up here.

But now the apartment had a different feel to it. After Scout left, he'd stripped the place of anything that reminded him of their whirlwind marriage and had gotten an interior designer to make the space over. In his attempt to scrub her memory away, the walls had been painted a stark white, and the comfy couch where they'd cuddled—usually stripping down to make love—was replaced with a black leather behemoth that was neither comfortable nor cuddly.

Everything was sharp angles, black-and-white. Modern monochrome.

He hated it. But maybe that was the point.

A knock at the door startled both him and Star. She jumped out of her bed and ran over to the entry, toenails skittering on the floorboards.

Bark! Bark! Bark!

"Such a good guard dog," he said with a chuckle as he headed toward the sound. Star was all bark and no bite. She was more likely to lick someone to death than to attack them.

When Lane got to the door, a strange sensation washed over him. Déjà vu, maybe? Intuition? He peered through the peephole and saw a flash of blond hair, which made his stomach clench.

No, surely not…

He shook his head. The anniversary was creeping up on him and messing with his head. He saw Scout everywhere he looked—on billboards, on internet ads, on the street. It was never her. Just a cruel reminder that he *really* needed to get on with his life.

As he wrapped a hand around the handle, he made a promise to himself. After he'd dealt with this surprise visitor, he was going to call his lawyer and start divorce proceedings.

Lane pulled the door open and was convinced that he'd been hit over the head. Either that, or the universe had decided now was the day it would well and truly screw with him.

Because Scout was standing there, right in front of him, and it took everything in his power not to reach out and poke her to see if she was real.

"Hi, Lane." Her soft voice was like a fist to his solar plexus. Adding to the impact was the fact that she looked incredible.

Somehow, even better than he remembered.

Her long blond hair fell around her shoulders in a thick sheet and her hazel eyes were wide and alert. It looked as though she might have come from work—a pair of dark jeans and high-heeled ankle boots making her already long legs look even longer. On top, she wore a white blouse with a hint of sheerness to it, enough that he could glimpse the straps of a camisole underneath, but the rest was left to his imagination. The fabric of the blouse was quite rumpled, which somehow made her look even sexier.

She looked older, wiser. More put together. But there were still hints of the woman who loved smoky bars and playing air guitar and the taste of a peaty Scotch in the details. Her boots had tiny studs on the heels, her nails were painted a glossy black, and there was a smudginess to her eye makeup that hinted at 3:00 a.m. bar crawls and making out in the back of a cab.

Hints of the woman who'd caused him to fall head over heels in a Vegas hotel room and declare his love at a tacky strip chapel, thinking it was the best day of his life.

Or maybe that was him seeing what he wanted to see. Remembering what he wanted to remember.

You do not want to remember that.

"What are you doing here?" He was so rattled that the question shot out of him sharp-edged with shock. There was an impulse to soften it, but he swallowed it down.

He had no reason to be soft with her. Not after the way things had ended.

"Actually," she said, drawing her shoulders back and sucking in a breath. It was like watching her slip on a layer of armor. "I need a favor."

"You need a favor." He sounded the words out slowly as if he were trying to translate them from an unfamiliar language. For a second he almost couldn't believe the audacity. She'd left him in the middle of the night, creeping out and leaving him to wake to a cold bed and silent apartment. Then she'd avoided his calls, responding only with a text to say they were over and she wouldn't discuss it.

That was it. Their marriage erased in twenty-four hours. And for what?

You know exactly for what…and the blame doesn't all lie with her.

He hadn't been willing to see it at the time, since hurt had blinded him and frustration had been an ever-present fog in his head. But later the truth had come to bite him in the ass.

"Can I come in?" She twisted the ring on her middle finger once, as if adjusting it. It was the only sign that she was nervous about coming here.

It was a small tell, but he knew all those details about her. The single twist was all she allowed herself. It was a tiny release of nervous energy before she put the mask back on. His gaze flicked up to her face, and for a second, her hazel eyes widened. She knew she'd slipped and he'd seen it.

But curiosity had gotten the best of him. What on earth could she possibly want from him now? Was she here to demand a divorce? Alimony? Half his shit?

There was only one way to find out.

4

When Lane stepped back and held the door open for her, Scout's knees wobbled. In relief? In regret? She had no idea. No matter how many times she'd played this moment in her head...this was *not* how she thought things would go down.

Her coming to Lane—voluntarily—to ask for help? Over her dead body.

But Scout knew if she could solve this problem for Isla *and* prove that she could not only think on her feet but put her personal feelings aside for the benefit of Paws in the City...that promotion might still be possible. And if the promotion was possible, then she could prove to her grandparents that she was a responsible adult and could be a good influence rather than a bad one. This was the thought she clung to as she stepped into Lane's apartment, almost gasping at how different it looked.

He'd clearly done a remodel, or at least had someone in to make some interior design changes, because it was...

So *not* him.

Before she had a chance to sit on the sofa, she looked down and saw Twinkle Stardust at her feet. The little white dog was staring up at her, almost in shock. At first she didn't move, only stared. But then Scout saw it—the faintest little wriggle of her tail, as if she were holding herself back from being too excited.

"Hey girl." She crouched down to pat the dog, but it skittered out of the way. The wagging stopped and Scout felt like she'd been lanced through the heart.

Lane had adopted Twinkle Stardust when she was barely a year old and Scout had moved in the year after. They'd spent weekend mornings cuddling in bed—all three of them. She'd walked the dog most days and they had formed an extremely tight bond in a very short period of time. Leaving her had been brutal. Scout thought about her often, since it was the first time she'd ever had a pet.

"We can sit here," Lane said stiffly. He motioned toward the couch, which looked about as comfortable as a block of lead. Rather than joining her, he chose to stand by the wall, leaning back against it with his arms folded across his broad chest.

Seeing him in the flesh...

It was like having every single one of the stitches on her heart ripped open.

He was the same, and yet not. His green eyes were as intense and beautiful as ever, and he wore his signature work uniform of dark jeans, sneakers and a black sweater. She used to call it his "Steve Jobs look" although he never wore a turtleneck. His dark brown hair still had the reddish gleam she loved, but it was a little longer than she remembered. It was almost like he'd chosen not to make time for a haircut—not forgotten, mind you. Because a man like Lane didn't forget things.

He forgot his vow to make you part of his life.

She perched on the edge of the sofa, tempted to keep fiddling with the ring on her middle finger but resisting. Outside the sky was a dusky purple. She looked at Lane, keeping silent until he eventually left his position on the wall and took the single seat adjacent to her. If you ignored the thick-enough-to-cut-it tension, the scene was so familiar it unsettled her down to her very core.

How many nights had they sat in this exact space, drinking Scotch and listening to music? How many times had they abandoned dinner to make love on the couch…or against the wall?

"Are you going to make me guess why you're here?" he asked, his gaze shifting over to the dog, who was watching them at a distance. The poor thing looked like she could sense the unease and was keeping the hell away from it.

Smart girl.

"If you're looking for a divorce, then I can make a time with my lawyer, because I'd prefer to do this with legal representation," he said.

Oof.

Why hadn't she asked for a divorce? Or more strangely, why hadn't *he*? For some reason, she'd never been able to work up the courage to reach out and suggest it. For months after she left, Scout had been waiting for an email or a phone call to start proceedings.

But nothing ever came.

After that year passed, she started to wonder why he hadn't initiated anything. Maybe it was because his meteoric rise in the tech community meant he had more to lose. More money. More assets.

But she had no interest in that. Scout was a lot of things—not all of them good—but she wasn't a gold digger. She'd left that relationship with exactly what she'd brought to it: nothing.

"I'm not…" She shook her head. "That's not why I came here, actually."

His eyebrow shot up. It hurt to see the suspicion scrawled across his face, but she couldn't really blame him. There was no trust left between them.

There's nothing left between you.

"It's about Twinkle Stardust."

His features hardened like concrete setting, and his muscles seemed to coil like he was bracing himself for something. "No."

"I haven't even told you want I want." Scout resisted the urge to fold her arms across her chest. Taking a combative posture wouldn't help the situation.

"If you're going to fight me for custody—"

"I'm not trying to take her away from you." She held up a hand to stop him. "Please, Lane. I know we don't have a relationship anymore, but I'm not a monster."

He loved that dog more than anything and he was the best dog dad out there. In truth, Lane's loyalty was both his best *and* worst quality. It was something she admired about him, but it also led to him shutting Scout out of his personal life.

"What could you possibly want with Star?" he asked. His posture had relaxed a little now, curiosity making him lean forward.

"It's kind of a complicated story, but I need a Bichon Frise for a photoshoot."

Lane blinked once. Then twice. "Come again?"

"Remember my friend Isla? Well, she started a social media

and talent agency for pet influencers. It's called Paws in the City, and I work for her."

"I've heard of it," he said. "I saw an article about the rise of niche talent agencies recently, but I had no idea it was Isla's business."

"She did it all on her own. Well, I helped." Scout nodded. It felt important to let Lane know that she wasn't simply riding on her best friend's coattails. Why? She had no idea. He probably already thought every bad thing possible about her. "And we have a client who has a Bichon Frise with very successful Instagram and TikTok accounts. She was booked for a promotional campaign with a pet brand and the photoshoot is coming up but...she's pink."

"Pink?" Lane frowned.

"Bright pink. Like, Barbie's Dreamhouse pink."

"Uh...why?"

"That's also a complicated story."

"Right. And you want Star because..."

"I need a doppelgänger to stand in." Scout glanced at Star, who had retired to her doggy bed and was watching them warily. "And she's perfect."

"Star isn't a model."

"I know, but she's fluffy and white and well-behaved. She looks exactly like the dog I need to replace." Scout bit down on her lower lip. "Like I said, she's perfect."

In the back of the cab, she'd tried to pull together a coherent argument for why Lane should help her. But now that she was here in front of him, facing the frosty wall of suspicion, her argument suddenly felt ill-conceived.

He had zero reason to help her.

She'd left him in the middle of the night after sticking a goodbye Post-it note to his kitchen table. Was it cowardly? Maybe. But at the time she'd felt so broken and sad that the only thing that would have made it worse was crying in front of him. All of Scout's life she'd had to be tough.

Tough when her mother disappeared for days at a time and twelve-year-old Scout had to try and figure out how to scrape together meals and get herself to school.

Tough when her grandparents had showed up in her life after more than a decade of being absent and imposed all these rules and conditions that made no sense to her.

Tough when she married Lane and he was too ashamed to introduce her to his family.

Tough, more than ever, when her impulsive marriage was the reason her grandparents wouldn't let Lizzie come live with her.

Anger and resentment simmered inside Scout, like a fire fanning to life. This was the only way she could untangle the mess she'd made of her life.

She couldn't lose this opportunity.

"You have no reason to help me," Scout said. "I know that. Frankly, I want to be here asking for your help as much as you want to give it to me. But I screwed up and I need to fix things with Isla and with our client. More importantly, if I can get promoted at work, then I can find a nicer apartment and have a better chance of convincing my grandparents to let Lizzie come live with me."

For a moment Lane said nothing.

He knew about her family situation—not all the sordid details but enough that he understood how much she adored her little sister and how it was a permanent tear in her heart to be away from her. He also knew how controlling her grandparents were and how they thought Scout made poor decisions and wasn't responsible enough to be a caregiver.

It was so uncomfortable to lay herself bare. To admit that she *still* hadn't figured her life out. She was twenty-six and still struggling to find her feet. But maybe if she appealed to the good, kind heart she'd fallen in love with. Maybe…

Maybe.

"Let me get this straight," he said, knotting his hands. "Your original dog was accidentally dyed pink and you need a replacement dog in the correct color so you can get a promotion in order to get custody of your sister."

She swallowed. "Yes."

"That's a lot of pressure for one dog," he said.

"It's a lot of pressure for one woman."

He scrubbed a hand over his jaw. Something flickered in his eyes—an understanding. Empathy. "I take it your grandparents are still trying to restrict access to Lizzie."

"They're moving to California," she replied, holding her shoulders back and promising herself she wouldn't crumble in front of him. "Norman is coming out of retirement. He got a teaching position at Berkeley."

She lowered her gaze to the modern black-and-white rug underneath his concrete-and-glass coffee table. Did all broken hearts have the dream of running into their ex when they were hotter/smarter/more successful than they were before? This was the antithesis of that. She looked up at him and held her back straight. There was no sense crying over how things were—that never helped anyone.

She had to *change* things.

"They want to take Lizzie with them."

He shook his head. "They're only hurting Lizzie by keeping you two apart."

The words struck her with force, and her response clogged the back of her throat. Even now, after all that had happened, he wouldn't take what could have been a very easy swipe at her. She had to give him credit for that.

"Thank you," she replied. "I appreciate it."

"But I don't know that I want Star being used to replace some pet influencer. She's well-behaved, but she's not trained to do anything like that."

"There's no training required, I promise. All she has to do is sit there and be her adorable self while someone takes some photos. That's it." Scout sucked in a hopeful breath. Maybe this might go her way after all. "Easy as pie. She'll be a natural."

Lane looked back over to Star's bed. She'd slumped down, her fluffy white head resting on the soft, squishy edge.

"One photoshoot?" he clarified.

He was considering it! She didn't want to get her hopes up, but perhaps being honest about the reason behind her request had worked.

"Just the one," she confirmed.

This would give Sasha Frise time to grow her fur back—after the color was shaved out—before they booked another job. The advertiser would be satisfied. The client would be satisfied. Isla would be satisfied.

And Scout's plans would be going in the right direction.

"I want to be there," he said. "At the shoot, from start to finish. I don't want her being in this strange environment and freaking out because she doesn't know anyone."

Scout tried not to feel hurt at being placed in the category of strangers Star would encounter, especially since today had proved she wasn't exactly great at taking care of people's pets. So she couldn't really begrudge Lane that opinion.

Besides, this wasn't the time for feelings or emotions. She was in solution mode.

"Of course. Absolutely." She nodded. "You can be there the whole time."

"Okay. You can borrow Star for one photoshoot. Email me the details and I'll make sure we're there."

Relief flooded through Scout's body and it was almost like

a wave of euphoria. So often in her life things didn't go her way, and she wouldn't soon forget the sweet, sweet victory of hearing yes instead of no.

"Thank you so much. You have no idea how much I appreciate this," she said.

Lane stood and jammed his hands into the front pockets of his jeans. He might have said yes, but the air around him was still cold and walled off. That brief flicker when he'd been kind about her grandparents? Gone. Maybe it was nothing but muscle memory. Phantom feelings.

It doesn't matter. This is about Star, not him.

She rose from her chair and clutched her bag in front of her, as if needing the physical barrier. For a moment she wanted to say more.

But no words came out. There was so much water under the bridge, and trying to say something now would be like trying to scoop it out one cup at a time. It was pointless. Futile.

She headed to the front door and Lane followed. The second she was outside, he closed it and flicked the lock. The sound triggered a memory of the night she'd left. She remembered standing in this very spot, door closed, key in her hand. When she'd locked it, the sound had felt like a gunshot. Like finality. She'd slipped the key into his mailbox on the way out of his building and walked into the cool night air with everything she owned stuffed into a suitcase.

In that moment, she never thought she'd be back.

You're not back. This is purely about your goals…and they don't include him.

As far as Scout was concerned, her goals would never include falling in love ever again.

5

The following day, Scout hurried up the stairs to the Paws in the City office. It was five past nine, and she was supposed to be on a call with their landlord to talk through some issues they'd had with the office. Namely, a shoddy heating unit that wouldn't fire up. And since the milder spring weather was only teasing them at this stage, she really wanted to make sure a technician was sent over ASAP.

The phone rang in the office as she jogged up the stairs to the second floor, but it cut out just as she pushed the door open. Shit. She could see Isla sitting in her tiny office—which had been used as a storage cupboard by the previous tenants—holding her phone up to her ear.

"Yes, that's right. The heater won't turn on." Isla nodded, her back toward Scout and the office's foyer. "No, we haven't had any power outages recently. Not to my knowledge anyway."

Crap. Scout let out a sigh and dumped her purse under the desk. She had been on her way to the subway station when a stranger stopped her to ask for directions—Scout had taken ten minutes to help the woman out, which put her behind schedule. Then, *of course*, the subway was having issues, forcing her to disembark early and walk the last few blocks to the office.

Thank God she'd decided to wear her winter boots for the slushy commute. Dropping into her chair, she yanked them off and slipped her feet into the cute stiletto ankle boots she'd brought to go with her outfit. Most of her clothes were from secondhand shops, since her budget didn't exactly allow for any Fifth Avenue sprees.

Hell, some years she'd barely been able to afford Nordstrom Rack.

"Okay, great. Three o'clock? Perfect. We'll make sure someone is here to let them in. Thanks so much." Isla came out of her office. As always, she looked chic and professional in a pair of gray trousers, a cream blouse and a powder blue blazer with vintage buttons. Her long dark hair was softly curled and she looked every bit the has-her-life-together boss that she was. "Good morning."

"Go on, say it. Good *afternoon*." She sighed. "Sorry I'm late."

"It's five minutes, Scout. I coped perfectly fine." Isla laughed. "Mrs. Nelson again?"

Mrs. Nelson was Scout's elderly neighbor who often needed assistance due to her family not being close by.

"No. It was a random stranger on the street that I had to help with directions," she grumbled in response as she tossed her boots into a canvas tote and slipped them under her desk.

"You're a bleeding heart, girl," Isla teased. "Anyway, that was the landlord. The technician is coming at three."

"I'll make sure they get access to whatever they need." She used her mouse to open up their shared work calendar on her computer.

"So, I talked with Gina on my way to the office this morning." Isla leaned against Scout's desk.

"And?" She tried not to get her hopes up.

"She's happy to use a replacement. It was quick thinking on your part, because she was so mad I was *sure* she was about to fire us." Isla let out a sigh. "It's not how I want to resolve this situation, because it feels unethical."

"Once we have the photos from the shoot, Gina can still post them to Sasha's accounts and uphold her end of the contract, which means the advertiser won't lose out," Scout pointed out. "In the grand scheme of things, does it matter that the dog is technically different when they look exactly the same and the campaign will still get the exposure it's paying for?"

"That's exactly what Gina said." Isla chewed on the inside of her cheek, as though still uncertain it was the right move. "But she'll need the replacement for more than the Lively Paws shoot."

Uh-oh.

"Really?" Scout cringed internally. She'd sold Lane on it being a one-time-only deal, and now she was going to have to ask for more. He'd probably think that she planned the bait-and-switch all along.

"Sasha is committed to some charity calendar that's being created to raise money for a nonprofit animal rescue center on Park Avenue. This was booked even before she signed on as a client with us."

Well, a charity event for a rescue center might not be *too* much of a hard sell. She already knew that Lane was a major donor for the place where he'd adopted Star and it was something he was passionate about.

"What's the other thing?" She was already trying to figure out how she was going to position this with Lane.

"A meet and greet."

"What kind of a meet and greet?" Scout asked warily.

"At an old folks' home."

"Wait, so I'm going to have to take the fake Sasha to a meet and greet with some sweet elderly people and *lie* to them." She groaned. This felt so much worse than swapping a dog out for a photoshoot. "I can't do that."

"Look, I don't like this, either," Isla said. "Part of me was hoping that Gina would chew me out and tell me it was a stupid idea, and then force us to move all her meetings around and maybe give her a few free months' services or something."

"But she's seen an opportunity to get paid without doing the work?" Scout guessed, thinking back to how Gina had seemed all too happy to let Scout take care of things while she went off for a smoke.

And look how that turned out.

"Whatever her reason, we're on the back foot. Do you think Lane will loan us his dog more than once? Because if we lose Gina as a client, then…" She shook her head. "That's going to set us back a lot. *She's* the one I use in all my pitches to new clients to show how well established we are, because Sasha is by far the biggest star on our books. Without her, we look a lot smaller."

"I'm sure it will be fine," Scout said with a confident smile that she hoped hid the uncertainty she felt inside. She had to fix this mess, no matter how humiliating it was to go groveling to Lane for help. No matter how she really didn't want to ask him for anything else.

Your ego is the least important thing in this equation.

"Great." Isla let out a sigh of relief. "Now, what do we have on the books today?"

Scout leaned over and brought up the shared calendar on her screen. "You've got a Zoom meeting at nine thirty with the business development manager for that new app, Connect Paw. And I'm doing a client assessment at the same time. Oh, it's with that sphynx cat. Lucille Bald."

Isla giggled. "How do they come up with these names?"

"No idea, but I do *not* possess that level of creativity." Scout shook her head in wonder.

They had come across some really creative names since opening the business. Of course there was the cantankerous Scottish fold, Isaac Mewton. They'd also met Droolius Caesar, the bulldog, Subwoofer, the teacup poodle, Spark Pug, who was an adorable snorting pug, and an Iguana named Lizzinardo Da Vinci.

"I'm glad you're doing that and not me," Isla said.

"Why?"

She wrinkled her nose. "Hairless cats creep me out. Plus, Theo once made a comment about how they look like a ball sack with legs and now I can't unsee that image."

Scout snorted. "I thought he was so prim and proper the first time I met him."

Isla flushed and ducked her head. "He is *not* prim and proper, trust me."

"Hey," she replied, holding up two hands. "I don't want to know what you two were up to last night."

"Actually, I wanted to talk to you about that, now that we've gotten all the business chat out of the way."

"If you got something stuck up there, you need to see a doctor," Scout teased. "I can't help you with that."

Isla swatted at her, and they both laughed. They'd been

friends for so many years that nothing—not even the weird stuff—was off-limits. "Not *that* kind of talk."

"Tell me quick," she said, fishing around inside her purse for her wallet. "I was going to do a coffee run for us both before the meetings start."

Scout was busy looking for the café reward stamp card in her wallet when she realized that Isla hadn't said anything. She looked up and her friend was holding her hand up at a very obvious angle, such that it was easy to see the diamond ring on her finger.

She'd been so stressed about being late and Isla's call with Gina that she hadn't even noticed it.

"You got engaged? Oh my god!" Scout jumped out of her seat. "Let me see, let me see."

Laughing a little giddily, Isla thrust her hand out.

"Oh, it's *beautiful*."

The ring was gold with a large oval diamond surrounded by a spray of smaller diamonds and flanked at the shoulders of the band with a ruby on each side. It had intricate detailing around the stones and was vintage perfection from every angle.

"It was Theo's mother's ring," Isla said, her blue eyes a little misty. "We honestly hadn't talked about it too much. I didn't want to push, because I know the idea of getting married without a single family member there to witness it will be really hard for him. But he surprised me out of the blue last night at home. We were eating a nice dinner and…he disappeared like he was going to the bathroom and he came back with the ring. I don't think he planned it at all."

"Aww." Scout pressed a hand to her chest.

She felt a pang there. A deep, old wound that she'd thought had healed was suddenly pulsing and raw again.

This is your best friend in the whole world. You must be happy for her.

She *was* happy for her.

Isla and Theo were the sweetest couple, and Scout knew her friend was truly, madly, deeply in love. Not to use a cliché, but there was a reason people phrased it like that. They deserved to have an incredible, fairy-tale happily-ever-after.

But it did remind Scout what she'd lost. What she'd probably never have again. And that wasn't simply because she was legally still married, either. Reopening her heart to that kind of pain and rejection could *never* happen.

"I don't think we're going to have a traditional wedding," Isla said. "Big parties aren't Theo's style and they're not mine, either. But we were thinking something simple, with a celebrant and the people closest to us."

"That sounds wonderful."

"Dani would shoot me if I didn't make her maid of honor, but I was hoping you might be our witness. You're like a sister to me and I want you to be involved, if you're comfortable with that."

Tears filled Scout's eyes and she threw her arms around Isla's neck. "Of course. I would be honored."

"Yeah?" Isla drew back and looked her in the eye. "I totally understand if the whole wedding thing isn't—"

"Just because I screwed up my own marriage doesn't mean I can't celebrate yours. So stop that shit right now, please." She gave her friend a gentle shake by the shoulders. "I am 100 percent here for you."

"Thank you. That really means a lot." Isla also looked misty-eyed. "Dammit! Now you're going to make me cry."

"Nope, no tears. This is a happy occasion." Scout waved her hand and grabbed her wallet. "I'm going to celebrate by getting us coffees. Vanilla latte for you?"

"Yes please. You're a gem."

Scout headed out of the office, and stealthily put an order

in at Milk Bar, Christina Tosi's famous bakery, for one of their delicious tiered cakes. She'd have it delivered to the office as a surprise that afternoon.

Regardless of her own thoughts on marriage, she would not make her best friend feel anything less than fully loved and supported. Scout would simply have to do what she did best—hide her scars away from the world.

Even if that was going to be extra difficult now that it looked like she'd be seeing Lane more than she'd initially hoped.

Lane jogged up the three steps and raised his hand to knock on the front door of his sister's home. It was getting dark out and the quiet Staten Island street was blanketed in soft purplish light. A warm glow spilled from the front windows, casting golden streaks across the doorstep.

Beth and the kids had moved in a few months back, after Lane had bought the 1970s home. Since separating from her husband, his sister had done her best to stand on her own two feet, and despite Lane offering repeatedly to set them up in a new place, she'd been reluctant to accept his help.

Money was strange like that. He'd always assumed that becoming wealthy would mean he could ensure his family had everything they needed—along with his love of tinkering with code and creating new things, Lane's driving force was to take care of the people he loved.

Family was everything after all.

But Beth had said she didn't want to feel like she was indebted to anyone—something she called a leftover of marriage to her controlling ex-husband. When the company she worked for went under and she lost her job, however, she finally relented. Together, they'd picked out the house with a separate bedroom for each of her kids and a nice kitchen.

Frankly, Lane could have afforded something bigger and in a better part of town, but Beth wanted to buy him out once she was back on her feet and a big house wasn't her style.

Neither was a fancy neighborhood.

The door swung open and his sister stood there, looking slightly frazzled as always. But a big grin stretched across her lips and she threw her arms around his neck.

"I'm so glad you could make it!" She planted a kiss on his cheek the way his mother always did. It never ceased to make him smile how alike they were. "I know it was a last-minute invite, but the kids have been hassling me for the last two weeks."

He glanced around the entryway. There were paint samples on one wall—four shades of cream that all looked the same to him but would no doubt be vastly different to his sister's keen eye. The house needed a little work, and Beth was excited to make the space her own. He'd given her carte blanche to get whatever contractors in that she needed—no need to worry about the cost. Thankfully, her love of interior design had won out over her stubborn need for independence.

"Where are the little rug rats?" he asked. But he needn't have. Because two seconds later, a small human wearing a princess dress came careening around the corner like she was auditioning for *The Fast and the Furious*. She slammed into Lane so hard he had to take a step back. "Ariella! My favorite niece."

"I'm your only niece." She giggled. But then her eyes went wide and she looked utterly horrified. "Unless you found another one?"

"No way. It's just you, baby." Lane bent down and scooped her up. She grinned, showing off two gaps from where her baby teeth had recently fallen out.

"That's a relief."

Beth rolled her eyes. "The girl could not possibly handle being upstaged, I tell ya."

A second later, another figure came waddling around the corner. Two-year-old Dante clutched a stuffed animal to his chest with one arm and extended the other out to his mother. "Up."

"Hey, big man." Lane leaned over as Beth lifted the little boy and he pressed a kiss to his forehead. "You're up late."

"He's going to bed right now," Beth said, looking down dotingly at her son. "Because otherwise you're going to drive Mommy bananas tomorrow."

Lane stifled a smile. Single parenthood was no joke, but Beth had blossomed once she got out of her toxic marriage. It was good to see her sounding so light and looking like a weight had been lifted off her shoulders. The house still had boxes dotted around and there was laundry flung over the back of the dining chairs, but she seemed so…free.

"Do you like my dress?" Ariella asked. She was wearing a pink frothy thing with a full skirt and puffed sleeves, and Lane was pretty sure it was shedding glitter all over his sweater.

"I *love* your dress," he replied. "Very stylish."

"I made Mommy put spaceships on it." She pointed to where a silver spaceship had been haphazardly sewn on to the fabric. Beth was a great many things, but she was not a seamstress. "Because I want to be a princess *and* an astronaut."

"That's a cool combination."

"I'm going to fight aliens with my princess powers!"

"Uh-oh. Watch out, aliens." Lane made his eyes wide and Ariella giggled.

"She got mad that Walmart only had space-themed things in the boys section," Beth said, a proud smile forming on her lips. "So I told her we could add patches of whatever she liked onto the dress."

"What else are you going to put on your dress?" Lane asked, tucking an errant strand of brown hair behind his niece's ear.

"Books," she replied with a serious nod. "And lemons."

"Lemons?"

She shrugged. "I like lemons."

Kids were so joyfully random. Beth went to put Dante to bed, and Lane carried Ariella into the kitchen, plopping her on the kitchen counter. Her little legs swung back and forth, her sock-covered feet bumping gently at the lower cabinets.

"What are we having for dinner?" he asked.

"Lasagna," she replied, although it came out more like *la-zanna*.

"Yum."

Ariella wrinkled her nose. "I prefer spaghetti because I get to twirl."

Lane was sure Beth preferred lasagna because Ariella *didn't* get to twirl. He'd seen the mess that kid could make with a single bowl of spaghetti and meatballs. "But it still tastes good, right?"

She shrugged. "I guess."

"How do you like the new house?" he asked her as he took a peek at the oven. A pan of lasagna was browning nicely and Lane's mouth watered in response. It had been a while since he'd had a home-cooked meal.

"It's great. I have my own bedroom!" She fired one of her adorable gap-toothed grins at him. "No more listening to Dante cry like a baby."

"Well, your brother *is* a baby still," Lane pointed out. "But I'm glad you like it."

"Mommy said I can paint it whatever color I like. I like purple and blue. They're my favorite colors." She tapped h chin in the exact same way her mother did when she thinking. "But I also like green and yellow. How do I choose only one color?"

"Maybe you could paint each wall—"

"Don't make me kill you, little brother." Beth appeared in the doorway, her eyes shooting daggers at him as she placed the baby monitor on the countertop.

"You could paint a stripe of each one on the wall to help you decide," Lane said, stifling a smirk. "The paint store will give you little pots of each color so you can see what they look like."

"That's a great idea." Ariella's face lit up and then she turned to her mom. "Can we do that?"

"Sure thing, honey." Beth pulled her daughter down from the countertop and blew a raspberry on her cheek. "Now, why don't you go and play in your room until dinner is ready. Uncle Lane is going to help Mommy set the table."

Ariella raced off, more than happy to be given an opportunity for extra playtime instead of having to help with dinner preparations. Lane raised an eyebrow. Usually Beth was big on making the kids assist around the house to teach them that they were all responsible for things like meals.

Clearly she wanted to talk about something important.

But then she asked, "How's work going?"

"Good." Lane cocked his head. "Busy, like usual."

His sister nodded and he could feel tension rising in the room, but he wasn't sure why. She reached into the cabinets and pulled out some plates for dinner. Four in total. One for him, Beth, Ariella and...

"Who else is coming to dinner?" he asked, narrowing his eyes.

Beth was facing the cupboards to get the water glasses down and she didn't turn around. "Todd."

Lane's jaw ticked as he felt every muscle in his body tighten.

He hadn't seen his younger brother in more than two years—not since the night Lane found out that his brother had taken a credit card out under his name and used it to rack up twenty thousand dollars of debt, most of it on a luxury hotel in Vegas and poker chips that he spent like water.

When Lane had asked him what the hell he thought he was doing, Todd had thrown it back in Lane's face by saying he wasn't the only one in the family who could go wild in Vegas. Bastard.

The event had caused an irreparable rift in his family. Lane wanted the debt repaid—more to teach his brother that actions had consequences than because he wanted the money back—but his mother had tried to claim that her youngest son had a gambling problem and needed their support.

Gambling problem, Lane's ass. Todd was simply looking for a way to make a quick buck. Too bad he was as good at poker statistics as he was covering his tracks, because Lane had turned up at the hotel and almost busted down the door when he figured out what was going on.

After it became clear that Lane wasn't going to roll over, Todd had taken off to god-only-knew where. But he'd returned to Staten Island a few months ago and Lane had done everything in his power to avoid him, including skipping dinner with his folks if Todd was going to be there. But Beth had been at him to see his brother, because she claimed that Todd was getting his life back on track.

The thought of looking his brother in the eye made him want to scream bloody murder, and he didn't want that to happen around the rest of the family. Especially not the kids.

"I know what you're doing, Beth. It won't work." Lane folded his arms across his chest. "I'm not looking to play happy families with that asshole."

He kept his voice low so Ariella wouldn't hear from the

next room. As much as he hated the guy, Lane wasn't about
to ruin Todd's relationship with his niece and nephew.

"You can't avoid him forever." Beth turned around and her
brows were furrowed. She had the same multitoned green
eyes and reddish-brown hair as Lane, which they got from the
Scottish side of the family. Todd, on the other hand, had the
cool gray eyes and dark hair from their grandfather's Welsh
heritage. "We're still a family."

"Are we? Because it certainly doesn't feel that way to me."

"Lane, come on." Beth looked at him with imploring eyes.
"Yes, he's made some mistakes—"

"Made some mistakes?" Lane gawked at her. "Are you fucking kidding me? The man committed identity theft to *steal*
from me, and when I called him on it, he invented a gambling
problem to weasel out of responsibility."

The worst thing of all was that if Todd had actually come
to him for a loan, Lane would have done everything in his
power to help the guy. That, in his eyes, made the betrayal
hurt even more.

Between his ill-fated marriage to Scout and the theft issues
with Todd, it was no wonder Lane never wanted to leave his
office to socialize with people. Why would he? Humans, as
a general rule, couldn't be trusted.

"He was in a bad place," Beth said. Turmoil gathered in
her eyes and in the crease deepening between her brows. She
hated nothing more than seeing people she loved fighting—
she was like their mother, in that way.

"He was *jealous*, Beth. He wanted what I had without putting in any of the blood, sweat and tears." The night he'd con-
fronted Todd in Vegas, Lane had felt the seething resentment
billowing off him. The green-eyed envy. "Which makes it
even worse. Do you know how many times I offered to set
him up with my contacts or make an introduction to some-

one who might offer him a job? But he never took it. Why? Because he's fucking lazy and he wants everything handed to him on a silver platter."

Beth's gaze dropped to the ground. As much as Lane hated to make his sister feel bad, she'd crossed a line tonight. Putting him and Todd in the same room wasn't magically going to fix things, and doing it behind his back simply reinforced why Lane handed out trust like it was more precious than diamonds.

"I understand you want the kids to have a relationship with him," Lane said. "I don't begrudge that at all. I'm *not* asking you to pick sides and I won't hold it against you for spending time with him. But don't try to force my hand, okay? That's not cool."

"Won't you give him a chance?" Tears swam in her eyes and it was like a knife through Lane's chest. He loved his sister more than anything.

But there were some concessions he couldn't make.

"No, I won't." He walked over to her and planted a kiss on her cheek. "Enjoy dinner. I'll say bye to Ariella on the way out."

He walked out of the kitchen to the sound of his sister quietly crying, and he stopped past his niece's bedroom to give her a hug and tell her he loved her. By the time he made it outside into the rapidly cooling night air, Lane thought he was going to explode. Fiery resentment flowed through him and he was pretty sure if he turned his wrist over, he'd see the emotion bubbling in his veins.

A car was parked behind his and a shadowy figure sat inside. There was no denying it was Todd, and Lane stared for a moment before walking to his car and yanking the door open.

As far as he was concerned, he no longer had a brother.

6

Two days later, Lane sat in the back seat of his private car, staring out the window, fairly certain he'd made a mistake. Actually, scratch that. He was *absolutely* certain he'd made a mistake. What the hell was he thinking, agreeing to get involved in Scout's problems? That was something you did in a real marriage.

Not in whatever the hell kind of sham on-paper-only, over-before-it-started marriage they now had.

Frankly, Scout was closer to being a stranger than she was to being his wife.

Yeah? So why have you been dreaming about her again, huh? Do you usually dream about strangers?

That was an unfortunate turn of events. He'd gone for

months without the dreams and then she'd shown up on his doorstep, looking like sinfulness itself, and *boom*! The dreams were back. Only instead of seeing young Scout with her baby face and freckle-dusted skin, now he saw her as she was today. Hair longer, eyes cooler and her body with new curves that turned his concentration to smoke.

There *was* one good thing that could possibly come of all this, however.

Earlier that morning he was so irritated that he'd fallen for her doe-eyed, heartfelt request like a complete and utter sucker, that he'd called his lawyer and started the ball rolling on the divorce paperwork. It was time to stop sticking his head in the sand. He had no idea whether there was anything suspicious about Scout suddenly turning up on his doorstep—though his gut said no—but while they were still legally married she *might* have a claim on his assets...assets like his business.

Rav had flipped when he found out that Lane had never actually divorced Scout. And with how well Unison was going—not to mention other projects they had in the pipeline—the longer he left it, the riskier the situation would become. He owed it to Rav and their staff to make sure the business was safe.

He'd use this whole ridiculous scenario as the catalyst to finally get off his ass and act. She might have convinced him to help her out of a jam, but he and Scout were well and truly over.

It was time to make it official.

"Ready for your fifteen minutes of fame?" Lane looked at Star's fluffy white face peering back at him from inside the dog carrier. "Bet you never thought you'd get a modeling gig."

Nothing. Usually when he talked to her there was some semblance of recognition. She was very animated—always tilting her head from side to side or yipping back at him in response. But she'd been acting strange ever since Scout showed up.

Earlier he'd found her gnawing on the leg of one of his dining table chairs, her teeth carving off the paint to reveal raw wood beneath. That was so unlike her.

Everyone deals with things differently.

No kidding. Lane wasn't the quiet, agreeable introvert he'd been back when he'd been swept away by a glimmering, vivacious blonde in a Vegas elevator. Back then he was an up-and-comer, but he hadn't developed his voice. He hadn't yet shed the computer-nerd awkwardness that had plagued him since he was a kid. The joke was on all the bullies who'd punched in his locker door and strewn his books across the hallway, however. Because Lane was now a *Forbes*-certified success story running a multimillion-dollar company and they were flipping burgers back on Staten Island.

Who was the loser now, huh?

The driver pulled the car to a stop in front of a well-presented house on a leafy, tree-lined Brooklyn street. This was where the photoshoot was taking place. Per her email, Scout was waiting outside to brief him about how the day would go. As always, she looked like a million bucks. Her blond hair was swept up with a few tendrils falling softly around her face. Her long legs were encased in a pair of tight black jeans capped with snake print ankle boots. On top, she wore a white T-shirt under a funky checked blazer. The sleeves were rolled back, and everything about the outfit screamed "effortless cool."

He supposed when you looked as good as Scout, any outfit would appear cool.

Can we not focus on how attracted you still are to her even though she broke your heart?

How was that even possible? Surely there was some evolutionary, biological wiring that *should* have prevented him from still being attracted to her. But apparently, at his core, Lane was simply a glutton for punishment.

"Come on. Let's get this over with."

Lane grabbed Star's carrier and got out of the car, pausing to thank the driver. He hardly ever used the service—still preferring to catch the subway around town like he had as a broke graduate in his early twenties—but today he was thankful that Rav insisted on keeping a driver on retainer.

"Hi, Lane." Scout waved and came over. She seemed a little stiff, as if she might be nervous. "I'm glad you found your way here."

Translation: I was worried you weren't going to show up.

He'd joked early in their marriage about needing to become "fluent in Scout-speak" because there always seemed to be some hidden message to her words. Not because she was actively trying to hide anything, but because she was often afraid to voice her desires and needs. He understood why—from what she'd told him about her family, they were as dysfunctional as it got—but it was part of the reason things never worked out between them.

Ultimately, without communication, their marriage didn't have a snow cone's chance in hell.

"Well, GPS exists for that very reason," he said drily.

"Right, of course." Her smile faltered as an older man with neatly styled silver hair and an expensive suit exited the house and walked up to them. Scout stuck out her hand, shoulders squared. "Mr. Daniels, so nice to see you."

"I'm looking forward to seeing the results of the shoot today," he said. "The marketing team wasn't convinced about having it take place in my home, but I told them I never want Lively Paws to lose the personal touch." He waggled a finger. "We might be a big business now, but when my father started Lively Paws, it was strictly a family affair and I want to keep that intimacy."

The man turned his attention to Lane, eyes narrowing.

"Have we met?" he asked. "You look very familiar, son."

"This is Lane. He's Sasha's handler." The words rushed out of Scout's mouth and a sick feeling settled in the pit of Lane's stomach. Only the pleading expression in her eyes stopped him from correcting her.

"Nice to meet you." Lane stuck out his hand.

The older gentleman shook it and continued looking at Lane like he was trying to figure something out. Then he shrugged and bid them both a good day as he got into a waiting car. Scout let out a long breath.

"You didn't *tell* them you were swapping out the dogs?" he said, swinging his head toward her. "I thought when you said you needed a replacement that Star would simply be standing in for a photoshoot. I didn't think you'd be expecting me to *lie*."

Pink colored her cheeks. "I know this isn't ideal. But the Lively Paws campaign is a *huge* gig for Paws in the City. It's one of the biggest campaigns we've booked, and it will mean huge exposure for us."

"That's no excuse for lying." Lane shook his head.

"What's the harm? The dogs look the same, and Lively Paws is still going to get what they paid for in terms of social outreach. Sasha's account will still feature all the images, and once she's no longer doing her best Pepé Le Pink impersonation, then she'll step back in. No harm, no foul."

"You're lying to your client."

"We represent the dog, not Lively Paws." She huffed. "One teensy little switch is all it takes to keep everyone happy."

"One *teensy* switch? That would be like turning up to a

movie starring Jason Momoa only to find out the leading man is actually played by Rob Schneider."

Scout folded her arms across her chest, and a smile tugged at the corner of her lips. "You really think Twinkle Stardust is the Rob Schneider in this scenario?"

"Metaphorically speaking. And it's just Star, okay?" He sighed. "I only use the full name around Ariella."

"Noted." She nodded. "Still being the world's best uncle, huh?"

She was trying to flatter him and it wouldn't work. "I'm not the world's best anything."

"So the *Forbes* '30 Under 30' is a scam then?"

"You know about that?" Since it had happened only a year ago, that meant she was still keeping tabs on him long after they should have forgotten all about each other. For some reason, that made warmth blossom in his chest.

"I was...scrolling." She waved a hand. "You know how it is."

"You have a *Forbes* subscription?" he asked, knowing the chances were slim. Scout had told him one time that she found financial news as interesting as cardboard-flavored oatmeal.

"No, I don't." Her eyes flicked back and forth across his face.

She'd been thinking about him while he'd been thinking about her. It was satisfying for some reason, because Rav always made him feel like a tool for moping when the anniversary of their wedding approached. His business partner had seemed certain that Scout had forgotten about him the second she'd yanked her engagement ring off.

Apparently not.

For a long moment, neither of them said anything. He wasn't about to let Scout off the hook so easily for not telling him the whole story.

"Fine. So we'll go in there and tell them we don't have a dog to shoot. Who do you think is going to lose out? The big company with the multimillionaire CEO and his collection of Rolexes and his big-ass holiday house in the Hamptons? Or the small agency run by two women and a struggling mom who's trying to make a living with her pet?" Scout said.

"Don't play the underdog card with me," he grumbled. "That's beside the point."

"Of course. Couldn't possibly bend the rules now, could we?"

Shots fired.

On top of the fact that their marriage was a totally ill-fated misadventure from the get-go, he and Scout could never see eye to eye on anything. She was ruled by emotion and empathy, and he was ruled by…well, rules. Obligation. Responsibility. The black-and-white comfort of right and wrong. There was no gray area, with him. No fuzzy space.

Something was either right or it wasn't.

For the short while they were married, he'd viewed this difference as a great positive. She helped him loosen up and he helped her to see that she could achieve anything so long as she understood the rules of the game.

Weren't differences the best thing about a relationship? He certainly thought so. Yes, they caused friction. But he'd never wanted to date a carbon copy of himself. That would be weird.

Scout, however, had clearly seen the differences as a problem. An insurmountable problem. An irreconcilable problem.

"Don't try and play this off as a typical Scout-bleeding-heart situation, okay? I know why you're doing this," he said, holding his ground. "You told me the exact reason why. There's a benefit for you and you're not willing to look past that."

Scout opened her mouth to respond, but the sudden sound cut them off. *Bark! Bark, bark, bark!* Lane set the carrier down and crouched so he could check on Star. She was yapping up a storm so bad he opened the door and scooped her up in his arms. But the barking continued, and he winced as she vented her frustrations right into his ear.

Stop arguing! Ugh, you humans are the worst sometimes.

"Shh." He patted her head. "Okay, okay. That's enough now."

"She doesn't like us fighting," Scout said, her expression softening. For a second he saw something real and raw flicker across her face, but it was gone in an instant. "Look, I agree that I should have been more up-front with you. And you're right, I *do* have something to gain. But I really am trying to do what's best for Isla and our client. It's not easy starting out in business, as I'm sure you remember. Or maybe you don't. Maybe you're too successful now…"

Her voice trailed off as if she was simply wondering aloud to herself.

"Of course I remember," he said quietly. "It wasn't *that* long ago."

He'd done the typical start-up thing—working out of his parents' basement, subsisting on packet ramen and energy drinks while pulling all-nighters. He'd walked instead of driving his car when he was low on gas. He'd sacrificed evenings out to save money. Having a successful business wasn't going to change *who* he was nor his values. And having more money than he'd ever imagined didn't suddenly mean he'd lost sight of what it meant to struggle.

"And don't give me this crap about the fact that Isla's dating someone rich, okay? She runs this business on her own." Scout made a noise of frustration. "It really bugs me when people say that. Like dating someone with money somehow erases all your hard work and sacrifice."

"I wasn't going to say that." He couldn't lie and claim the

thought hadn't crossed his mind—but in many ways, Isla, Scout and he were all cut from the same cloth. They'd come from little and took pride in standing on their own two feet, neither one of them looking for a handout.

He respected it, because he'd been that way, too.

"I've heard it a few times now and it always gets under my skin." She sighed. "I'm sorry I wasn't fully transparent about this situation. That wasn't cool. But if I promise that nobody is going to be hurt by a little white lie, then will you pretend to be okay with this for the next few hours...please?"

Lane glanced at Star, who was giving him some serious side-eye action.

You got yourself into this mess, bud. I was perfectly happy staying home with my toys.

Was it worth screwing up the day for everyone who was waiting for them inside—not to mention Isla and her client— for the sake of being "honest" about something that probably didn't matter in the grand scheme of things? Not really. As much as lying of any kind got under his skin, he understood that Scout was used to operating in survival mode. She'd spent so much of her life doing whatever she could to make it through the day.

And he really did believe that she thought she was doing the right thing by her friend and boss. But he was going to get out of this situation as quickly as possible. Hurricane Scout had blown through his life and made a mess of things once before. It *wouldn't* happen again.

"Fine," he said with an air of reservation. "I'll keep my mouth shut."

"Thank you, Lane." Relief washed over her face and the worry was replaced with a bright smile. "I really appreciate it."

He mumbled something along the lines of "you're welcome," because he felt like she'd bowled him over again. Scout tended to have that effect.

"Great. And the same deal goes for the next two events," she said, the words tumbling out in a rush. "You're the best, Lane. I owe you one!"

Wait, what? Two more events?

He opened his mouth to protest, but Scout had already skipped ahead to the front door of the house, leaving him gaping after her. Five years might have passed, but not much had changed.

Scout walked toward Mr. Daniels's home with her shoulders squared and her head held high. But on the inside she felt a little tendril of shame unfurling. She'd sunk pretty low, throwing the extra events at him like that and not even giving him a chance to say anything about it.

But it wasn't like she was trying to scam anyone to make a quick buck. It wasn't even that she *liked* lying—far from it—but the reality was that she'd told many lies over the course of her life in order to save a relationship.

Like how she pretended to respect her grandparents when she was around Lizzie, so she didn't damage their relationship.

Like how she'd pretended not to be hurt all those times her mother left her alone, hoping that one day she might come back for good.

Like how she'd tried to give Lane the benefit of the doubt when he didn't want to introduce her to his family, hoping maybe he was simply nervous about telling them he was married.

How many of those have actually paid off, huh? Now Lizzie thinks you'd rather work than see her, your mother kept abandoning you until the day she died, and Lane made it clear he was happy to keep you as a dirty little secret.

Although she wasn't sure she could blame the demise of her marriage *all* on Lane, because there had certainly been other circumstances at play. But it stung even to this day that he'd been happy to kiss her like mad in the middle of a Vegas casino floor for all to see, but the second they'd arrived back in New York, it was like he was ashamed of her.

And it wasn't only that he hadn't introduced her to his family and friends. He'd also asked her not to accompany him to a big awards gala for his work. *And* he'd told her not to post images of them online until he'd thought about how they should handle the news.

You should be used to people being ashamed of you by now.

Shaking off the thoughts, she strode into the house and refocused on work. There was a flurry of activity surrounding a photographer and his assistant. The latter of the two came over to her and Lane, a big smile on his face. The set seemed relaxed and organized, which was a relief after the chaos of the last one.

"You must be Sasha and company," the young man said. He was stylish, with fitted pants, a brightly patterned shirt and well-groomed facial hair.

"I'm Scout, from Paws in the City."

"I'm Kenneth." He stuck his hand out to Scout. "This is such an honor. I've been following Sasha Frise for months, and I swear, it's some of the most creative content on the internet. You've done well signing her. I predict she's going to blow up in a big way."

"This advertising campaign will certainly help." Scout swallowed and tried to fight the churning sensation in her gut. Why did it feel like everything was a house of cards right now? Like one wrong gust of wind would blow everything down around her?

Lane came forward with Star still in his arms. Damn. What

was it about a big, hunky guy cuddling a small dog that made her insides twist and turn? Clearly Kenneth had the same reaction, because Scout didn't miss the way his gaze traveled over Lane in open appreciation.

Trust me, Kenneth. I know exactly how you feel.

"This is Lane," Scout said, brightly. "He's helping out today."

Keep it vague. Keep it generic. That was her motto. The less detail she gave about things, the less it could come back to bite her in the ass.

"Nice to meet you." Kenneth beamed.

"Nice to meet you, too." Lane smiled back and it lit up his whole face. God, how she'd missed that smile.

When they'd met in that Vegas elevator, she had been attracted to him instantly and seemingly without reason. He was so *not* her type. If there was a literal antithesis of a bad boy it was Lane Halliday in his mid twenties. He'd been lanky as a bean, had his shirt tucked in and wore thick-rimmed glasses. The computer-nerd vibe shouldn't have done it for her.

Hell, she'd made a joke about him wearing a pocket protector, to break the ice, and he'd gone on a five-minute monologue about how useful they were.

But his green eyes—with shifting shades of sea foam, moss and emerald—were like nothing she'd ever seen before, and the shy smile he aimed in her direction was a ray of sunshine.

Now he'd gotten LASIK and ditched his glasses. In their month together, she'd taken him shopping and it seemed he was sticking to the fashion rules she'd taught him. And the lankiness was gone, replaced with broader shoulders and a slight muscular bulk that filled out his shoulders and arms and thighs. He'd been working out and it showed.

She gulped. "Well, yes. Lane if you want to put St—Sasha down then we can get started."

The words came out in a rush.

Did you really think you'd suddenly stop being attracted to him simply because you left?

Scout wasn't sure what she thought anymore. Because a month ago, her marriage to Lane was firmly in the back of her mind. She'd not only swept it under the rug but bolted down the edges of said rug and placed a coffee table on top of it. Seeing him had brought it all rushing to the forefront of her mind.

All these years later, her heart still galloped when she saw him. Her palms still got a little sweaty and her skin tingled in anticipation. Time had dulled the edges of her pain, taking those sharp lines and softening them. It was almost like she'd forgotten how bad it hurt to have her heart broken.

Well, you can't forget. Because you're not strong enough to make that mistake twice.

7

"You can pop Sasha down here." Kenneth motioned toward a flat surface, over which a towel had been thrown. A young woman stood there, presumably to prepare Star for the shoot. "I'm assuming you have her costumes?"

"Yes." Scout handed over the bag that had been supplied by Gina.

Thankfully Isla had taken one for the team by going over to pick them up, because Scout wasn't sure she would be able to face the woman again.

"We've got three different outfits, depending on what vibe the art director is looking for."

"Leave me to it," Kenneth said with a nod. "We'll have this darling little fluff looking like a million bucks in no time!"

After Lane placed Star down, looking more than a bit nervous about leaving his baby with a stranger, the dog made a slight growling noise when the woman went to touch her. Scout's eyebrows shot up and Lane looked equally surprised. She wasn't sure she'd heard Star growl, *ever*.

The dog was usually the canine embodiment of a marshmallow.

The groomer didn't seem fazed, however. Instead, she cooed in calm tones and Star sat her butt down, her pink tongue lolling out of her mouth. Crisis averted.

When it was clear she was in capable hands, Lane relaxed. Scout went to speak with the art director and photographer to make sure everyone was on the same page. She snapped a few behind-the-scenes photos to share on the Paws in the City social accounts. But after that, there wasn't much for her to do.

It was strange to attend one shoot, let alone two in such close succession. Sometimes Isla would make an appearance if there was a business connection to be made or if the client specifically requested it. But most of the time she only popped in to show her face, if she turned up at all. However, it didn't feel right to leave Lane by himself when he was doing her a huge favor.

You sure it's nothing to do with the fact that you've got a penchant for emotional self-flagellation?

There was a Scrabble-winning word if she'd ever heard one. Her grandfather would be so proud.

Lane walked over and stood beside her, looking like he was unsure of what to do with himself.

"So..." She rocked back on her boots, trying to think of something to say.

"So." Lane's eyes drifted to her and the corner of his lips tilted up into an amused smirk.

"This is awkward," she admitted, and to her relief, Lane

let out a soft chuckle. "I thought about trying to say something smooth to pretend like it wasn't, but the air is so thick I could chew on it."

She sensed some of the tension leave his body and he leaned back against the wall of the expensive Brooklyn home. "I guess there's no point pretending a giant elephant isn't staring us down."

Especially since ignoring potential problems had kind of been their MO when they were living together. Turned out problems only got bigger when you left them to their own devices.

"How are…" She searched for a topic of conversation that didn't feel fraught, but not being able to talk about his family or hers, nor his business, left precious few conversations topics available. "…the Yankees?"

"That's the best you could do?" He raised an eyebrow and Scout cringed. "Really?"

She sighed. "I'm trying, Lane."

"You don't need to try. I'm perfectly capable of being civil for an hour or two."

"But not much longer than that?" she teased softly.

"Set your timer." He snorted. "And the Yankees are doing okay. The new outfielder we got in from Toronto is batting two-eighty and seems solid in center. Which is good, because we handed over pitching prospects for him and our newest starter's ERA is in the toilet. And don't even get me started on the bullpen."

Scout blinked. "I literally have no idea what you just said."

"Hey, you asked." Lane shrugged. "I take it you haven't watched a single game in the last five years?"

"Not a one."

He'd taken her to the season opener at Yankee Stadium not long before everything went to hell. The whole time Scout had pretended to know what was going on, using terms she'd heard from any and every sport to make him laugh.

Thankfully she didn't need to dwell on the bittersweet memory too long, because the groomer was carrying Star out to the area set up for the shoot.

"What the hell is she wearing?" Lane said under his breath, and Scout clamped a hand over her mouth.

The little white dog was dressed up as her doppelgänger's style icon, Fran Fine. The outfit was a totally over-the-top sequined leopard-print dress, which left half her back and her hind legs free. Star's fur had been teased and sprayed to resemble the big, poufy hairstyles from the show—no wig today— and she wore a matching glittery, leopard-print headband and gold chain around her neck.

As she was carried past, Scout could swear that the dog shot daggers at them.

"She does *not* look happy." Scout cringed.

"No shit. You've dressed her up like she's going to turn tricks for dog treats on some street corner."

Scout snorted and tried to cover it up with a fake cough when the photographer's assistant looked over at her. "Stop it. She looks cute."

"Cute," he scoffed. "Right."

The groomer set Star down and the dog wandered around, sniffing and exploring the area. There was a model with great legs, wearing a pair of bright red stiletto pumps, who would be photographed with the dog but only from the knees down. The dog would be the star of the show.

No pun intended.

"You wear that outfit and see if you feel cute." He narrowed his eyes at Scout.

"Do you dare me?" The challenge fired out of her mouth before she had a chance to think about it.

It was a game she'd liked to play with him. After they'd returned home, it became very clear that marrying someone on a whim was so *not* Lane's style. He made every decision with cautious consideration—right down to what brand of coffee to buy—and she'd taken it upon herself to bring more spontaneity into his life.

The rule was, if one of them dared the other, then they *had* to do it.

It had led to them eating all kinds of adventurous foods and doing silly things like yelling at the top of their lungs in the middle of Wall Street. The game had turned sexy more often than not, since they'd barely been able to keep their hands off one another, and Scout had dared him to make love to her on balconies and in alleyways and in the semi-anonymity of a nightclub.

For a time, she'd thought he'd loved that about her. But he'd thrown her spontaneity back in her face right before they broke up, calling their marriage "reckless" and "risky."

Lane didn't reply. So Scout turned her attention toward the shoot, where a makeup artist was crouching at the human model's legs and dusting shimmery powder along her skin. The groomer positioned Star at the model's feet and held a small treat in her hand, asking the dog to sit and stay. For a moment Scout worried that Star might not respond—either because of being called Sasha or because she might not be trained— but the little white dog did everything that was asked of her.

"You've trained her well," she said, glancing over at Lane. He had his arms folded across his chest, and Scout tried not to notice how the pose made the muscles in his arms look extra delicious.

"She's a smart cookie." A look of pride washed over his face. "I taught her to sit, stay, beg, roll over, play dead, shake and high five. We've been working on getting her to jump over a stick."

"Wow. That's very impressive."

"It's training." He shrugged. "Clear communication and a handful of treats, and I could teach her almost anything. She's extremely well-behaved."

It was easy to see. She sat quietly while the groomer fussed with her fur and while the photographer set up behind his camera. "She's lucky to have a dog dad like you."

Lane looked over at her, something flickering in his eyes. But like most of the time with him, it was difficult to tell exactly what he was thinking. "Thank you. That means a lot."

Scout snatched her gaze away, her heart thudding unsteadily. Dammit. How did he *still* have that effect on her? Even after all that had happened, there was a goodness in Lane. An honesty. Plenty of guys in his position would *never* have even opened the door to her, let alone agreed to help.

Stop thinking it means something. Because you know that when push came to shove he wasn't the man you hoped he would be.

A camera flash went off and the model changed position slightly. Star's eyes were fixed on the treat, patiently sitting until she was told she could have it.

The camera went off again. Everything was going smoothly, and Scout finally felt some of the anxiety she'd been carrying around all week leave her system. Seeing Lane was tough on her heart, but he really *was* being civil. Nobody had taken one look at the dog and spotted the swap. Star was being a champ and doing everything asked of her.

Maybe this will turn out okay.

And for the next fifteen minutes it seemed like it would… until it didn't.

Without warning, the model shrieked and stepped backward, wobbling on the towering heels as she bumped into a sprawling kitchen island. All eyes zeroed in on the sudden commotion. Scout frowned, trying to figure out what had happened. And then she spotted it…the yellow puddle on the pristine white tile.

"Did she…?" The model's French accent was filled with disgust. "That horrible little creature pissed on my foot!"

Kenneth went to fetch some paper towels, and the groomer tried to scoop Star up. But she was *not* having it. Star began to bark like she'd been possessed by a demonic force and then she took off like a rocket. As she raced around the side of the kitchen island, she skidded across the tiles like a rally car driver and disappeared into another room.

"Crap." Lane took off after Star.

"What's going on?" An older woman appeared in the kitchen, dressed in tailored navy pants and a white silk blouse. Her hair fell in a neat silver sheet around her shoulders.

"I'm so sorry, Mrs. Daniels." The art director rushed forward to greet the wife of the Lively Paws CEO. "We had a small accident with our model."

"Not with me," the model replied haughtily. "This is why they tell you never to work with children or animals."

"Our canine model," he replied stiffly. "But please don't worry. We'll get everything back on track in a moment."

Scout's eyes darted to where Lane had gone, following Star into another room of the house, and she decided to slip away to make sure everything was okay. The last thing she needed was to have jumped over *all* these hurdles, only to piss off the advertiser's wife at the last minute.

Mrs. Daniels was involved with the family business and had a reputation for ordering heads to roll when she wasn't happy. Which was exactly how a spot had opened up in this campaign. Apparently the last spokesmodel had chewed on her kitchen table.

"Lane," Scout said in a stage whisper as she walked into a sunny living room. "What are you doing?"

He was on all fours with his ass in the air. Usually, Scout would take a moment to enjoy the view—because Lane's ass was peach-emoji perfection—but currently she was too worried about getting Paws in the City fired.

Lane looked up. "Star's hiding under the couch and I can't get her."

Groaning, Scout dropped down and looked under the couch. Star was small and she'd tucked herself way back into the corner of the room, out of arm's reach. She appeared to have gotten some fabric in her mouth and was guarding it like Golem with his treasures.

"Come here, girl." Scout tried to reach toward her and was rewarded with a rumbling growl.

"She *never* does this." Lane huffed. "I swear, she was a little angel until you turned up on our doorstep."

"Me? How the hell is this my fault?" Scout hissed, trying to keep her voice down.

"I'm not saying it's your fault, but I noticed the timing. You turn up, and all of a sudden, Star starts acting weird. She was chewing on my furniture this week and now the growling and peeing on people." He shook his head. "She hasn't so much as tried to pee on a potted plant at the office, so why is she doing it now?"

"I don't have time to play canine therapist, okay? We have to get her out and get back to the shoot." She glanced over her shoulder. "Do you have any treats on you?"

"She's already had a few from the groomer. You know, it's not good to overfeed dogs with treats, it can lead to health conditions." His tone was deadly serious and Scout wanted to shake him. Lane's rigid adherence to rules and ideas was sometimes endearing, but often times infuriating. "But no, I don't have any."

Shaking her head, Scout lay on her stomach so she could slide farther under the sofa. "Hey there, cute pie. Come on, you don't want to hide under this dusty old couch."

The dog growled again, baring its small white teeth. Whatever she'd gotten a hold of looked like something red and silky. A handkerchief, perhaps? Praying that she wasn't going to end up getting bitten and needing a tetanus shot, Scout made a grab for the dog, who skittered along the back wall and out of her grasp.

"Is she under there?"

The voice of Mrs. Daniels froze Scout on the spot. Crap.

"She's a little jumpy today," Lane replied. "Sorry for the chaos. We'll get her out and make sure things run smoothly from now on."

Bless him. Scout couldn't placate the woman *and* fetch the dog at the same time. She reached again for Star and narrowly missed grabbing on to her sequined outfit. "Come on, girl. *Please.* You're killing me."

"Try getting her to go out the side," Lane suggested. "I'll wait there and grab her."

"Good idea."

Scout wriggled on her stomach, knowing she looked like a feral lizard, and tried to herd Star out the right side of the couch. Sweeping her arm toward the dog, it had the intended effect and she scooted out between the legs of the couch and right into Lane's waiting arms.

Flopping down for a minute to catch her breath, sweat beaded along Scout's hairline. Unfortunately, moving backward to get out from under the couch was *way* more awkward than going forward and she bumped her head while extricating herself. It was only when she finally sat up and swiped the back of her hand across her forehead that she realized the room had fallen completely silent.

Lane was holding Star in his arms, his eyes wide. Dangling out the side of Star's mouth was not a handkerchief.

"Where did she find that?" Mrs. Daniels pointed. Her face was almost the same shade of red as the silky fabric.

"Uh…" Lane looked at Scout like a deer in headlights.

Mrs. Daniels marched forward and snatched the thing from Star's mouth, unperturbed by the dog's growling. Hanging from the crook of the woman's finger was a lace-trimmed thong in a bright shade of cherry red, very much *not* the size that Mrs. Daniels would wear.

Oh shit.

"Hang on. *What* happened?" Isla shook her head.

It was several hours later and the three of them—Isla, Scout and August—were getting drinks in Midtown. The place was dimly lit and stylish, with a long, curved bar and stools accented with gold. Low lounge music played in the background, and Scout had just ordered her second martini. It felt like even a bottomless pit filled with alcohol wouldn't be enough to numb her current frustrations.

"So, it turns out that Mr. Family Values CEO was getting it on with someone other than his wife." She scrubbed a hand over her face. "And that someone left their very red, very lacy thong under the couch."

Isla's eyes widened. "Oh no."

"Oh yes." She shook her head. "And Mrs. Daniels seemed to care more about the fact that they might have damaged the new upholstery on her couch than the fact that her husband was cheating on her. Like, I get it, those stains are hard to remove. But come on!"

August snorted. "Can we please not talk about semen stains?

I want to order snacks soon and I'd like to keep my appetite, thank you very much."

"That's truly bizarre." Isla wrinkled her nose. "Of all the things to focus on..."

"Part of me wonders if that was a diversion so she didn't seem vulnerable." Scout reached for the martini as the bartender slid it toward her. She didn't even have the heart to return his interested stare, despite him having that rough-and-tumble look that she liked.

And the lack of interest is totally because of a crappy day in the office and nothing to do with finding out you're still hopelessly attracted to your estranged husband? Hmm?

"Definitely possible," August said, nodding. Her bright red hair was pulled up into a poufy ponytail and she was dressed simply in black jeans and a white T-shirt, in contrast to many of the other bar patrons. But that was August in a nutshell, practical to boot. "I can only imagine how it must have felt to have such a thing come out in front of all those people while trying to save face. Even thinking about that gives me hives."

That was one thing all three women had in common—they loved working *behind* the scenes rather than being in the spotlight. The thought of having to be "on" and "well-behaved" all the time made Scout want to flip the bird and lock herself away in her apartment.

No, thank you.

No wonder she hadn't lasted long adhering to her grandparents' strict house rules.

"So that's when she kicked you all out?" Isla asked.

"Yeah. I thought she was going to chase us out with a broom if we didn't pack up fast enough."

Isla reached for her wine and took a long gulp. "Now I know why you wanted to go over this in person. What a disaster."

"The art director called me when I was in a cab on the way over here. They'll go over the photos they already took and determine if we need to reschedule." Scout plucked the olive out of her martini and stuck it into her mouth, yanking the toothpick out. "Hopefully they've got a shot they can use."

"The show must go on, luckily for us."

"Don't worry, I'll be hounding the guy for an answer. I won't let us lose this job."

"I appreciate it." Isla shook her head.

"What a jerk, though." August made a sound of disgust. She was still nursing her first drink, something pink and fruity that looked like it had half a mint bush sticking out the side of it. "I hate those people who act so high-and-mighty about their moral standing and then do the exact opposite behind closed doors."

"I could not agree more." Scout circled her finger around the rim of the cocktail glass. "If you're so dissatisfied that you need to go elsewhere for sex, get a divorce and move on with your life."

Isla raised an eyebrow. "That *does* seem like good advice."

Scout bristled, knowing exactly what was coming next. Isla had been vocal about Scout initiating divorce proceedings for some time, believing it was holding her back from living her life. But it wasn't. She had nothing to do with Lane and didn't want anything from him. Moreover, she had zero desire to ever get married again, so until the day *he* found someone new, what was the harm in leaving it alone?

Usually, thinking about Lane moving on only produced numbness in response. Today, however, it made her martini taste sour.

"I'm clearly missing something," August said, swirling her straw through the slush in the bottom of her curved cocktail glass.

Isla shot Scout a look. "I was simply speaking about people who should get a divorce and move on with their lives…"

August's eyes shot up. "Um, what?"

Scout narrowed her eyes at Isla. "Just because you're my
boss doesn't mean I can't tell you to shut the hell up if we're
out of the office."

Isla nodded. "Fair."

"You're married?" August asked, her eyes wide. "I had no
idea."

"It's a long story," Scout grumbled. "The TLDR version
is that I fell head over heels for a dude I'd known for five seconds, got married in Vegas and then when we came back here
reality settled in and…it was crappy."

"Reality is a bitch," August mused sympathetically. "I can
attest to that."

"How so?" Scout was keen to shift the spotlight away from
herself.

And as much as August had shared a lot about her business plans and her dreams in the past few months that their
friendships had all blossomed, she didn't talk much about her
personal life. All Scout knew was that she had a strained relationship with her family.

Welcome to the club.

"The fantasy in your head almost never matches up to how
things turn out in real life," August replied, staring into her
drink for a minute. "And people end up becoming someone
other than who you thought they would be."

Cryptic, much?

"How was it, seeing him?" Isla asked, letting August off
the hook.

"Confusing." It was the only word that seemed to fit the
messy tangle of emotions in her gut. "I really thought I was
over him."

Isla raised an eyebrow. "But?"

"That feeling I had when I first met him, it's still there." She drained the remaining half of the martini in one fell swoop, but the alcohol had lost its potency. Droplets clung to the glass and caught the light, winking at her. Mocking her. "I'm still attracted to him. I'm still *intrigued* by him. It's like there's a bit of code left inside me that reminds me of all the good things, when I know it's safer to remember the bad."

August reached out and placed a hand on Scout's arm, squeezing. "I'm sure you had good times. It's not wrong to remember those things."

Only the memories of the good times were far too tempting. They whispered to her that she should forget about the bad, that maybe she should have tried to make it work. That maybe she could have had it all. That maybe she still loved him.

You don't still love him.

"The good times weren't enough," she said resolutely. "And mistakes have consequences. *That's* what I need to remember. I'll have to see him for these other events, and then, that's it. I'm grateful he's helping me out, but I can't let myself get messed up thinking about what might have happened if I'd stayed."

Because Scout could put up with a lot of things—but being made to feel like she wasn't good enough by someone who was *supposed* to love her wasn't one of them.

Her grandparents had only ever seen her as a carbon copy of her mother. Trouble. A train wreck waiting to happen. And she'd proved them right by getting married to a veritable stranger at twenty-one and springing it on them after the fact. They'd wrenched everything from her that day—any hope of her caring for Lizzie, any hope of a reconciliation with them, any hope that their opinion of her would ever change.

It was the lowest of the low. Rock bottom. Scout was *far* from perfect, but she wasn't a bad person. She wasn't careless or reckless or destructive. She'd loved Lane, and marrying him had felt right.

But when Lane had said those words—words she'd heard *so* many times before—he'd crossed a line. And she'd given up far too much for a man to do that to her.

That was worth remembering.

"Are you okay to go through with this?" Isla asked, her blue eyes swimming with concern. "I can take over if you need me to. And don't give me any crap about me being the boss, okay? We're in this together and if you need my help, then I am here for you."

"Thanks. But it's fine. I can handle it." She drew her shoulders back. "I made this mess and I'm going to clean it up."

As much as she appreciated that Isla was making the offer from a good place, Scout was determined not to accept it. She had to prove why she deserved a promotion and that meant handling tricky situations on her own. After all, if she crumbled at the first sign of pressure would Isla trust her with things in the future? Would her grandparents ever trust her to take care of her little sister?

No.

Being weak was not an option. Nothing—not even the unsettling attraction she still felt toward Lane—was going to stop her achieving her goal.

8

It turned out they *didn't* need to reshoot the Lively Paws campaign, thank goodness. But Scout had still sprung the extra events on Lane without giving him much of a say in the matter, while he got nothing in return. Because she knew he wouldn't refuse.

Lane was wired to help people. In fact, during their first week back in Manhattan together she'd commented that it seemed like his brother was taking advantage of Lane's generous nature.

And now she was doing exactly the same thing.

The least she could do was say thank-you. She'd logged off early from work with Isla's permission and had gone shopping for a collection of Lane's favorite things.

Dill bagels from his preferred bodega. A bottle of the Scotch he liked in a cool limited-edition bottle. A paperback from his favorite sci-fi author. Fancy coffee beans from a local roaster. Chocolate truffles from Jacques Torres. And Lane's ultimate guilty pleasure—Cool Ranch Doritos, which Scout thought were an abomination to taste buds everywhere.

But she bought three bags to show him she was serious.

She packaged all the items in a gift bag from a funky boutique stationery store and headed to Lane's apartment on foot. The plan was to leave the gift bag with the concierge in his building, because she knew he wouldn't be home from work yet. Was that a chicken move? Maybe.

But was it sometimes smart to be a chicken? She certainly thought so.

Seeing him twice in a short space of time had unlatched something inside her. The first six months after Scout had walked out had been torture—she'd cried a lot, mentally beating herself up for being so stupid. But eventually the tears had stopped and she'd put Lane out of her mind as much as possible.

Only now it had become clear that "putting him out of her mind" was nothing more than suppression. The thoughts and memories hadn't vanished, they'd simply been shoved into a box. Seeing him had it all flooding back to her.

Snatches of them in bed together, with Lane's wicked smile and wandering hands. Cuddling on the couch with him and Star, feeling as though she belonged to a proper family unit for the first time ever. The day she got married in a second-hand wedding gown, with no one around, but still feeling like she was truly loved.

"Stop it," she said, as she turned a corner onto the street where Lane's apartment building stood tall and proud, like a gleaming trophy of steel and glass. "Just drop the gift bag off, get through the next few weeks and then go back to pretending it never happened."

Squaring her shoulders, she lifted her chin and walked toward the building. Heavy glass doors slid open to the vestibule and she jabbed the button for the concierge intercom.

"Delivery," she said, and the second lot of doors slid open.

The building was much nicer than the one she lived in currently and had a single reception desk, behind which the head concierge manager sat, wearing a uniform of a white shirt with a black blazer. He looked up as she approached.

"I'm delivering this for Mr. Lane Halliday, apartment 1709," she said.

"I can take that off you now." A deep baritone came from behind Scout and she knew without turning around that it was Lane himself. "It'll save Mr. Schultz the work of putting it into the system."

Dammit. She'd been hoping to butter the man up from a distance, not turn herself into butter from the sound of his voice.

Scout turned and produced her best, most-practiced, professional smile. "I didn't come up because I assumed you'd still be at work."

He was wearing a pair of dark denim jeans and sneakers, along with a soft black sweater that perfectly fitted his muscular chest and arms. The dark outfit made him seem even taller and longer limbed, and his green eyes shone without competition from any other colors.

"So you *do* remember that I'm a workaholic," he said, the corner of his mouth lifting slightly. "And you were hoping to avoid me."

"No," she said, feigning insult. "Not at all. It's only that I know I'm already asking a lot given how busy you are, and…I didn't want to impose."

He raised an eyebrow. "Since when do you care about imposing?"

She sucked on the inside of her cheek. He was, of course, referring to the fact that she used to be the kind of woman who'd crash a party without thinking twice—like she convinced him to do in Vegas. They'd snuck into someone's fancy gala, after swiping some guest lanyards from a table, and had a wonderful night of free champagne, canapés and wild sex in a private bathroom.

"Maybe I've changed," she said primly.

"Hmm. Shame."

The concierge cleared his throat behind Scout, and the noise made her jump.

Skittish, much?

"Why don't you come up for a bit?" Lane suggested. "There's something I wanted to talk to you about anyway."

"Okay." The word slipped out before she could even think about the consequences, and she trailed after him as he headed toward the elevators.

The heels on her ankle boots clacked against the polished tile-covered floor, and the mirrored panels surrounding the elevator doors reflected her image back tenfold. Her hair was pulled into a ponytail, and she'd done little more with her makeup than smudge some eyeliner into her lash-line and swipe some glossy lipstick across her lips.

If she'd known that she was going to see Lane, then…

Then, nothing. You're not here to look good.

The elevator doors opened to reveal an empty carriage. Being alone with Lane in the small space reminded her *way* too much of that first night in Vegas—the way she could feel the heat of his gaze warming her up, despite the fact that she was wearing a scrap of sequined fabric that could only hope to be a dress when it grew up.

She hadn't even wanted to go on that trip, but an old friend from high school was marrying some rich dude ten years her senior and he was paying for everything—flights, accommodation, room service. Scout had never been out of the state before. It seemed too good an opportunity to pass up, even if the rest of the women who were going were frivolous and vain and called Scout "a loser" behind her back. Isla had stayed home to look after Dani, and the very first night, Scout had regretted going with all her being.

She was heading back to her room after breaking away from the bachelorette party, feeling demoralized and alone. When she'd stepped into the elevator, there was this shy, nerdy guy staring at her like he'd seen a living goddess, and she'd teased him for it.

Instead of being insulted, he joked with her, espousing the virtues of pocket protectors. Then he asked her what she was doing.

"Going back to my room," she said with a sad sigh.

"It's not even ten," he scoffed. *"You can't call it quits yet."*

"I can," she replied stubbornly.

"Okay." He nodded, stuffing his hands into his pockets. *"But have you drunk out of a fishbowl yet?"*

She laughed, surprised by the unexpected question. *"No."*

"Then, I'm sorry, ma'am. You can't go back to your room yet." His green eyes twinkled. *"It's a local Vegas law, subsection 450, that hot women in sequined dresses are not supposed to go to bed until a minimum of one fishbowl cocktail has been consumed."*

"Subsection 450, huh?" She didn't want to smile, and Lord help her, she tried to stop it, but the straight-faced guy in the elevator made her feel tingly and warm all over.

"Subsection 450, part A recommends that fishbowls be consumed with a partner," he added.

"It's only a recommendation?"

"Of course. It wouldn't be right to force a woman to share a fish-bowl against her will... But it is recommended."

"Do you know anyone who would be up for sharing one with me?" she asked, feeling shy all of a sudden. Scout had never been short of male attention—she'd inherited her mother's shiny blond hair, long legs and big hazel eyes, after all—but most of the time pickup lines felt skeezy and gross.

But maybe that was because nobody had ever led with an offer of a fishbowl before.

"Scout?" Lane's voice popped the memory, like piercing a bubble with a pin.

"Huh?" She shook herself. "Sorry. I, uh... What did you say?"

"I asked how you were doing."

The elevator dinged and the doors slid open. Scout stepped into the hallway, feeling well and truly rattled.

Note to self: no more elevator rides with Lane.

Lane watched as Scout marched on ahead of him toward his apartment's front door. Her ponytail swished like a band of gold silk against her back and it was impossible not to admire the sway of her hips and backside, encased in a short black denim skirt, her long legs protected from the cold by a pair of thick tights.

"Oh fine, busy. You know how it is," Scout said, laughing, but barely any sound came out. "Work, work, work."

Maybe she *had* changed, because the Scout he knew had once told him he should work to live, not live to work. He wasn't sure he would ever agree with that sentiment, but after the words had come out of her mouth, she'd started crawling down his body and he could very well have been swayed.

He grabbed his keys out and let them into his apartment. Like last time, it was odd to see a relic of his past against the modern backdrop of his new life. The two things didn't fit well together.

"So," he said, tossing his keys into a bowl. "You first. To what do I owe the visit?"

"I, uh… Where's Star?" Her eyes darted around the apartment, worry streaking across her face. He wanted to think it was because she was concerned about the dog's well-being, but more than likely it was because Star was her way out of the problem she had with her client.

"Custodial visit," he said. Shock registered on her face and it took him a second for the penny to drop. "No, not like that. I'm not with… Star is at Beth's house. I made an agreement with Ariella where she gets to spend one night a month with Star."

His niece adored the little dog and the feeling was mutual. And while Lane didn't like to ever leave Star with anyone, Ariella had literally drawn up a proposal in crayon about why she was responsible enough to have Star one night per month, including such items as how well she took care of her Barbies, that she always cleaned up her room when asked *and* that she tolerated her baby brother, even though he was an annoying crybaby.

With such compelling arguments, how could he possibly refuse?

"Oh sure. I mean, it's your business. I'm sure you've had loads of girlfriends since me and I don't care at all." The way the words tripped over themselves indicated that maybe that wasn't entirely true.

It shouldn't have made Lane feel good, but it did.

"Anyway," she said, collecting herself. "I realized that I sprang the request for Star to attend the extra shoots in a pretty crappy manner and you're basically getting nothing from helping me. So I wanted to show my appreciation."

She thrust the gift bag toward him and he took it, curious. Peering inside, the contents made his heart thump unevenly in his chest.

"You remembered that I love all these things." He frowned. How was that even possible? They'd been together such a short time and he wasn't even sure he'd ever mentioned his favorite author.

Yet there was a brand-spanking new copy of the latest book in the series sitting right there. As far as he knew, it wasn't even out yet, because he'd put his name down for a copy at his local bookstore, and they hadn't rung him. He picked it up, eager to read the blurb.

"Yeah, I did." She looked excited as she pointed to the book. "That one wasn't even on the shelf. I knew it was coming out in a few days and I convinced the guy to sell it to me early."

He had to laugh—the woman could be highly persuasive when she wanted to be.

"And Cool Ranch Doritos. I haven't bought these in ages!"

"I would have thought you'd be more excited about the fancy chocolates or the Scotch." She shook her head, laughing. "Well, I always did say that you—"

"Had the palate of a five-year-old," he finished with her.

Silence settled over the room as he held the gift bag in his hand, feeling more like it was a grenade rather than some pretty paper and ribbon. The thoughtful gesture touched him.

But at the same time, it rattled him, because it didn't jibe with the image of Scout in his mind—which was one of a woman who'd flitted away, without giving him a second thought, and who probably never loved him like she'd claimed.

Yet now he held a care package of his favorite things, curated so perfectly he wasn't even sure his own sister could do a better job.

"How did you know about the book?" he asked. "I don't remember doing much reading when we were together."

Too busy making love every chance we got.

"I went through your bookshelves one time," she said. "I was looking for something to read while you were out, and I noticed you had a lot by this one author. All the spines were cracked and the pages were dog-eared, which told me you'd read them more than once."

She'd paid attention to the details of him.

"And I got the box of truffles without any of the fruit-flavored ones, because I remembered you don't like mixing fruit and chocolate." Her hands knotted in front of her.

How did he reconcile this thoughtful, soft version of her with the sequined vixen in the Vegas elevator? With the bride he'd carried over the threshold? With the woman who'd broken his heart when she left and wouldn't return his calls?

"Thank you," he said, nodding. "Do you want to stay for a drink?"

She hesitated for a moment before answering, "I can't. I'm actually meeting Isla for a bridal gown fitting."

"She's getting married. Wow." He nodded. There hadn't been anything in the press about Isla's engagement to Theo Garrison—aka New York royalty—but he figured that's probably how they both wanted it.

As someone who'd spent some time on Manhattan's Most Eligible lists himself—which was about as far from the truth as it could be—he understood that feeling of being an animal behind glass. It wasn't fun.

"I'm thrilled for her." Scout smiled, but it felt a bit brittle. He knew she cared for her best friend like they were sisters, and any reservations would be more about her feelings on marriage itself. "It's going to be something classy and intimate. Well, not as intimate as *some* weddings, I guess."

Lane laughed. "You mean intimate but not quite a celebrant-and-a-single-witness-off-the-street levels of intimate."

"I still think it was a great wedding," she said quietly, her gaze catching his. There was a tenderness there, layered with regret and confusion and perhaps even a little hope.

You're reading too far into it, seeing things that aren't there.

Hadn't he done that before, been blinded by potential rather than focusing on what was in front of him? With Scout, and then with his brother? Been too naive, too trusting.

Or maybe he could have seen what was going on, but instead he'd chosen to stick his head in the sand.

"I did, too," he said, placing the gift bag down.

There were so many things he wanted to say. To ask.

Why didn't you give us a chance to work things out?

Why didn't you take my calls?

Why were you so afraid of what everyone would think?

The last question was directed at himself—because he *had* been worried about what everyone would think. His parents. His siblings. The tech journos who'd tipped him to be the next big thing. The investors who had high hopes and higher expectations.

He'd worried that turning up married to a girl he met in Vegas would signal that he wasn't ready to go big. Wasn't responsible enough to run a company. Wasn't smart enough to soar.

In the end, his fear had come back to bite him in the ass, because he'd delayed introducing Scout to his family, and when he'd tried to explain why the marriage would be perceived as risky and reckless, she'd snapped.

He thought it was just an argument. That he'd wake up in the morning and kiss her and apologize. That he'd have time to think through how to manage his image while introducing Scout into his life.

But by morning she was gone.

"I can hear your brain working overtime from here," she said.

"I never did know what to say around you."

She shook her head and wrinkled her nose. "Are you kidding? A guy who opens with important information about Vegas law subsections and fishbowls knows *exactly* what he's doing."

"I was a tool."

"You were different."

He took a step toward her, drawn by an invisible force that he'd felt the second they met. It wasn't love at first sight. Connection at first sight, maybe. Potential at first sight. But it had turned to love so sharply and so strongly it was like being in the eye of a tornado, the world whipping around him while he stood there, trapped and terrified and mesmerized.

The urge to kiss her was like horses dragging him forward, need pulsing through his veins with a mixture of fantasy and memory. Her lips parted and her eyes drank him in, lashes touching gently with each blink.

"What did you want to talk to me about?" she asked, her voice breathy.

"Uh…"

This is what she did to you last time. You were dumbstruck. Suckered in.

Never again.

Reality rushed back with force, almost knocking him off his feet. What the hell was he thinking, wanting to kiss her? He was supposed to be asking for a divorce. He *would* ask for a divorce.

No backing down.

She blinked, as though she felt the change in the air and wrapped her arms around herself, going into protection mode.

"I spoke with my lawyer," he said, unable to think of a way to broach the topic without coming across like an asshole. "About, uh, finalizing things. Between us."

"Oh, of course." Her face returned to the bland mask he'd seen earlier. "Good idea."

"Good idea?"

"We should definitely get divorced. I mean, I thought…" Her expression faltered for a nanosecond, just long enough for him to glimpse the vulnerability inside her. "I was expecting you to send papers after I left."

"I've been busy." It was a terribly weak excuse.

"Me too." She nodded. "And so we're clear, I don't want anything from you. Whatever I need to sign so that the legal aspects are taken care of is fine by me. I won't make things difficult."

Lane waited for relief to wash over him, but he felt surprisingly sad. It was going to be over in the most official way possible. "I appreciate it."

"Anyway, I have to run. I really hope you enjoy the goodies, and thank you for agreeing to let me use Star for a few extra days." The smile was bright, like artificial lighting. "Toodle-oo."

Toodle-oo?

He watched as she exited his apartment for the second time, a sense of vacancy and emptiness growing inside him. He should be happy. This was exactly what he wanted and it seemed like she wasn't going to put up a fight.

But for some reason, getting everything he thought he wanted felt a whole lot like getting nothing at all.

9

Scout hustled out of Lane's apartment building and into the street, her cheeks burning and tears stinging her eyes. What the hell was wrong with her? She *knew* that getting divorced was the best thing to do and he had every right to ask for it. Heck, he was doing her a favor by getting the ball rolling so she didn't have to.

She should be dancing in the street!

Instead, she wanted to thump her fist against the wall. The excitement on his face when he'd looked through the gift bag had filled her with such joy. She hadn't been prepared for it. That genuine smile was like pure gold, because she knew Lane didn't open up to many people.

And she had been one of the precious few in his inner circle.

"Not anymore," she said to herself as she headed toward the bridal shop to meet Isla.

On the walk over, her phone rang and a picture of a gap-toothed Lizzie flashed onto the screen. Shoving aside her problems, she swiped her thumb over the screen to answer the call.

"Hey girl! How's my favorite little sister?"

"Scout."

There was sniffling on the other end of the line, and her heart plummeted. She knew exactly what conversation they were about to have. "What's going on?"

"Grandma and Grandpa told me that we're moving to California, but I don't want to move!" she wailed. Then there was more sniffling. "That's so far away. I don't want to change schools. I like it here and all my friends are here. And then, how will I see you? I asked if you were coming and they said no. Why can't you come? Don't you want to live close to me?"

If Scout had thought nothing could be as painful as the day she left Lane, this moment proved that wasn't quite true. It felt like her chest was being cleaved in half.

"Of course I want to live close to you," Scout said, fighting back tears. "I promise we'll work something out."

"How will we work something out?" she said, her voice wobbling. "They told me this was not negotiable."

Scout could practically hear her grandfather's voice saying those words. "Let me talk to them, okay?"

"Do you think I could come and live with you?" Lizzie's voice rose to an excited pitch. "I know your apartment is small, but I don't take up much space. We could even share a room!"

"We're not sharing a room," Scout said with a laugh. As much as she loved her little sister, she could think of nothing worse than sharing a room with a teenager. "But we can explore some options."

In the background, she heard "who's that?" in a harsh, feminine voice.

"Don't say anything to Grandma and Grandpa yet, okay? Let me have that conversation with them."

"Okay, Scout. I love you."

"I love you, too, sis."

She ended the call and let out a sigh. Talk about a roller coaster of emotions. She was desperate for a glass of wine and a brainstorming session. If she had any chance of convincing her grandparents that she was finally ready to look after Lizzie, she really needed to think through how she was going to present the idea to them.

But first, wedding dress shopping.

As she double-checked the address for the shop on her phone, she rounded the last corner and almost walked right into Isla and Dani.

"Hey, you two!" She brought Dani in for a squeeze, and the teen hugged her back.

She was a year and a half older than Lizzie, and was quickly blossoming into a young woman.

"I am *so* excited," Dani announced with a grin. "Isla asked me to be her maid of honor. I've never been in a bridal party before. Actually, I've never even been to a wedding!"

Scout caught Isla's eye, and her friend looked as happy as happy could be. The three of them walked, chatting about all the details Isla and Theo had planned for the wedding, until they arrived at the bridal boutique.

In the window, two glossy white mannequins wore exquisite wedding dresses in polar-opposite styles. One had a full skirt with a cinched waist and a delicate lace bodice. The other was sleek and minimal in a pale ivory silk, with spaghetti-thin straps and a draped neckline.

"Wow." Dani pressed her face to the window. "I bet these are expensive."

Isla shot Scout a look. "The second you say the *W* word, *everything* is expensive. I was happy to get a dress on consignment."

"Let me guess. Theo insisted." Scout smiled.

"You know it."

Isla's fiancé had probably never even touched a secondhand item in his entire life. If some rich people had grown up with a silver spoon in their mouths, then Theo had grown up with a platinum, diamond-encrusted spoon in his. But he was generous and wanted Isla and Dani to have the best of everything. No expense spared.

Isla rang the doorbell, which was a mother-of-pearl button, inlaid in a filigreed silver casing. God, even the doorbells screamed luxury here. No doubt the attention to detail was meant to reassure brides that every aspect of their shopping experience would be carefully managed, with no detail too small to warrant a luxurious touch.

A second later, the door was opened by a woman with silver hair pulled up into a plump bun and pink lipstick artfully applied. The shade perfectly matched the floral print on her blouse, which she wore over navy slacks and sensible black shoes. A tape measure was draped around her neck.

"Isla Thompson?" She smiled, her eyes darting between Scout and Isla until Isla raised her hand. "I'm Marnie. I'll be looking after you all today."

"Nice to meet you," Isla replied. "This is my sister, Danielle, and my best friend, Scout."

"Please, come in."

The inside of the bridal store was everything the window display promised—ornate, high quality, decadent. Rows of frothy white gowns lined the main room. There was a pedestal in the center, which had a large gold-framed mirror in front of it. Several more mirrors were dotted around, as if trying to catch the light at varying angles. Several cabinets were filled with twinkling jewels and other bridal accessories.

"It's so sparkly in here," Dani breathed. "Oh look! They have tiaras."

Scout tried not to scrunch her nose. She couldn't exactly claim they were tacky when she'd gotten married in a Vegas wedding chapel, now, could she? Still, having seen several women she'd worked with get married over the years, she got the impression that some people wanted the Disney Princess experience for their big day more than they wanted the marriage itself.

Bitter, much?

"I have some selections pulled, based on the preference form that you filled out, Isla," Marnie said, gesturing to a rack that was sitting in an archway with a heavy drape drawn to one side. Presumably that was the changing area. "We'll start there, but if none of those options work, then that is totally fine. We can look at anything that takes your fancy."

Isla suddenly looked a little pale, but she mustered a smile. "Great."

"You'll know when you've found the right dress. I always say that my brides fall for their dress like they fall for their husband or wife." Marnie ran her hand over a small rack of gowns, pushing the hangers to one side as if looking for a specific dress. The metal hangers made a soft *clink, clink, clink* as she selected option number one. "It's all about listening to your gut. If you've got butterflies in your tummy, then that's a very good sign."

Pass me a bucket.

"This one is our newest design. I'll hang it in the change

room here, and you come in when you're all set." Marnie nodded and then left Isla to have a moment to get ready.

There was a bottle of champagne chilling in a bucket with
a few glimmering flutes sitting neatly on a tray next to it.
There was even a special blue bag from Tiffany, waiting patiently, with a handwritten tag hanging off the side that had
Isla's name written on it in perfect calligraphy.

"This is *a lot*," Isla whispered to Scout.

"The doorbell outside was a lot. This is…something else."

For two women who'd grown up the way they both did—
never being certain of what the next day would bring—being
in a place like this was strange and unsettling. Scout could
only imagine what Isla must feel like, being swept up in Theo's
world.

It felt like they'd landed on some alien planet. An alien
planet with *a lot* of sparkles.

"Please don't let me walk out of this place with a dress that
makes me look like a marshmallow." Isla grimaced. "And
don't let me look at the price tags, either, or else I'll puke."

"This is supposed to be fun," Scout reminded her as she
watched Dani out of the corner of her eye. The young girl
was stuck in a trance by something shiny in one of the cabinets. Such a magpie, that one.

"It *will* be fun on the day. It's just everything else…" Isla
sucked in a deep breath. "I know, I'm being ridiculous. Anyone else would be thrilled to have a blank check to buy the
dress of their dreams. I'm being ungrateful."

"You're entitled to feel your feelings, okay? Your mother
ran off and left you alone because she wanted to get married
to some guy, so I'm not surprised that you feel a little squirrelly about the whole wedding thing."

Her shoulders dropped. "You're so right. That *has* been
playing on my mind."

"How's Dani taking it?" Scout lowered her voice. "Is she coping?"

Isla nodded. "She's a trooper. Theo is really good with her, too. He makes sure that she always feels included in whatever we do and that she's part of the decision-making process for the house. They even have a movie night together once a week when I go to yoga."

"He's a good egg."

"He really is."

"You're marrying the right guy." Scout grabbed her friend gently by the shoulders. "The wedding is going to be intimate and beautiful. Marriage didn't ruin your family. Your mother's selfishness did. More importantly, you're not her."

"Thanks, Scout. I needed to hear that." She drew her shoulders back. "Okay, this is supposed to be fun. It *will* be fun."

"That's the spirit. Now go try on a stupidly extravagant dress."

Scout settled on the couch with Dani, enjoying the way the young girl yammered on about ballet and school and what TikTok accounts she was currently obsessed with. She pulled out her phone and made Scout watch silly dance routines. She was a sweet kid. Good-hearted, like her big sister.

"Are you ever going to get married one day?" Dani asked suddenly.

Scout blinked. God. How was she supposed to answer *that*? Dani had been eight or nine when Scout had gotten married, and even though she was close with Dani, she'd never gotten the chance to introduce Lane before it all fell apart.

"Are *you* going to get married one day?" Scout parroted.

"Probably. I mean, what's the point of life without falling in love?" Dani looked up at her, blue eyes wide with curiosity.

"Love comes in many different forms. It's not always romantic. Friendship is love and family is love. And you can have love for a job or a dream, like you do with ballet."

"Yeah, sure," Dani said with a bit of signature teenage drawl. "But they don't write ballets about falling in love with work, do they? Or even friendship. It's always about romance."

"Not everything in a person's life should be about romance. We're more than our relationships."

Maybe that's why her marriage with Lane had suffered—because Scout didn't have anything else except him and Lizzie. But Lane had a career and a future and a family he was loyal to. His refusal to let her be part of all that had cut so deep because it had shown her how little her own life contained. When she walked away, there was barely anything left.

"Ladies, prepare yourselves." Marnie scurried out of the changing room. "This is dress number one."

Isla came out looking like a deer in headlights. Scout's mouth popped open. The dress was…

Hideous.

Even Dani—a girl who could fill any kind of pause with a mile-a-minute chatter—was stunned into silence.

The dress was white with a simple square-necked bodice and floor-length skirt, which was capped with a ruffle that looked better suited to a bed skirt than a couture dress. Sheer organza sleeves might have been cute, if it wasn't for the strange volume at the shoulders that made it look like she was getting married at a renaissance fair.

This whole frou-frou thing was so *not* Scout's jam. It wasn't Isla's, either.

"I know the sleeves are a little out there, but mutton sleeves are one of the hottest runway trends this year."

"Mutton sleeves?" Isla squeaked. "Uh…"

The poor thing was too sweet to say that she hated the dress and would rather set it alight than wear it a moment longer.

She might not be the matron of honor, but Scout could still step in and help a sister out.

"As much as this dress is—" *think, brain, think* "—so innovative and fashion-forward, perhaps a simpler style might be better? It's going to be quite a small and intimate wedding after all. I think a dress like this begs for a large audience, don't you agree?"

Isla shot her a grateful look and Marnie nodded. "I understand completely. Let's try another one."

As the woman ushered Isla back into the change room, Dani and Scout exchanged a look.

"No amount of love is worth looking like *that*," Dani said, wrinkling her nose like she'd smelled something particularly offensive.

Scout chuckled. "What happened to 'it's always about romance,' huh?"

"I'd rather die single." Dani looked her dead in the eye. "No boy is worth those sleeves."

The chuckled turned into a full-blown belly laugh and Scout had to dab a tear from her eye. "I couldn't agree more."

It felt good to release some of the tension of the day. They might not write ballets about female friendship, but Scout wasn't sure she'd survive without hers.

An hour and a half—and five dresses—later, Isla had picked her gown. It was a pale silver, instead of white, and had a simple yet modern sleeveless design with an open back and a neckline that cut straight across the collarbones. She'd avoided Marnie's upselling techniques, opting to go without a veil or extravagant jewelry. Instead, she selected a simple pair of pearl earrings and an art deco–inspired clip for her hair.

Now the three women were sitting in a cafe. Dani had a pair of headphones on while she watched something on her cell and sucked on a drink that looked like it was made of blended My Little Ponies.

"That first dress, though." Isla groaned. "When I wrote on the form that I liked 'interesting details,' I did *not* mean mutton chop sleeves or whatever the hell they were called."

Scout snorted. "What were the designers thinking?"

"It was uncomfortable, too. So itchy." Isla shuddered. "Anyway, thank you for stepping in and saying something. I was so dumbfounded I couldn't speak."

"Hey, you know I'm always there to piss people off if necessary."

"You don't piss people off." Isla pulled a face and took a sip of her hazelnut latte. "And don't give your family as an example because your grandmother was born with a pole up her ass."

"They're moving to California." Scout blurted the words out before she could think about whether she was ready to talk about it. "And they're taking Lizzie."

"They're *what?*" The utter panic on Isla's face made Scout feel reassured that she wasn't overreacting by wanting to go all mama bear on the situation. But as tempting as it was to drive to her grandparents' place and have it out with them, she had to be strategic.

If there was one lesson she'd learned living with them in her teens, it was that arguing did not get her anywhere.

"Tell me you're joking," she said.

"I wish." Scout filled Isla in on the conversation with her grandfather.

"So, what are you going to do?" Isla asked.

"I don't want her to go, obviously."

"Understandable." Isla sipped her drink. "Did you say anything?"

"Not at the time. I was...stunned. But I'm going to ask

them if they would consider letting Lizzie live with me." She sighed. "I know it failed hard the last time I tried, but… people our age have babies all the time and manage to keep them alive. I can handle a thirteen-year-old who knows how to make her own snacks."

"Of course you can. I mean, teenagers come with their own sets of problems, for sure." Isla glanced at Dani, who was oblivious to the conversation going on around her. "But Lizzie is a good kid."

"Exactly."

"I think you'd do a better job raising her than they would," Isla replied, with a wrinkle in her nose.

"You think?" Scout asked.

"Yes. Because you're a better person than either of them will ever be," Isla replied fiercely, her voice rising with each word. "You were still a child when they kicked you out. And for what? Breaking curfew? Smoking? God, even underage drinking doesn't warrant you putting a child out on the fucking street."

A few people turned their heads and Dani pulled one earbud out to see what was going on, but Isla waved at her to keep watching her video.

"Sorry," she said. "It gets my goat, even now. I'm still so *mad* they treated you like that."

"I appreciate you being in my corner," Scout replied. "It means a lot."

"Always."

"I try so hard to be civil with them for Lizzie's sake. If it wasn't for her, I'd never see them again." She sighed. "But I don't want her to forget about me."

"She won't. She loves you."

One good thing she could say about her grandparents was that, while they kept a tight grip on how much time she spent with Lizzie, at least they hadn't poisoned her sister's mind and made her think Scout was a bad person. Small blessings.

"Does she know yet?"

"Yeah. They broke the news today and she called me wanting to know why I couldn't move with them." Scout scrubbed a hand over her face. "The kid knows how to tug on my heartstrings, that's for damn sure."

"So you're going to talk to them about her staying here. Have you got a strategy?"

"I'm going to present them with all the reasons why it would be better for Lizzie if she remained in New York." Scout sipped her coffee and churned through the plan in her head. "Such as her being able to stay in school with her friends and the teachers who know her."

"You think they'll go for that?"

"No," she replied honestly. "But I have to try."

Scout wasn't going to bring up the part of her plan that involved getting promoted at work so she could find a nicer apartment with a second bedroom. The last thing she wanted was for Isla to be guilted into giving her something. That wouldn't be good for their relationship nor for Scout's self-esteem.

"I could move closer to her school so she can walk there herself every day. All I have to do is feed her, put a roof over her head and make sure she has enough sex ed so she doesn't get pregnant."

"Don't even joke about that." Isla cast a glance at Dani. "There was a girl at Dani's school who got pregnant last year. I had to have the whole birds-and-the-bees talk with her while she made gagging sounds at me for twenty minutes."

"You're a responsible big sister."

"So are you, Scout. I know your grandparents have piled a whole lot of doubts into your head over the years, but you're an excellent influence on the people around you." Isla reached for her hand and squeezed. "You're smart and creative and hardworking."

They were *not* words Scout associated with herself. After all, if she was so smart she wouldn't have accidentally dyed a dog pink!

"I can see you trying to come up with an argument to refute me," Isla said. "But I won't hear it."

"I'm not perfect."

"Nobody's perfect, girl. Get that through your skull. We *all* have our flaws, trust me."

Still, Scout could stand to tip the balance more toward her good points versus her bad points. And she was determined not to screw up this time. The Hot Mess Express had pulled into its final station! She was going to shed that image once and for all.

As of right now, Scout was officially getting her life on track. She was going to get her promotion—legitimately— then convince her grandparents to let Lizzie stay with her in New York *and* she was finally going to get divorced from Lane.

10

Lane sat in his office, leaning back in his chair and staring up at the ceiling while his head of programming, Mark, talked through a coding problem. The team was getting ready to issue an update for their Unison app, and it was the first time that Lane had been totally hands-off. It had taken a lot of prodding and poking from Rav to hire someone to oversee the coders so Lane could take a step back and focus on the bigger picture.

Frankly, Lane was more comfortable in the weeds. The sixty-thousand-foot view was Rav's bag. But they'd agreed that if they wanted to expand the business, Lane needed to be focused on what Unison 2.0 would look like, what other products they could launch and what up-and-coming tech developments they wanted to jump on.

Besides, the guy sitting in front of him was an MIT grad with some serious skills. Lane trusted him to do his job.

"I'm sure there's a more elegant way we can approach this new functionality. Because at the moment, it feels a bit like we're bolting it into the side rather than seamlessly integrating it," Mark said. "The last thing we want is a jarring user experience."

"Agreed," Lane replied. "I wonder if—"

"Lane?" His assistant, Julie, poked her head into the office. "Uh...sorry to interrupt. We've had an incident."

In the tech world, the word *incident* meant something serious—usually a data breach or system failure or a service outage, something that could result in major reputational damage and regulatory fines. But if that was the case, it wouldn't be his executive assistant delivering the message.

"It's Star." She cringed. "I had her sitting at my desk after her walk, and she crept away when I wasn't looking."

He pushed up out of his seat, worry flashing through him like lightning.

"She's okay," Julie assured him. "But she's...stuck."

"Stuck?"

He stalked out of the office and it didn't take long to figure out what had happened.

Rav had insisted on making their office an "innovation garden" where ideas could be planted and grown. He'd taken the model of Silicon Valley start-ups, where the office was a place people *wanted* to be. They had a world-renowned chef running the cafeteria, where staff got all meals for free, and a "creative thinking zone" filled with leather beanbags and whiteboards and net hammocks...which was what his dog was currently stuck in.

"Oh Star," he groaned.

"I tried to help her, but she nearly took my hand off." His

operations manager, a whip smart woman in her forties, motioned to the dog. "Be careful."

"She won't bite me," he said, as he went over to her. "How did she even get in there?"

The dog had somehow gotten her legs tangled up in the netting and was whining miserably. She looked up at him with her soulful black eyes, begging him to help. A ripple of murmuring went through the office, but no one offered any suggestions.

Not once since they'd opened this office had she *ever* done something like this.

"What is *wrong* with you lately?" He went to untangle her, and she growled at him. Lane blinked in surprise. "Excuse me. Do you want to look like a fly trapped in a spider's net the rest of your life?"

Star whined.

"No growling." He gently touched her and she wriggled, further entangling herself. "Hold still."

Untangling the poor dog was like trying to solve a Rubik's Cube that was fighting back.

"Lane?" Mark came up beside him. "I've got a meeting with the development team in five. We need to finish up."

He could feel the man's impatience radiating off him. Lane knew some people in the office thought it was weird he brought his dog to work. Hell, there'd even been an article or two written about it in tech media and on some social platforms.

Search Reddit and you'd find more than a handful of threads about how it wasn't "masculine" for a guy like him to have a small fluffy dog glued to his hip. This was usually followed with speculation about his sexuality. Lane believed that love was love, and as far as he was concerned, people should be with whoever they wanted, and fuck anyone who had a problem with that.

He also strongly believed that the idea a man would be considered weak because he cared for animals was about the dumbest thing he'd ever heard. But empathy, he'd realized, was in frighteningly short supply. Especially online.

"I am presently in the middle of something," Lane said, as he continued working to free Star. "So have your meeting with the team and we'll catch up later."

Mark huffed. "You really want to delay making a decision on this because of a dog? Can't your assistant take care of it?"

The guy was smart. He was also relatively new, which meant he'd possibly mistaken Lane's quiet and introverted nature to mean he was a pushover. Most people in the company deferred to Rav as the big boss, because he had a larger-than-life personality to command that respect. And yeah, in the past, Lane had let people treat him in a less-than-stellar way.

These days, however, Lane was *not* a pushover.

"Let me give you a tip," he said, turning around to face his employee. Mark was dressed in jeans and sneakers with a button-down shirt, and had one of those irritating hipster beanies that slouched at the back of his head like a sad Santa hat missing its pom-pom. "Look at the priorities of the person who signs your paycheck. If you can't possibly understand why they care about something, then maybe you're working in the wrong company."

He wrinkled his brows. "You mean that I should care about dogs?"

"You should care about how you treat those around you, human or otherwise. Because I don't tolerate assholes in my company." He looked the guy up and down. "Are you an asshole?"

"What? No," Mark spluttered.

"Then don't tell someone else how to manage their time," he said. "The world will not fall apart if you have to wait an hour to get an answer from me. Have the meeting with the team and then come and find me. And remember, I'm your boss."

Suitably chastised, the guy turned and headed out of the room. Shaking his head, Lane turned back to Star.

"I don't want to leave you at home by yourself all day long, but I can't have you causing chaos in the office." He extracted one of her paws from the netting. "I especially can't have you accidentally guillotining off a body part with this netting."

A few seconds later she was free, and when he picked her up, she nuzzled into the crook of his neck.

"First growling and now you're snuggling. Women." He rolled his eyes and Star snorted, as if saying "ugh, men" in response. "I don't know what is up with you at the moment. You've been acting so strange."

Lane headed into his office and closed the door behind him. When he put the dog down onto the floor, she trotted straight toward her bed and jumped into it, curling up into a ball and promptly falling sleep. Shaking his head, he dropped onto his desk chair and glanced at his laptop screen, but the words swam in front of him.

Concentration wasn't coming easy of late.

Scout turning up on his doorstep—and then proceeding to unsettle him to his core—definitely had something to do with it. But on top of that, Beth appeared to be on a glue-the-family-back-together mission and, like how she did most things, was trying to steamroll her way toward a resolution. Last night, when he'd gone to collect Star from her place, she'd voiced her opinions again about him giving Todd a second chance.

Not. Going. To. Happen.

Todd was no longer a part of his life and he wasn't looking

to change that. He didn't blame *only* his brother for what happened, because there were definitely more factors at play. Like how Lane's mother had constantly given in to her youngest son from day one. Like how Beth had covered for him over and over to prevent conflict in the family. Like how Lane had ignored Scout's comment about Todd seeming to take advantage of his time and money.

She'd only been around for a month, had only ever heard him talking to Lane on the phone, and she picked it up immediately.

Maybe you should have listened to her more and been more concerned with her feelings than what your family would think of the marriage.

His laptop screen went dark and he angrily jabbed at his mouse to turn it back on. The words and numbers still swam, however. What was the point of getting wrapped up in all this? Mistakes had been made, and now everyone had to wear the consequences. He would have nothing to do with Todd, no matter what his sister said. As for Scout…yeah, he should have handled things differently. But that didn't excuse her walking out.

A marriage wasn't supposed to crumble at the first test.

His lawyer was sending over some draft paperwork for the proceedings early next week, and now Scout knew the divorce was coming. She hadn't exactly seemed upset by it or shown any resistance at all. Her promises that she didn't want a complicated process were reassuring, too.

"Lane?" Julie poked her head into his office again, worry creasing her face. "Can we talk for a minute?"

He sighed and looked at his computer. Work was piling up, but it was clear he wasn't going to be productive today anyway. "Sure, come in."

Julie shut the door behind her and took one of the seats on

the other side of Lane's desk, where Mr. Impatient had been sitting a moment ago. She was a few years older than Lane, in her mid thirties, and had worked for him ever since they moved the company into a proper office four years ago.

"What's going on?" he asked, concern building behind his chest. Julie wasn't the kind of employee who needed to talk about much—she was super independent and efficient, anticipating his needs better than even he could do himself. "Is everything okay?"

"It's about Star," she said, glancing over at where the little ball of fluff was curled up asleep. "She's..."

"Acting strange, I know." He nodded.

Julie let out a relieved sigh. "Okay, so you *have* noticed it, then. I was wondering how to broach the topic."

"You know you don't have to walk on eggshells around me."

"Don't I?" She cocked her head. "You bit Mark's head off in front of everyone and that is so *not* like you."

Lane didn't want to feel a pang of guilt over the incident, but he did. "I won't have someone who's been here for five minutes telling me how I should run my business."

"Fair."

"But I also could have had that conversation in private," Lane conceded. "That was not my finest moment."

He tried so hard not to be like the bosses he'd worked for in his youth. Lane had spent time working at a computer repair place on Staten Island, being underpaid and underappreciated, while he created programs on the side in his own time. When he and Rav started their company, they made a pact that the people would be as important as the product.

"You're a good man, Lane. Everybody knows it." She wrung her hands. "But I think Star needs some help."

He scrubbed his hands over his face and then raked them

through his hair as he leaned back in his office chair. "I went to pick her up from my sister's place last night, and Beth told me that she'd literally ripped the head off one of my niece's dolls. She never does stuff like that. I know I trained her well, so I don't think a lack of training is the issue."

Were pet psychologists a thing? It felt like one of those ridiculous bougie services that people used when they had more money than sense. And Lane might have plenty of money, but he would always have more sense.

"She also snapped at a child in the park on her walk today *and* she tried to pee on someone in the elevator," Julie said.

"Jeez, Star." He looked at the dog and shook his head. What had happened to his sunshine-y ball of fluff? "What are you doing, girl?"

"Look, I may have overstepped here but..." Julie held up her hands. "I made you an appointment with someone who deals with this kind of stuff."

Lane raised an eyebrow.

"Her name is Sylvana Adonay and she deals with animals who are having uncharacteristic behavioral issues." Julie placed a business card on his desk and slid it forward.

The card had clearly been designed to show exactly how expensive it was to print—plush textured cardstock, gold embossing, elegant font.

Adonay Pet Communication Consulting.

Communication consulting? Maybe they didn't like to use words like psychologist when it came to pets.

"You were supposed to be meeting with the reps from Apple this afternoon, but Rav requested we move the meeting to next week because something came up. I called Sylvana to see if that slot happened to be free and she'd also had a cancellation, so I grabbed it." Julie looked at him with her please-don't-be-mad expression.

But she needn't have bothered; Lane wasn't mad. He wanted to understand what was going on with Star so he could fix it and get his furry best friend back to normal as quickly as possible.

His gratitude toward Julie wore off, however, when he headed into the building where Sylvana Adonay's business was located. He stepped into the elevator with Star, praying that she didn't try to piss on anyone, as there were three other people in there with them.

One of the elevator passengers was a woman in her fifties, wearing a ruby red wool coat over a black dress and a pair of expensive-looking high heels. She smiled down at Star and then looked up to Lane.

"Let me guess," she said. "You're going to see Sylvana?"

"I am," he replied. "That must be an easy guess when there's only one pet-related business in the building."

"True." She nodded. "You're making the right decision. Sylvana helped me *tremendously* with my darling Prince. He's a pug. Such a charming breed. But he had a very difficult time after my husband passed."

"I'm sorry to hear that."

"Don't be. My husband was a horrible man. But animals don't know that, do they? All Prince knew was that Gary fed him and cuddled him, never mind the fact that he screwed anything that breathed."

Yikes.

Lane glanced at his phone, eager not to be part of this discussion anymore. Mercifully, the numbers on the elevator screen climbed higher and higher. Just as they reached the floor he wanted, there was a ding and the doors slid open.

"Good luck!" the woman called. "If you're lucky, she'll do a reading on you, too."

The doors slid closed and Lane turned back, frowning. A reading? What did that mean?

The floor was quiet and a frosted glass door had the words Adonay Pet Communication Consulting etched into it. A lot of pet businesses had a very kitsch feeling to them, with cutesy pictures of animals and their owners, but this place could have been a legal office or a high-end accounting firm. In fact, it looked like one of the wealth management offices that he'd visited recently.

He pushed the door open and stepped into a soothing space decorated with shades of ivory, sage green and a soft ocean blue. Several black-and-white pictures of owners with their pets hung on the wall, although they weren't happy snaps. They looked more like professional portraits.

He leaned closer. Was that...?

"Yes, that's Tippi Hedren." A voice came from behind him. "She's a huge animal lover."

"And a lover of huge animals," Lane said, turning.

A woman stood there, smiling. She wore a long dress the color of a pale winter sky, and the upper half of her body was wrapped up in a fluffy shawl in a slightly deeper gray. Her dark hair was loosely swept back and she appeared to be in her sixties, possibly older. She looked as though she could have been an actress or model in her youth.

"Apparently she still has a number of lions and tigers at the sanctuary where she lives. Not bad for someone in their nineties." The woman extended her hand. "I'm Sylvana Adonay."

"Lane Halliday." He glanced down. "And this is Star."

"It's a pleasure. Please, come through to my office."

Lane followed Sylvana through the doorway and Star trotted happily with them. Would she even believe he was having issues with the dog? It seemed like Star had developed a bit of a Jekyll-and-Hyde situation. One minute, she was all snuggly and cute, and the next minute, she was decapitating Barbie dolls.

Sylvana crouched in the middle of the room and held a hand out to Star, who went over for a sniff. "I'm going to unclip her leash, is that okay?"

"Sure."

Sylvana unclipped the leash from Star's collar and Lane wrapped the length up and stuffed it into his jacket pocket. The dog gave a happy little shake of freedom and allowed Sylvana to run a hand along her back. He had no idea what to expect with the appointment, but he'd been increasingly frustrated with Star's sudden personality transformation.

"I, uh...I haven't taken her to an appointment like this before. Could you tell me a little about the process?" he asked.

"Sure, take a seat." She motioned to one of a small cluster of chairs in the corner of the room. "How did you come to find out about my services?"

"I didn't, actually. My assistant made this appoint for Star, after she had a few...unusual instances of bad behavior in my office."

Sylvana nodded. "Right. Well, as a pet communication consultant I establish a connection with the animal to determine how they're feeling and what they're thinking. A sudden change in behavior is always caused by something, usually an upheaval of some kind, and once we determine what the cause is, then I will work with the animal to soothe them."

"How exactly do you establish a connection with the animal?" Lane asked, suddenly having a weird feeling in his gut.

Sylvana offered a serene smile. "It's a psychic connection."

Lane blinked. "I'm sorry... A *psychic* connection?"

"Yes."

Julie had sent him to a fucking pet psychic.

He closed his eyes for a moment, wondering how on earth

he was going to deal with this when he got back to the office. Lane had no love for people who preyed on those seeking certainty during difficult times. After his grandfather had died, Lane's mother had gone to see a psychic to deal with some unfinished business.

The woman had taken her money, given her a couple of platitudes and told her that if she wanted to "maintain a connection" with her father, then it would be best to start a payment plan. They were crooks, the lot of them.

"I can see that you weren't quite aware of what my services entailed," Sylvana said.

"Did you use your psychic powers to deduce that?" he asked, folding his arms over his chest.

"It's written plain as day all over your face." She didn't seem offended. "Can you go into this with an open mind? I'm already getting a sense from Star as to what the problem might be."

Lane didn't move. Part of him wanted to grab Star and get the hell out of there, because there was as much chance of him taking advice from a "psychic" as taking advice from a person dressed as a unicorn in Times Square. But the other part of him—the part that felt hopelessly untethered and unsettled—was desperate for anything that might help.

And he was here now; the time and money were already wasted.

"Really?" he asked skeptically. "And what might that be?"

"You spend a lot of time at work," Sylvana said, holding up her hand before Lane could interject. "Work is something that's incredibly important to you and she knows that."

Did she know who Lane was? It would be easy enough to look him up, since Google had everything documented about his life.

Even if she didn't, it wasn't a stretch to assume a guy in his

thirties who could afford such a frivolous service as a pet psychic was someone with an all-consuming job. And wasn't that
how most psychics worked? They read external information
and cultivated a heightened sense of perception to make ob-
servations that felt accurate.

But he'd like to see her guess his social security number.
That would make her psychic.

"But she had someone else once who spent a lot of time
with her," Sylvana said. Lane stilled, narrowing his eyes at her.
Mistake! Now she's going to read your face and know she's right.

"You're the sole person in her life right now and she misses
her other person." The psychic leaned back in her chair and
knotted her hands in her lap. She looked serene, almost too
serene. "Now, I'm not saying you're not enough for her. She
loves you dearly, and I could tell as soon as you walked in that
there was a great bond between you. But it's like she's realized
lately what she has been missing."

Scout.

He didn't want to think about her right now. Because it
was the exact conclusion he'd drawn himself—that Star and
Scout had grown super close when they first got married, and
now seeing her again after such a long absence had upset Star.
It reminded her of what she'd lost.

Of all the days that poor little ball of fluff had waited by
the door, scraping with one paw and crying for her friend.
He'd started taking her to work more regularly then, because
she didn't cry there.

"That someone was also very important to you." Sylvana
kept her eyes on Lane, but she must have spotted that he wasn't
wearing a wedding ring. Maybe she'd hedged her bets and assumed that a guy his age would have had at least *one* serious
relationship before. "Someone you also miss."

"What's her name? Tell me that and I'll be impressed," he

said. God, he sounded like a dick, but this woman had caught him off guard. Her words had hit home and that pissed him off.

"I don't need to prove my abilities, Lane. You're here for a reason."

"I'm here because my assistant set this appointment up. Honestly, I don't believe in all this. I don't read star signs, I don't think you can look into a cup of tea and read the future. I don't think you can get certainty from a deck of cards." He shrugged. "Call me a skeptic. But you haven't told me anything that wasn't an educated guess."

Sylvana looked at Lane like he was the subject of the meeting, rather than the dog. It was like being scanned by a laser, read up and down with every little flaw picked over. Uncomfortable under her scrutiny, he glanced over to Star. She'd become particularly enamored with a potted plant and was trying to jump up and catch one of the leaves.

"You were married," Sylvana said suddenly.

"Wrong."

"Hmm. *Still* married, but long separated."

He was tempted to look down at his hand and see if there was some kind of permanent indent from the wedding ring he'd worn for too short a period of time, but he didn't want to give her the satisfaction.

"You worry too much about what people think," she said.

"I really don't." He wasn't sure if that was a lie or not. He'd certainly cared in the past and he told himself he no longer cared... But was that the truth? Or had he simply withdrawn so much from the world that he'd stopped giving people the chance to think anything about him because he was more ghost than man?

That's a sad fucking assessment of your life.

But it was true. He'd retreated into himself, retreated into his work, using it as a shield from the ugly bits of his life that he didn't want to acknowledge.

"I didn't come here for me," he said, frustration creating a roughness in his voice. "I came here for Star. I want to know how I can help her."

"Help yourself," the psychic said. "She takes her cues from you. If you're happy, then she's happy."

"I *am* happy."

But the words couldn't have felt further from the truth. He was alone, his family was fractured, and his work, while fulfilling, was starting to feel like a poor substitute for a life. Having Scout come to his house, the overwhelming attraction he felt toward her and the shock at how well she knew him, it had kicked up his emotions like sediment on the ocean floor disturbed by a wave.

And wasn't that Scout in a nutshell? A wave. A force.

"You have an unresolved issue that she is picking up on. If you want to fix this problem with Star, then first you need to stop lying to yourself. Because she knows how you're truly feeling, whether you can admit it to yourself or not," Sylvana said, looking at him with an intensity that made him feel like an interrogator's lamp was being shone in his face. "And then you need to make peace with what happened in the past."

Lane pushed back on his chair, shaking his head. "This is a waste of time."

He picked up a bewildered-looking Star and marched out of the office, annoyance rippling through his body.

You're only annoyed because she's right. The second Scout walked out you gave up on everything that wasn't work, and now you know what you've been missing.

11

"This idea was freaking *genius!*" Isla looked at Scout, a big smile slipping across her face. "Good job."

They were standing in a warehouse in Brooklyn which was being set up for the Pets of Park Avenue charity photoshoot, although everyone was jokingly calling it the "hot guys and dogs" project. The proper name was much classier, of course. But when you boiled it down, it really was about famous pets and hot male models.

Talk about a goldmine.

As soon as Gina had sent the information through, and Scout had started looking into the event, she knew this was the perfect opportunity to get Paws in the City involved... and not just because Scout needed to bring Star here as Sasha's replacement.

She'd contacted the woman running the charity to ask if they could volunteer at the shoot as well as donating to the cause itself, on the proviso that they were allowed to pitch their services to anyone who seemed interested. That way, they could potentially identify another big client to add to their list.

Isla had loved it! Thankfully, the woman running the charity was thrilled with Scout's ideas, too.

"This is *exactly* the kind of stuff we need to be involved in," Isla said. "Who knows? Maybe this whole thing with Gina might be a blessing in disguise."

"Are you saying I should dye more of our clients pink?" Scout said with a wink.

"Don't even joke about that. My stomach can't handle the nerves." Isla waved both hands back and forth. "But seriously, this is the kind of business development we need more of. If there were two of us looking for these opportunities, I feel like we'd be growing even faster."

Scout suppressed the bubble of excitement in her stomach. "Now that I've connected with the shelter, I'll ask if they know of any other initiatives we might be able to support."

"Great idea."

The two women stood by a trestle table where they had promotional items set up. Scout and Isla had spent the previous evening sitting on the floor of the office, packing gift bags, which included some Paws in the City–branded cookies for the humans and a little packet of fancy organic pet treats for the dogs.

Scout had also leaned on their contacts to get more goodies, like discount vouchers for a fancy Manhattan pet salon, a free day at an upmarket doggy-daycare place and handcrafted leather collars in an array of bright colors from a local designer. They had extras on hand, if anyone got a size or color that didn't suit their pet's style.

The guest list for the day was mighty impressive. Along with Sasha Frise—or rather, her doppelgänger—Isla had also convinced Theo to let his pampered dachshund, Camilla, be part of the shoot since his grandmother had been a big advocate for animal charities. There was a New York fashion-week regular, Minnie the Italian greyhound, who had more Instagram followers than most models who walked the runways. Plus there were a few celebrity men who'd agreed to model with their pets, including successful Broadway producer Wes Evans and his adorable husky puppy, Lamington.

"This is going to go bananas. I can feel it." Isla was practically buzzing with energy.

"Right? I put an order in for fifty calendars. I figured we could give them out to people who come in for a meet and greet at the office, as a way of showing the kind of work we're involved in."

Isla snapped her fingers. "You're on fire with the good ideas right now! I love it."

"Thanks." Scout beamed. "I can see so many opportunities for us to help animal-based charities with our work. I know we're still establishing ourselves, but I feel like this could be a big pillar of the business moving forward."

For a moment she worried that maybe she'd overstepped, since charity work wasn't something that would bring in a return necessarily. And so many small enterprises failed in the first five years of operation, so suggesting they take nonpaying work might not be a smart business move.

Scout often wondered if this had been her biggest problem in life—focusing on the priorities that felt right in her heart but that didn't always make the best sense in her head.

But Isla nodded enthusiastically. "Totally. I mean, we need to make money, too, of course. But I've always wanted to do something that brought joy to the world, and helping animals absolutely fits in that category. Why don't we get out of the office for lunch one day next week and brainstorm some ideas?"

"I'd love that."

Confidence buoyed by her boss's support, Scout noticed that Latoya, the woman who ran the charity, was headed their way.

"These look incredible. Thank you so much." Latoya gestured to the gift bags, a big smile on her face. "You ladies have really come through. I can't express my gratitude enough."

"It's a fantastic cause," Isla said. "We're thrilled to be part of it."

"And the personal donation from you and Theo…" She pressed a hand to her chest, her eyes turning misty. "That was so incredibly generous, thank you."

"We're both longtime animal lovers, so it's something close to our hearts." Isla winked at Scout, who had to stifle a laugh.

She knew that Theo wasn't exactly a *longtime* animal lover. When he'd first ended up with his late grandmother's Dachshund—hidden in the fine print of her will—he'd been less than thrilled. But Isla had helped him come around to the sassy little dog *and* to the idea of love.

"We've got the models coming in blocks so they don't have to be here all day—and so it doesn't look like we're running a menagerie." Latoya laughed.

"That is a *very* smart idea," Scout said, shuddering at the memory of the chaotic shoot that had started the whole doppelgänger thing.

"I've got the fliers you printed up dotted around the catering table and in the greenroom, so there's plenty of opportunity for people to read up on Paws in the City," Latoya added.

"And we are ready to answer questions and hand out gift bags." Scout grinned.

Latoya was drawn away with a question from one of the

makeup artists, and Isla glanced over to Scout. "What time is Lane coming in with St…Sasha.?"

"Nice save," Scout teased, keeping her voice low. "I think he's in the last block."

You don't think, *you know. Because you looked at the damn schedule, like, fifty times so you could count down the minutes until he arrives.*

Scout had tried to tell herself it was because she was excited to see Star again…but that was only partially true.

Isla's eyes searched Scout's face. "Are you…?"

"I'm fine." She tried not to be annoyed at her friend checking in, because she knew Isla only ever wanted her to be happy.

"You know what *fine* stands for?" Isla teased with a smile. "Fucked up, insecure, neurotic and emotional."

Scout snorted. "I'm only one of those things. I'll let you figure out which one."

"I know you're Miss Independent and all, but I'm here for you if you need me."

"Thanks. I appreciate it, but I really am fine—in the traditional sense." She nodded, though it felt a little harder to convince herself than Isla. "We're getting divorced, so I need to get used to seeing him because I'm sure we'll have to sign papers and stuff."

"Really?" Isla blinked. "You're getting divorced."

"Why do you sound so surprised?"

"Maybe because I've asked you about it a bunch of times, and you keep doing your best impression of an ostrich." Isla cocked her head like she always did whenever she was thinking something through. "And now you mention it out of the blue."

"It's the right thing to do," she said. The words sounded rehearsed, robotic. And there was a dark tendril of doubt unfurling in her stomach. "We have no ties to one another, so what's the point of staying married?"

"Who brought it up?" Isla prodded.

"He did."

Her expression was difficult to read. "If you need a hookup for a good lawyer, just say so. Theo knows some people."

"Theo knows everyone." Scout laughed. "For a hermit, he's quite connected."

"Tell me about it. But seriously, don't think you need to do this on your own, okay? You have people around you who care, so you don't need to act like a monolith."

"It's not going to be that complicated. I don't want anything from him, and there's nothing he can take from me, because I don't have anything to give. Simple."

It sounded so sad when she said it out loud. But there was no point dwelling on the negative. Getting divorced *was* the right thing to do. The logical thing to do. The smart thing to do.

And it was the very opposite of what her former-hot-mess self would do, which was sign enough.

"Did he say why he wants to make it official now?" Isla asked.

"Who knows? Maybe he wants to move on with someone else." The thought hit her square in the chest, but she chose not to linger in it. After all, *she* was the one who'd left. "I guess I want to move on, too."

Now it was Isla's turn to raise an eyebrow. "Really? You want to get back into the dating scene?"

"Why do you sound so shocked?"

"You always tell me men are more trouble than they're worth," Isla said, and it was true. "And it's not like you've even looked twice at a man in...forever."

"I've dated plenty," Scout grumbled.

"Oh yeah, like who?"

"I went to dinner with that guy from the gym."

"What was his name again?" Isla asked sweetly, although Scout knew she was asking to prove a point.

Scout glanced at her friend. "James."

"You sure about that?"

No, she wasn't. She was sure it started with a *J*, though… maybe.

The truth was Scout *had* been on a number of dates, but even if they cleared the hurdle of date number one, they all ended up the same way: with her never taking the guy's calls ever again. Most of them didn't deserve to be ghosted— although one or two of them *absolutely* did—and in another life, she might have given them more of her time.

Yet anytime a man even *thought* about trying to get close to Scout, she snapped shut like a mousetrap. The last five years had been an emotional wasteland. Perhaps it might make more sense if she still loved Lane—which she absolutely, 100 percent, most definitely did not. But the sad fact of it was that her persistent single status came down to one thing and one thing only.

She was terrified of having her heart broken again.

In her eyes, there was a three-strike rule on heartbreak. Her mother had broken it once, her grandparents had broken it a second time and Lane had broken it a third.

So she was *done*.

No more letting people in. No more letting people know the real her. No more trusting anyone. Whatever weak sparks her poor, battered heart were able to produce were reserved for Lizzie first and Isla second. That was it. Her heart was officially closed for business.

Forever.

So why did the thought of signing divorce papers fill her with rain clouds and gloom? Scout wasn't sure she wanted to know the answer to that question.

★ ★ ★

By the time they got to the last block of bookings for the shoot, Scout was drained. Her feet ached from standing for so long and her face was sore from overly bright smiles. She'd sold her heart out today, trying to plug Paws in the City to all the owners of the adorable and famous pets that had come in. She'd even tried to spread the word with the models, in case they knew of anyone looking for representation.

So far, nothing more than a half-hearted nibble of interest. But she wasn't going to give up!

As she approached the table where the last remaining swag and promo items were stored, Isla was talking to an attractive man with a small husky puppy. He was tall and fair-haired with a warm smile and model-like features.

"Scout, this is Wes Evans." Isla motioned to the man. "Remember that modern dance production Theo took me to a few months back? *Out of Bounds*? He's the producer."

"Lovely to meet you." Scout stuck out her hand and he shook it. "Congratulations on the success of your show. It's getting rave reviews."

Scout wasn't much of a theater buff, but even *she* had heard about the unique dance production taking Broadway by storm. Apparently it had started as a small local production, then had gone overseas for a while, and now it was selling out a full-size theater back in New York.

"Thank you." He beamed. "It's been a long road to get there. Cracking Broadway is no easy feat."

"I can only imagine." She looked at the adorable black-and-white puppy squirming in his arms. It had the most intense blue eyes that Scout had ever seen. "And who is this beautiful little critter?"

"This is Lamington. My wife is Australian and she wanted to name him after something from home." He scratched behind the little guy's ear. "It's a good thing he's cute, because I found him with another one of my sneakers this morning. He thinks they're all chew toys."

"Oh no! But he really *is* cute." Scout reached in for a scratch and the puppy tried to gnaw on her finger. "I don't suppose he has an Instagram or TikTok account?"

"This is going to make me sound like a total Luddite, but I don't do social media. Honestly, I had my time in the spotlight for a while there and I am *so* glad that's over." Wes laughed. "Thank God I've got a marketing person to handle it all for work."

Her heart sank. She'd been *sure* that today would be the opportunity for her to snag an exciting new client and prove to Isla that she had the right business development skills to be an account manager.

"Well, if you ever feel like your little one could be a star, we'd love to help you out," Scout said with a smile.

Isla slipped a business card into the goodie bag, along with a few extra doggy treats since they had leftovers, and then handed it to Wes. He bid them both a friendly goodbye and headed outside.

"No luck so far," Scout said sadly. "And we've only got two more people in this last block, one of them being Lane."

"It's okay. Growing a business is a lot like growing a garden. You have to plant a lot of seeds and not all of them will bloom." Isla patted her on the back. "But you never know, we might hear from someone after the campaign launches. Besides, I'm glad we can support such a wonderful cause."

Isla seemed so happy, it was like sunshine was bursting out of her pores. Scout remembered feeling the same in the early days of her marriage. It was blissful. Like each step you took was cushioned by clouds.

"What?" Isla asked when she caught sight of her friend looking at her.

"You're beaming."

"Am I?" There was no containing the grin on her face.

"You've got that pre-wedding glow about you." Scout made a circular motion with her hand. "It's sweet, in a sappy Hallmark kind of way. Who would have thought sparkly vampire-magnetism guy would turn you into a sunbeam?"

Isla snorted. "I told him recently about how you used to refer to him before we started dating."

"What did he say?" she asked.

"He wasn't sure whether it was a compliment or an insult."

"A compliment, obviously." Scout laughed.

Out of the corner of her eye, she spotted Lane arriving through the front entrance. Star was sitting inside a dog carrier while Lane chatted with the woman who was checking people in and out of the photography venue. The girl flicked her hair over one shoulder, laughing at something he said.

"You're staring," Isla said, slinging an arm around Scout's shoulders.

"No, I'm not. I'm being observant." Her cheeks warmed. Damn Isla and her persistence; that woman was like a dog with a bone sometimes.

That's why she's successful. Maybe you should try it.

But before she had the chance to ponder on that for too long, Latoya came over to them, looking rather frazzled. She ran a hand over the top of her long, dark braids.

"Everything okay?" Scout asked.

"Our final model just called. He was in a car accident." She blew out a breath. "He's fine, thank God. But he's stuck waiting for the police and dealing with insurance."

"Oh no!" Isla sighed. "I'm glad he's okay, but that's terrible timing."

"Right?" Latoya made a frustrated sound. "I don't suppose you have any human talent on your books?"

"We're strictly a pet agency," Isla said with an apologetic tone. But then she glanced at Scout, her blue eyes twinkling. "However, we do know *someone* who might be able to stand in…"

Oh no, she didn't.

"Really? That would be amazing." Latoya's eyes brightened. "I'd owe you."

Isla looked at Scout without saying a word. Not that she needed to—Scout knew *exactly* who she was talking about. She tried to shake her head, but with Latoya watching, she didn't want to seem unhelpful.

When Latoya's phone rang and she excused herself to take the call, Isla motioned to Lane, who was heading toward them.

"Can you ask him?" Isla said. "He's here and, well, he fits the part, right? He's in *great* shape."

Scout sighed. "You really want me to ask my current-but-soon-to-be-ex husband to take his shirt off for the camera? Seriously?"

"I can ask if you don't feel comfortable," Isla said. "I feel bad for Latoya. It's stressful organizing these things and we have the means to help."

"Too bad Theo already took Camilla back home," Scout muttered, knowing full well there was zero chance he would have agreed to the request. The man was stubborn like that. Lane, on the other hand, was a sexy marshmallow of a man and was wired to say yes. "What's one more request, right? He's already planning to divorce me, so it can't get any worse."

She headed over to Lane, leaving Isla with a puzzled expression on her face. She *hated* having to ask Lane for something else—it felt like she'd done nothing but ask, ask, ask and take, take, take. And she knew this would be a big one.

Lane, like her, had never enjoyed being in the spotlight, even if his success dictated it.

"Hey." He smiled shyly as she approached, which made her feel even worse. "I've got one dog ready for action."

"That's great." Scout bent down to say hello to Star, who looked at her warily through the bars of the dog carrier as if to say, *Keep your distance, human.* "Actually, I may need another teensy favor."

She waited for Lane to roll his eyes or frown or judge her in some other way, but to his credit, he didn't. "What do you need?"

Oof. This man. He'd always been like that, wanting to help others. But he wasn't going to like her request. "I need you to be a model."

"I'm sorry, what?" He blinked.

"The last model for the day got into a car accident on the way over and so the shoot is down one hot bod."

Lane's eyes narrowed as he looked over to where the second-to-last shoot was taking place. A ripped guy with caramel surfer hair stood cradling a corgi named Cookie Bakewell.

Yes, Cookie Bakewell. She was a former dog model, with a YouTube channel where she helped her owner bake healthy dog treats.

"What's the catch?" he asked warily.

"Just that it's a topless shoot," she replied with a nervous laugh. "Because people give up their money real fast for a hot dude with a cute dog."

He blinked. "Seriously?"

"Seriously. And don't even *think* about trying to chastise me for it being sexist. It's for a good cause and everyone who's participating is doing so voluntarily, so I get a free pass."

Lane looked at her like he wasn't so sure about that. "That means I can say no, right?"

She nodded slowly. "You can."

"Then, I'm saying no."

"It would really help everyone out," she pleaded. "They'll barely even need to retouch you."

"Scout…" He let out a groan. "Don't try to flatter me into this."

"I'm sorry. But it would *really* help the charity out of a bind," she cajoled. "The calendar is going to raise funds for the animals at the shelter so they get new beds and toys and more staff to keep them happy and healthy."

It was a low blow, playing to his animal-loving nature. And she knew it would hit him right in the soft spot, that part that made him such a good dog dad.

He let out a growl of frustration. "I swear, Scout. One of these days I'm going to say no to you."

She clapped her hands together. "You're the best. Thank you! Latoya will be so grateful and so will all the animals. You won't regret it."

"I already do," he muttered.

It was going to take a hell of a lot more than a gift basket to make it up to Lane this time.

12

Lane winced as a fine mist hit his bare chest. He was standing with arms spread out to the side. The makeup artist in front of him—one of a team of two—was a woman dressed in black from head to toe. She had hair that started out dark brown and ended in a bright lime green, which matched the almost glow-in-the-dark liner on her eyes.

"You're not going to make me look like a Ken doll, are you?" he asked, watching her work.

She moved a small silver airbrush gun back and forth, gently coating his bare chest in a shade that more closely resembled a man who saw sunlight, rather than the pale shade of a man permanently attached to his laptop.

"Not at all." She smiled up at him. "The lights are harsh in here, so I'm making sure they don't wash you out."

"That's very kind of you, but I know I look like I'm related to Casper the ghost."

She laughed. "You're definitely not the palest guy I've worked on, but you're up there."

"I appreciate the honesty."

"The makeup will help bring out your muscle definition. The bright lights make everything look flat and two-dimensional, which would be a shame."

Was she flirting with him?

"And I'm not being kind this time." She smirked before dropping her head to focus on her work. "Turn around."

Lane did what he was told, staying in his scarecrow position. In truth, he felt like the *last* guy who should be stripping down to model for any kind of campaign. Growing up, he'd always been the scrawny kid in his class. He'd been on the shorter side and skinny as a rail—all gangly limbs and pointy elbows—until he was seventeen. His body took its sweet time before he had a huge growth spurt and he'd never been particularly sporty. In fact, he'd only taken up CrossFit for something to keep his brain occupied after Scout left.

Frankly, he found a lot of CrossFit folks to be drinking the Kool-Aid—like they saw it as their job to spread the good word of their lord and savior, the burpee. But the exercises were challenging and it was one of the only times Lane could truly shut off his brain.

Turned out it was difficult to overthink things while flipping giant tires and feeling like you were about to pass out from exhaustion.

So he might have the kind of physique they were looking for, but he definitely wasn't eager to rip his shirt off at every opportunity.

"Almost done," the makeup artist said. "Then I'm going to apply a little powder and do some touch-ups by hand."

Lane nodded, his gaze roaming across the room. There was one other male model finishing up shooting with a small, furry dog. That guy *looked* like a proper model. He knew the poses and everything. Lane would probably stand there stiff as a tree trunk.

Ugh, why did he have this compulsion to say yes to Scout?

He glanced over to where she was chatting with a guy dressed in jeans and a T-shirt so tight it looked spray-painted on. The dude was barely able to keep his tongue in his head while Scout handed over what appeared to be a goodie bag.

It pierced him like a lance. The jealousy—so swift and sharp and ugly—wasn't an emotion he was too familiar with. Lane genuinely believed there was no point dwelling on what other people had. Success wasn't pie. It wasn't a limited re-source. And people who thought they had to snatch it out of someone else's hands were not the kind of people he liked to surround himself with.

But in that moment—that petty, green-eyed moment—he very much wanted to snatch Scout's hand out of the guy's grip.

That's super caveman. Gross.

Yeah, but it was how he felt.

The makeup artist continued her work. Apparently Lane didn't need to change clothes because the jeans he was wear-ing were fine and the makeup artist had gotten him to pro-tect them from the airbrushing by tucking some tissues over the waistband.

A woman with a tablet approached him. "Lane Halliday? You're up next. I'll get you to stand over there," the woman said, pointing. "I'll ask the groomer to bring Sasha over as soon as she's done."

He had the urge to correct the woman over his dog's name, but he caught his tongue. Star was here as a doppelgänger today, not as herself.

"Try not to scratch yourself or disturb the makeup if you can help it," the makeup artist added. "But we can do a touch-up, if necessary."

Lane nodded and then headed over to where the woman with the tablet had told him to stand. This whole thing felt so *far* out of his world. Sure, they'd done a photoshoot for *Forbes* when he and Rav had landed on the "30 Under 30" list. But other than that, he avoided having his photo taken unless absolutely necessary. Plenty of the articles about Unison and his company featured photos of Rav, only. Or they used some of the older shots that were still floating around.

In fact, the last photos he'd had taken professionally were...

His wedding night. The memory of it slammed into his chest like a wrecking ball. Scout had worn a white dress that she'd found at a vintage shop, with her hair long and flowing. In typical Scout fashion, she'd snuck into a fancy restaurant and plucked some flowers from one of the tables, sticking them in her hair while her eyes sparkled like diamonds and mischief.

And when the celebrant had pronounced them man and wife, she'd kissed him with the kind of passion he'd never known was possible. She'd tasted so sweet that he hadn't even realized how close he was flying to the sun.

"Lane?" A female voice snapped him out of his thoughts. Scout walked over, hand raised in a shy wave.

She looked gorgeous, as usual, in sleek cream pants, high-heeled boots and a black silky top. Her hair was drawn back into a low, fat bun at the top of her neck. Everything about her screamed polished professional. Lane's laser eye spotted where she'd patched a belt-loop on her pants, because the thread was a slightly different shade of cream.

She'd spent a good portion of their marriage patching things or altering them to suit her style, and she'd never once let him leave the house with a loose button or frayed seam. Appearances were important to her, he'd learned. She'd told him once that she'd been badly bullied as a child because her mother dressed her strangely and kept her hair in an unflattering bowl cut.

Once she'd had control over her appearance, she'd grown her hair long and developed a keen eye for fashion. He suspected it was, at least originally, a tactic to avoid ridicule.

"I figured I should come over and see if you're okay," she said. Her tone was only half joking.

"I feel like I'm in one of those dreams where I'm suddenly sitting in the school cafeteria half naked. You know, every nerd's nightmare." If clothes were her mask, self-deprecation was his.

"You look…great."

This time he got the impression the words weren't meant to butter him up. Not if the shade of her cheeks was anything to go on.

"What did I say about flattery?"

"You never were good at receiving compliments." She lowered her eyes for a moment, but then she jerked them back up. "No matter how hard I tried."

"I'd say two played very well at that game, back then."

"Touché." She was very studiously looking at his face, as if chanting "don't look down" in her head. "We've been on the back foot from the beginning, haven't we?"

"Do you mean today or…since Vegas?"

"Today. I wasn't…" Scout flushed harder and it looked beautiful on her. The pink brought out smudges of green in her hazel eyes. "Anyway, I told the photographer that we wanted something a bit mysterious for you, so you don't have to have your whole face on display."

She delivered the change in conversation as skillfully as a master magician performing a sleight of hand. Impressive.

"Thanks for that. Rav would have a field day otherwise," he quipped drily. "The last thing I want is an article blowing up online with a picture of me half naked."

"You don't need to worry about that." The flush turned from pink to red. "I mean, you've clearly been working out. Hmm, that sounded creepy. Shit."

The curse word was muttered under her breath as she dropped her eyes to the floor. It was so vulnerable and endearing that Lane felt a piece of the ice around his heart melt away. *These* were the moments he'd lived for when they were married—when she was put into a position where she couldn't keep up her shield.

"I started doing CrossFit," he said casually, not wanting to make her more uncomfortable than she clearly already was. "Just on the weekends. Rav said I needed a hobby."

"And you chose flipping tires? Interesting."

"The cross-stitch class was already full."

The corner of her lip twitched. "Do you even know what cross-stitch is?"

"It's a delicate art form of crossing stitches," he said with all the bravado of someone who had no idea what he was talking about. "It was started in ancient Greece by Zeus himself."

Scout snorted. "Glad to see you're still as full of it as always."

"That'll never change."

When he smiled at her and she smiled back, he felt a warmth inside him that was strange and unfamiliar. Not new, but forgotten. Despite everything that had happened between them, it was clear he couldn't shake how much he liked her as a person. How much he *still* liked her.

She was funny. Sweet. So sexy.

She walked out on you in the middle of the night. She shattered your trust.

Over time it felt like his anger toward Scout and the breakup had lost its edge some. He was older now, wiser. He understood that they were ill-equipped to have married so young and without their families' support—with her so emotionally damaged and him so naive about the world. In a lot of ways, they couldn't be blamed for the fact that it all had crumbled.

If they'd married later, he would have handled things differently. He wouldn't have worried about what his family thought of the marriage or what the press might print with a clickbait headline or whether the investors would be concerned about his level of responsibility.

He would have stood proud with his wife by his side instead of hiding her away at home while he tried to figure it all out on his own. That mistake was entirely on him.

It was really freaking hard not to stare at Lane's abs.

She could tell from the moment he answered his door that he'd changed physically. But it was one thing to see it hidden behind a piece of clothing and quite another to look at those V muscles pointing toward what she knew was heaven.

Stop mentally undressing him.

Was it still mental undressing if he was already half naked? That sounded like a potential loophole, and boy, did Scout love a loophole.

"You haven't changed much, either," he said, shaking Scout out of her inner struggle.

"That a question or a statement?" she asked, cocking her head.

"Statement." Lane's green eyes held hers, as if daring her to look away first.

"And you base that on what, exactly?" For some reason, it made her feel a little defensive. He didn't know what she'd been up to all this time. He didn't know how she'd struggled to get motivated to start her days, how she'd tried so damn hard to be positive for her sister and for Isla, even though it felt like her life was running through her fingers like sand.

All he knew was that she'd left. And he probably hated her for it.

"Well, you start putting up walls around you the second it feels like someone is looking too close," he said quietly. "That's the same."

Lane never needed to speak up. Never needed to yell. She knew some people mistook his reserved nature and quiet ways as a sign he wasn't confident. More fool them. He was the most assured person she'd ever met. So assured, in fact, that he never felt the need to project how he felt onto others.

He'd said to her once, "Only those who lack security in who they are, need to shout about themselves." And she believed it.

"Why are you looking closely?" she asked, choosing to switch up her tactics and go on the offensive.

"Because, despite knowing better, I am still fascinated by you."

Scout's breath stuck in the back of her throat, his words hitting her heart like a sledgehammer. No man had ever made her—the real her—feel so utterly seen the way he did. It had been more intoxicating than any of those fish-bowl-sized cocktails they'd drunk that first night in Vegas.

For someone who'd been either ignored or misunderstood her whole life, Lane's understanding of who she was… Well, it was like coming alive.

But before she could even think about how to respond, the photography assistant walked Star over. She was dressed as Sasha Frise in one of her signature spangly outfits, complete with black Fran Drescher wig, sequined red booties and a leopard-print top.

The look on Star's face said there was a high chance of her murdering Lane in his sleep.

This is war, human! I will never get over this betrayal.

"If you can hold her leash for a moment," the photography assistant said. "We'll get everything set up for you."

Star looked up at Scout, but immediately, it was like some of the light dimmed in her eyes.

This was a dog, not a projection of her own guilt. An animal didn't know right from wrong. So, then why did it feel like Star was a far cry from the affectionate ball of fluff who'd snuggled in her arms as a puppy?

She probably doesn't even remember you. You're a stranger to her now.

That made her heart sink, because she'd mourned losing Star almost as much as losing Lane. She'd mourned their happy little family for months and months, because it was the first time she'd ever felt part of a unit. The first time she'd ever felt like a puzzle piece that slotted seamlessly into a beautiful picture, rather than being a square peg in a round hole.

Scout and Star stared at one another.

"You can pat her if you want," Lane said.

"I don't think she wants me to pat her."

Ugh, why was she getting so hung up on this? It wasn't like it mattered whether one dog liked her or not. Scout was *great* with animals. Even the aloof sphynx cat had come around to her in the end.

"Go slow," Lane said encouragingly. "She's been a little strange lately, but I think it's the change in routine."

"You're trying to make me feel better."

"Maybe."

"Why?"

"Reflex, I guess." He shrugged and a smile tugged at the corner of his lips.

"Kindness is a hell of a muscle memory to have. I always liked that about you."

It would be easy for Lane to be a dick—he was at the top of his game, with one of the hottest tech companies of the moment under his control…and yet he demanded nothing. He still worked as hard as he had when he started out. He didn't expect anything, didn't believe that he was better than anyone else.

"Funny. That's what I liked about you, too," he said.

She wasn't sure what to make of that. Or how to react. Instead, she crouched and slowly extended her hand to Star. The little dog looked at her, and then at her hand, and then back at her as if to say, *Are you for real now?*

"Hey, Star," Scout said softly. "I've missed you, sweet girl."

The dog stuck her face forward a bit and sniffed. She still wasn't exactly leaping into Scout's arms, but she wasn't growling, either. That was a win, right?

You do not need to win over your ex's dog. That's sad.

But then a tiny pink tongue swiped at her fingers and Scout felt like part of her heart had been healed. Why did it feel *so* good to be accepted by a small furry creature? Maybe other people weren't like that. Maybe they wouldn't care.

But she did.

"I'm sorry I had to leave," she whispered. "But I thought about you every day."

Star looked up at her with glossy black button eyes and Scout swore she heard her say, *I missed you, too.*

The photography assistant waved over to collect Lane and Star. "We're ready for you now."

Tempting as it was to stay and watch Lane have his photo taken, Scout felt it was better for her sanity to *not* do that. Ever since she'd visited him with the gift bag, she'd felt the connection between them. It was like a candle that suddenly flared to life after Scout was convinced she'd blown it out.

Even after he'd brought up the divorce, it flickered.

It was a cruel joke from the universe. A reminder of what she could never and would never have.

Scout stayed far away from Lane's shoot, fussing over the extra goodie bags they'd made in case there were more people at the event than anticipated.

"Looks like Lane is finishing up," Isla said, stifling a yawn. It had been a *long* day. "I might hand the extra bags out to the grooming and makeup staff."

"That's a nice gesture."

"Sure, if we overlook the fact that I don't want to trek all this stuff back to the office." Isla laughed. "We're going to a fundraiser for Dani's ballet school tonight and I *really* wanted to have time to refresh myself properly in between."

"I'll bring our stuff back to the office," Scout offered.

"Oh my gosh, no. That was *not* me trying to guilt you into doing it." Isla shook her head. "It's totally out of your way."

"Please." Scout waved a hand. "I don't have anywhere to be tonight. I'll bag it up and take a cab. It's a good excuse to get something from Vincent's for dinner."

"Are you sure?" Isla frowned.

"One hundred percent. Why don't you go now? I'll off-load whatever I can and pack up the rest. Then I'll bring it back to the office. That should give you an extra forty minutes at least to chill before you have to head out."

"You're the best." Isla gave her a hug. "I don't know what I would do without you."

Scout made a scoffing sound. "You'd be fine."

Isla pulled back and nailed her with a hard stare. "Do you seriously have no idea what a blessing our friendship has been to me? Especially these last few years. I would have drowned with the stress of worrying about Dani and my career. If it wasn't for you, I'd probably still be working reception at the dog grooming place, dithering about whether or not to strike out on my own."

"You only needed someone to believe in you."

"Yeah, I did. And that person is you." Isla squeezed her shoulder. "I will *always* be grateful that you gave me the push to bet on myself by opening Paws in the City. It changed my life. Our friendship means the world to me."

Scout found herself a little choked up with emotion. "It means the world to me, too."

The women hugged and Isla said her goodbyes before heading home. Scout offered the extras around, and most people were excited to take some of the goodies. She was taking a quick inventory of what was left when Lane approached.

"Hey, you got your shirt back," she teased. "Good for you."

"That is about as much public nudity as I need for the rest of my life," he joked back. Star was still on her leash, sniffing around.

"Let me get you a goodie bag. I'll throw in a few extras for Little Miss Well Behaved." She reached for some of the bagged doggy treats. "These are all organic and made by a small woman-run business. She'll love them."

"Thanks."

When Scout handed the bag over to Lane, her fingers brushed his, and she sucked in a breath at the electricity that shot up her arm. He must have felt it, too, because his eyes locked on to hers. She wanted to drown in those beautiful green pools.

But then he cleared his throat and tore his gaze away. "Are you done for the day?"

"Almost. Isla's got an event for Dani's ballet school tonight, so I offered to take everything back to the office."

"I can take you," he said. "Rav engaged a private car company for us and I don't use it much, but I can call them to come pick us up. It'll save you waiting for a cab."

"Oh." She blinked. "That's very nice of you."

"It's nothing," he mumbled.

Part of her felt like she should refuse—he was simply being polite, because that's the kind of guy Lane was. Also, being in a confined space next to him would probably cause her imagination to run around like a toddler hopped-up on red food coloring. But the other—louder—part of her wanted *very* much to spend a few extra moments with him.

Plus it was the fiscally responsible thing to do.

Fiscally responsible. Sure. Like you don't have a work credit card to charge the cab to. Uh-huh.

"That would be great, thank you." She nodded, feeling as giddy as a schoolgirl about to spend some time with her crush.

How did he make her feel like that—like she was young and naive and like she'd never been hurt before? His attention applied a filter to her scars, blurring them so that she wondered if they ever really existed.

Which was dangerous. Because her heart showed the aftermath of a lifelong battle, and those scars would never disappear.

13

Lane and Scout sat in the back of the private car, Manhattan rolling slowly by as they trudged through traffic. It would probably have been quicker to take the subway—which is what Lane had been planning to do originally. But she'd looked so tired when he approached her after his shoot was done. There was a weariness to her posture, like something was weighing her down.

And it poked at an old wound. An old urge. He'd made the offer to help before thinking about what kind of signals it might send.

What signals do you want *to send?*

He wasn't even sure anymore.

This would be the *perfect* time to bring up the fact that his lawyer had already pulled the divorce documents together. All he had to do was find out who would be representing her so they knew who to contact to get everyone in a room.

Now, it was just the two of them. Well, and the driver... But he'd undoubtedly heard worse. Still, every time he thought about how to phrase it, his mouth wouldn't cooperate.

She already knows it's coming. What's the problem?

Still, Lane took the easy option and kept his mouth shut. The ride home was filled mostly with small talk, although Scout showed a genuine interest in what he was doing with Unison and the company's plans for the future.

And he was more than happy to hear about how she wanted to help Isla grow Paws in the City into something big and successful. Back when they'd been together, work was very much a necessary evil for Scout. She'd never had ambitions of her own. Never had dreams of any kind.

For a guy who'd grown up with his eyes laser-locked on the future, he found it hard to understand...until he heard the history with her grandparents. Then he knew the reason she didn't dream was because they'd made her believe she didn't deserve to. So it was good to see her being passionate about a job. Although he knew that her plans for getting promoted had as much to do with applying for custody of Lizzie as enthusiasm for her career.

The driver pulled to a stop, inciting honks from the people behind them because it wasn't exactly a place to park. But that was Manhattan for you. People liked to honk, so why not give them a reason?

"Thank you *so* much for the lift," Scout said, gathering her things. Then she hovered for a moment, her eyes shining with sincerity. "It was really nice to see you, Lane."

"I'll give you a hand to take everything up," Lane said. He leaned forward to speak to the driver. "Give us a second to grab everything from the trunk. But then you can go. I'll make my own way home from here."

"No, you've done enough," Scout protested, but Lane was already securing the dog carrier and getting out of the vehicle before she could say anything further.

When he peered down to check on Star, she looked at him as if to say, *What. Are. You. Doing?*

He had no earthly idea.

From the back of the car, he grabbed a tote and a light but awkwardly shaped bag containing a dismantled pull-up sign and then closed the trunk. As the driver merged back into traffic, causing yet more horns, Lane joined Scout on the sidewalk.

"Do you always have to be a hero?" she asked. There was no sting to her words, no hint of sarcasm at all.

"I'm not a hero."

"Sure, you are. You're always trying to help people."

"I guess that makes you a hero, too."

She shot him a look that said *yeah, right.* "Come on, let's get this stuff upstairs so you can get on with your night. Got anything fun planned?"

He opened his mouth to say he was thinking about heading into the office for a bit, but then he snapped it shut. Would that make him seem like a loser?

"Going on a date, perhaps?" she asked cheekily.

Oh, she was *fishing.* Interesting. There was no logical reason that should give Lane a little ego boost, but it did.

"Why? Is that what *you* have planned?"

Her eyes narrowed slightly as though she was thinking about what move to make next. They carried the bags and promo items toward a small building with an entrance that was no more than a single door. It immediately led into a stairwell.

"Ladies first," Lane said. Which was a mistake.

Because now he had a whole flight of stairs to watch Scout's ass—which was heart-shaped perfection—sway in front of him.

"You didn't answer my question," she said, throwing a look over her shoulder.

"You didn't answer mine."

A loud sigh came from the dog carrier as if Star was saying, *Ugh humans, so pathetic.*

"No, I don't have a date tonight," she said, as she reached the top of the stairs. There was a small landing and two doors bearing business logos, one of which was Paws in the City. Scout unlocked the door. "I was planning to spend this evening on the couch with a good book."

"That sounds pretty similar to what I have planned," he said. "Well, plus a little cuddling with Star, of course."

"I thought you might have someone waiting for you to come home." She pushed the door open, revealing the Paws in the City office, which was tiny but well styled. Despite the size, it had an airy, welcoming vibe and he knew that Scout would make her clients feel at ease.

"If you want to ask me something, then ask," Lane said, setting Star down in her carrier and off-loading the bags and items onto the floor. "Don't beat around the bush."

"I don't have anything to ask. I thought, since you'd brought up the…" She smiled and shook her head. "Never mind."

"You're nosy," he said.

"Hey, you said I could ask." She folded her arms across the front of her silky black top. "And yes, I'm nosy."

"Why do you even care?"

"I honestly don't know." The way she said it struck him in the chest. "I guess I'm still fascinated by you, too."

Oof.

He shouldn't want to hear those words—*his* words— reflected back at him.

Scout sucked on the inside of her cheek like she was trying to squash another nosy question. He decided to put her out of her misery.

"I'm not seeing anyone."

But why, exactly? That was the million-dollar question.

Because no other woman ever made me feel the way you do.

Scout's hazel eyes darted across his face like she was trying to look inside him. Or maybe, trying to find a way in. For a moment, with dusk shimmering through the office windows and the flush of pink spreading across her cheeks like watercolor paint, he thought good and long about kissing her. He thought *hard* about kissing her. About lowering his head to those sweet glossy lips and coaxing them open with his own.

He thought about pressing her back to the office wall, bracing one hand on either side of her head and capturing her mouth so rough and so ready it would make them both gasp for breath.

Get out of here. You're supposed to be getting divorced, for crying out loud.

But he couldn't seem to back away.

"Why?" she asked.

"It didn't feel right." That was the most honest he could be right now. Maybe ever. "It *doesn't* feel right."

"Lane..." She took a step toward him. "What *happened* to us? It felt like everything was great and then *poof*! Shit storm."

"It was always going to end that way." He shook his head, hating himself for getting so tangled up in her. She'd had that effect on him from the very first night in Vegas—the way he'd kissed her then, so desperate. So full of need.

It was like he'd found something he didn't even know he could have.

"We made everything..."

"Complicated?" she supplied, quietly.

"Complicated is one way of putting it," he said, shaking his head. "Fucked-up would be another. A complete and utter disaster."

"It really was a disaster, wasn't it?" For some reason, she laughed and he found himself laughing, too. "It was a how-*not*-to guide for getting married."

"We made every mistake in the book." He scrubbed a hand over his face. The laughter had eased his tension a little. Now that they'd acknowledged the elephant in the room, things were a little easier. A little more relaxed.

"Rule one, don't kiss someone you just met in a Vegas hotel elevator. Tick. Rule two, don't throw away a job opportunity to stay with that same person in said Vegas hotel for another two weeks. Tick." She counted the items on her fingers. "Rule three, definitely *don't* marry that person on the last day of your vacation. Tick."

"Rule four," he added. "Don't be worried about introducing that gorgeous woman to your family."

She blinked. "I don't know if that was a mistake. They probably would have hated me on sight."

Would they? He had no idea. He'd never given them a chance to get to know her.

"Some days I wish we'd never left that hotel room," he said, shaking his head.

"We can't exist in a bubble, as much as I think that sounds wonderful."

A moment of connection and understanding passed between them—mistakes had been made on both sides. He was different now, and the Lane of today would handle things differently if they could do it over. He got the impression that she would, too.

If only they'd been a little older and wiser. If only they'd been better equipped for the harsh realities they'd faced back home. If only they weren't quite so damaged by their flaws and shortsightedness.

"It was pretty great in that bubble, wasn't it?" he asked.

Scout looked up at him, her eyes shimmering. "I think those two weeks with you in Vegas were the best weeks of my entire life."

Something snapped inside Lane. The tether that held him to his values—always being responsible and doing what he thought was best and making sacrifices left, right and center—suddenly disintegrated, and he stepped forward into Scout's space. Her head tilted up to him and her eyes grew wide, but there was no ounce of hesitation. No ounce of resistance.

She pressed her hands to his chest and curled her fists into his sweater, tugging him closer. *Yes.*

"Please," she whispered.

He angled his head down and her hungry kiss enveloped him, hot breath filling his mouth where a protest should've been. He crushed her to him, one arm snaking around her shoulders so that there was nothing between them but the clothes on their bodies.

But even that felt like too much to him.

A groan passed between them as their tongues met, and she melted against him. His tongue danced with hers, probing and exploring her with a gentle yet insistent curiosity. She tilted her head back, inviting him in. Inviting him to capture her. His fingers wrapped around the back of her neck, holding her in place, and her nipples beaded as she rubbed against him and he almost went weak at the knees.

It had been a long time…a very long time.

He didn't mean for it to happen—he absolutely had *not* come here looking to get mixed-up with his soon-to-be-ex wife—but once he started he couldn't seem to stop. She made him hungry. Ravenous. The sweet taste of her and the willing way she opened to him tempted Lane to keep pushing. To keep taking.

She rubbed against him, her hands sliding up his chest to clasp behind his neck and drag him closer to her. She pulled him back, stumbling until her back hit the wall of the office so that he could pin her there. He forgot that he was supposed to have stopped loving her.

But it was as if time had been rolled back to that moment in the elevator—and in his hotel room, and later, his apartment—where he'd been struck by her. Bowled over by her. Over the years he'd tried his best to harden his resolve to forget her. To scrub her from his brain.

But this proved that all he'd done was bury those feelings. They weren't gone. They weren't dead. They were *dormant*. Waiting.

They were revived.

He dropped one hand to her hip. Her flimsy top was a tease, the uneven texture of her lace bra almost visible through the silky fabric. The swell of her breasts pushed forward, barely contained. He wanted to rip the line of buttons open so he could expose that beautiful, smooth skin.

Her thumb traced the shell of his ear as they kissed, her lips leaving his mouth to sear a line down his neck. She devoured him. Hot, open-mouthed kisses burned the hollow at the base of his neck as her fingers drove into his hair.

Lane's body screamed for more, and the throbbing below his belt heightened to an unbearable state as she slowly writhed against him. Scout had never made him fail to feel like the only man in the world. The way she turned her attention on him—the blooming, sensuous bundle of heat—whipped him into a frenzy.

It felt so good he couldn't tear himself away. Her hair was silk in his palm, threads of pure gold silk that caught the light.

Her skin was satin and her body was perfectly soft and curved. He slipped one hand under her top, finding the flat plane of her stomach and sliding up, up, up.

"Lane," she gasped as he cupped her breast, flicking his thumb over her hardened nipple. "Yes."

The way she said yes tripped something in his brain. A memory of them in bed together, not long before everything imploded, was like a siren song of warning. Lane stiffened, his mouth freezing against hers. She pulled back immediately, the shutters going down as her eyes lost their sparkle and her luscious lips pressed together.

God, he *hated* that look on her. Every time she shut down like that, it was another lash over his heart.

He took a step back. "I'm sorry."

"I'm..." She shook her head. "I got caught up."

"Me too."

They were both breathing hard, staring at one another like they were playing a game of chicken. Who would make the first move? Who would flinch first?

"I should go," Lane said, and she nodded.

"Thanks for...helping out."

He wasn't sure whether she meant with the lift or carrying things in or letting her borrow Star. It didn't matter. He should *not* have kissed his estranged wife under any circumstances.

Deciding it was probably better to extract himself as quickly as possible, he picked up Star's carrier—not missing the way the little white dog judged him through the thin bars like she knew he was being an epic fool—and he got the hell out of there.

14

"Please be home, please be home." Scout huddled deep in her coat as she walked up to her grandparents' house. The night was cold and the wind whipped her hair and stung her eyes.

She hadn't called ahead—best not to give them time to gather their arguments against her. Heck, an hour ago she hadn't even planned to come and see them tonight. But in an effort not to think about the fact that she'd kissed Lane—or had he kissed her? Did it even matter who'd made the first move?—she'd tried to watch a movie. After starting half a dozen different things on Netflix and not being able to get into any of them, she'd started scrolling Instagram.

While watching the stories section, she'd seen an update

from her sister. Lizzie was at a birthday party sleepover with some friends, which meant her grandparents would be home alone. It would be the perfect time to talk to them about their move and about Scout wanting to keep Lizzie in New York.

They wouldn't be happy about this conversation, but at least if they were alone—without prying teenage ears—they could lay everything on the table. Despite what Scout's relationship with her grandparents was like, she was happy that they loved and sheltered Lizzie. But tearing her away from Scout and all her friends... Well, she couldn't allow that to happen.

Shivering, she hurried up toward the front door and jabbed the doorbell. Her hands were white from the cold since she'd left on such a whim that she hadn't checked her coat pockets for gloves. Bouncing up and down on the spot, she waited. Footsteps sounded inside. Even footsteps.

It was her grandmother.

She caught fuzzy shapes through the curtains on the front window. A second later, the front door swung open and a woman several inches shorter than Scout stood there, worry splashed like red paint across her face.

The expression hardened in an instant. "Scout. What are you doing here?"

If Scout's grandfather was coolly detached and emotionally oblivious, then his wife was his opposite. Joyce Myers had been a teacher, also, but at a Catholic girls' high school rather than a university. She had the severe look of someone who was used to keeping people in line and, even now on a night at home, was dressed impeccably, hair styled, with pearls in her ears.

"If you wanted to see Lizzie, she's—"

"I know she's not home," Scout replied. "I came to speak to you and Norman."

Her grandmother looked at her, mouth flattened into a thin line. For a moment Scout thought she might be turned away.

But then the older woman stepped back and held the door, motioning for her to come inside.

Soft jazz music floated in from the back part of the house and the scent of something cooking wafted from the kitchen— a roast. It was a little past seven and most of the house was in darkness because the ceilings were high and Joyce hated her husband getting up on a ladder to change light bulbs. So she tried to keep them alive as long as possible.

She cared more about the damn light bulbs than she ever did about you.

In the back room, Scout's grandfather sat with a book in his hands, feet resting on a small pouf and his slippers neatly on the floor next to him. A fireplace crackled and there were two wine glasses on the coffee table, with remnants of a dark red liquid in the bottom. The image might exude class, but Scout saw a few cracks in the facade—a threadbare patch in the rug, over which a side table had been placed to mask it. There was a small bar cart, but most of the decanters were empty or close to it, and the sofa looked sad and faded. The cushions had lost their shape and there was a section of fraying on both arms from wear.

Was her grandfather going back to work because they needed the money?

"Scout?" Her grandfather lifted his head up from his book. "Lizzie isn't—"

"I know," she said. If this wasn't their relationship boiled down to a single encounter, she didn't know what was. The fact that they couldn't even comprehend that she would be there to talk with them spoke volumes. "I wanted to speak to you both about your move."

The air in the room was cold and harsh like ice, despite the glowing warmth of the fireplace. They must have known this was coming.

"Sit." Her grandmother pointed to the couch and Scout did as she was told, though part of her wanted to stand, simply to defy them.

Pushing their buttons is a bad idea.

Scout had gone over this conversation nightly since Lizzie called, swirling the arguments around in her head to find the best phrasing and best angle. But in her mind, they always rejected her. It was all she'd ever known, so how could she imagine anything different?

Still, she had to try.

"Lizzie called me last week after you told her about the move," Scout started, folding her hands neatly in her lap. She'd changed her outfit five times before heading over, trying to find the right combination of armor to seem as responsible and grown-up as possible, but all while looking like it wasn't an act. "She was really upset."

"Of course she was upset," her grandfather said, sliding a leather bookmark between the pages of his novel and setting the book down on the table beside him. "She is a teenager and she's attached to her friends. She doesn't want to leave them."

Scout tried not to bristle. *She doesn't want to leave me! Can't you see that?*

"I'm concerned about the effects of such a big upheaval for her," Scout continued, undeterred by her grandfather's ignorantly hurtful comment. "She's at an age where she's trying to figure everything out, and moving her across the country and forcing her to start over could be detrimental."

"People move all the time, Scout." Her grandmother waved a hand and Scout noticed how claw-like her fingers seemed. Her arthritis must be getting worse. "Of course we would have preferred not to disrupt her teen years, but the move is necessary."

Necessary. That didn't sound like it was simply a job opportunity that had intrigued her grandfather enough to come out of retirement.

"I have no doubt at all that you want what's best for her." Scout's throat thickened, but she cleared it. There was no point getting emotional now, as it would only fuel their belief that she wasn't adult enough to handle important situations. "*That* love has never been in question."

For a moment she wondered if her grandmother winced, but maybe it was simply a trick of the light flickering from the fireplace.

"But it's not the only option," Scout continued, keeping her voice steady and her posture ramrod straight. "I'm old enough to take care of Lizzie. I have a good job and there's a promotion on the horizon, and I've saved enough to look for a place with a second bedroom. I'm happy to move here to Brooklyn so she can be close to school and I'll commute to Manhattan for work."

She laid out each element of her proposal clearly and succinctly, without her voice wavering even once. In the face of people that made her instantly revert to rebellious teen, it was quite a feat.

"Scout…" Her grandmother let out a long sigh. "We've been over this before."

"Years ago," Scout pressed. "That was a different time."

"You told us you were responsible then, and look what happened! You went to Vegas for a bachelorette party and you came back married to a stranger, and you wanted me to let *my* granddaughter live in a home with someone you picked up in a seedy casino." Her grandmother's voice was diamond hard. "He could have been anyone!"

"He was a good man."

Is a good man.

"Not good enough to stick around."

Her grandparents didn't know the particulars of the split, and Scout was in no hurry to correct them. As far as she was concerned, it was none of their business. "I was young then."

"You're young now," her grandfather replied. "And it's not only age, Scout. It's maturity. Marrying a stranger like that shows you have poor judgment."

Her heart hammered behind her rib cage and her cheeks filled with prickling warmth. Shame. It felt like a cactus under her skin and acid in her veins.

"Are you divorced yet?" her grandmother asked, folding her arms across her chest in a smug way that said she thought she knew the answer.

"Actually, I spoke with Lane recently. We're drawing up the paperwork to make the split official."

And yet you still kissed him like your life depended on it.

Ugh. She did *not* need to think about that right now.

For a moment she was greeted with surprised silence. Then her grandmother nodded. "That's good."

"Have you got a lawyer?" her grandfather asked.

"Not yet, but—"

"I'll call Bill tomorrow," he said, referring to the man who'd managed a whole host of legal things for the family over the years, including the will that Scout was no longer a part of. "He owes me a favor and it would be better to have someone you can trust to represent you."

She wanted to argue, but why? Because that's how they always made her feel. Like a naughty child. There was no other reason to argue, because playing along would work in her favor. It would show them she'd changed, even if it grated against every part of her to let them have a hand in it.

"Okay," she replied. "Thank you."

Norman and Joyce looked at her as if they were trying to

figure out whether an alien had taken over their granddaughter's body.

"And you've been working steadily?" her grandmother asked.

"I have. I'm an office manager for a talent agency, but my boss has been talking about making me an account manager so I'd have my own clients and opportunity to help grow the business." The words came out as she'd rehearsed them. Of course she left out the bit about Isla being her boss, because her grandparents would assume it was a pity job, even though it wasn't. "I've been there six months and I really like it. I was even thinking I might go back to school and do something in communications or something like that."

That wasn't *strictly* true, but it wasn't totally untrue, either. Scout had thought about what might happen beyond Paws in the City, and if she wanted to continue working in the industry, then additional education might be required. Did she *want* to go back to school? Uh, no. But she might do it if it felt necessary.

"That's very good thinking." Her grandfather nodded. "Education is important."

"I will be a good influence on Lizzie, I swear." This, at least, she could say with every molecule of sincerity in her heart. "I've got my life together. I'm fixing my mistakes and I'm laying down the foundations for my future. I've *changed*."

Joyce looked over at Norman, and something passed between them, but Scout knew her grandparents wouldn't be convinced by a single impassioned speech and an olive branch. It would take more. But she had her foot in the door now.

"Let us talk it over," Joyce said, standing. "This is not what we had in mind."

"But you'll consider it?" Hope flooded through Scout's body. "Really?"

"We make no promises." Her grandfather was already reaching for his book and Scout realized she was being dismissed. "But we'll talk it through."

"Thank you." Scout stood. She hadn't even changed out of her coat, because not once had she imagined that she might stay a moment longer than was necessary. Nor had she felt welcome to stay a moment longer than necessary. "And I appreciate you asking Bill to help with the divorce paperwork."

Without waiting for one of them to see her out, Scout left of her own accord. It was a small act of independence, but she would take whatever she could get right now. Not receiving an outright no was the best she could have hoped for. There was still a chance she could convince them yet!

"Star, no! What did you do?"

Lane stood in his doorway, blinking at the wreckage that had befallen his living room. His pillow and two T-shirts were strewn across the floor, clearly dragged from the bedroom where the trail of destruction began with an overturned laundry basket. The pillow had been torn open and feathers littered the space like oversize flakes of snow, and a scarf hung over a lampshade on the table next to the couch, which was an impressive feat given the dog's height.

Star sat in the middle of it all, her sweet face and black-button eyes staring back at him without any malice at all. Her pink tongue lolled out of her mouth and she wagged her tail, happy to see him.

Hi, Dad! I'm glad you're home. I got bored, so I decided to redecorate.

He'd only been gone for fifteen minutes—just long enough to grab a few groceries from the bodega downstairs so he could make dinner, because he'd felt like something home-cooked.

In that time, the dog had seemingly demolished anything she could get her paws on.

You have an unresolved issue that she is picking up on. If you want to fix this issue with Star, then first you need to stop lying to yourself.

The psychic's words danced in his head, and that only cranked up his frustration. He *wasn't* lying to himself. He was happy with his life. With his job. With Star.

Well, *usually* he was happy with Star.

"Don't wag your tail at me," he grumbled, setting the bag of groceries down on the kitchen island and scrubbing a hand over his face. Then he went to pick up his pillow, and as he lifted it from the ground, even more feathers fluttered out.

Star immediately bowed her head, knowing she was in trouble.

"I'm not angry, I'm…" He sighed. "You don't understand a word I'm saying anyway. I can talk to you as much as I want and it doesn't mean a goddamn thing."

He set about cleaning the apartment by stuffing the pillow into a garbage bag and picking up all the loose feathers, which Star thought was a very fun game indeed. She raced around the room, kicking the feathers up and barking at him, while her tail was a blur behind her.

"This isn't playtime." He sounded like a complete grouch. Was it so bad that his dog was being a little naughty in the grand scheme of things?

He picked up one of the T-shirts and saw perfect canine teeth–sized holes in the fabric. The scarf also had a few threads pulled, which distorted the check pattern. It had been a gift from his mom some years ago—a congratulations for selling his company—and he knew the scarf had been more than was really in her budget.

For a moment Lane stood in the middle of the room, feeling totally and utterly lost. Star had turned into a demonic little creature he barely recognized.

"What is going on right now?"

You need to make peace with what happened in the past.

But did he? His life had been going on perfectly fine without either a wife or a brother the last couple of years. Wasn't that the definition of peace?

Then Star did something strange. She walked right over to the front door and flopped her furry little ass down, raised one paw and scraped at the door like she'd done for months after Scout left.

Maybe Lane had made peace with the past, but what about Star? Was she missing Scout? Was it lonely just being with him?

He didn't want to think that the psychic's words had any influence on him at all, but…

God, what did he have to lose? The next attempt to fix the issue with Star would be seeing a dog trainer, and that was a big-time investment. Maybe he could call Scout over and see how Star reacted.

Without digging too far into whether this issue was more about Star or about him, he grabbed his phone and called Scout. She picked up on the third ring.

"Hello?" She sounded a little breathless.

It immediately sent him back in time to the way she panted his name when he made love to her. He thought seriously about hanging up and claiming it was a butt call.

"Lane?" She sounded clearer now. "You there?"

"Hey, uh…" Shit. What the hell was he doing? "I, um, I need a favor."

"Well, I certainly owe you a few at this point, don't I?" She laughed and the sound was like liquid gold. "What do you need?"

"Can you come over? It's to do with Star."

He sensed the tension over the line before she spoke. "Is she okay?"

"Yeah, she's fine. It's nothing serious, but her behavioral issues are getting worse and…I'm at my wit's end."

"I don't know what I can do to help, but I'm happy to try," she said.

"Have you had dinner? I was planning to make some pasta and…" He swallowed. "It's easy to make extra if you're hungry."

"You know what? I'm actually *starving*."

It made him smile because Scout had always been starving back in the day. The woman had a metabolism like a pro athlete, and she never shied away from something tasty. He'd always suspected it had come from her growing up with food insecurity. Lane had loved to cook for her, because it was a way he could show her what she meant to him. A way for him to provide her with the security and comfort her mother never had.

"Great, I'll get it on now."

"And I'll pick up some wine on the way over. See you soon."

Lane ended the call and stuffed his phone into his back pocket, feeling excitement unfurling in his stomach like a flower opening up to the sun. But he tamped the feeling down as quickly as it began.

This was about Star. About figuring out what she needed.

It was nothing to do with him.

15

For the third time in as many weeks, Scout found herself on Lane's doorstep. She knocked, shook out her hair, which had been dampened with the fine mist of rain outside, and bounced up and down on the spot. Footsteps approached and the door swung open, allowing the scent of onions, mushrooms, garlic and chili flakes to waft out.

"Hey, come in." He stepped back and smiled. This time there was no suspicion in his face, no reservation. "Dinner is about five minutes away."

"That smells incredible." Butterflies tickled the inside of her stomach. "Here, I got something for us to drink."

She thrust the bottle into his hands as she stepped inside, pausing to unzip her ankle boots and shrug out of her coat.

She hung the coat on a hook mounted to the wall, right next to his. The image made her breath catch—her bright red coat next to his dark one was so familiar.

"I'll grab some glasses." He headed into the kitchen.

"Where's Star?" Scout asked, looking around.

"She is currently in a time-out in my office." He got out the bottle opener and eased the cork out of the wine. It made a glugging sound as he poured it into two stemmed glasses. "I came home from getting ingredients for dinner to find that she'd decided to destroy the house."

Scout raised an eyebrow and looked around the apartment. As usual, it was neat as a pin. Unlike the reputation that a lot of men had when they lived alone, Lane kept his home fastidiously well-ordered and tidy. To him, destruction could mean that she'd knocked a cup over and spilled some water onto the ground.

"What did she do?"

"Where to start? She tore my pillow to shreds and sprayed feathers all over the room. She put holes in two of my T-shirts, threw laundry all over the bedroom and damaged a scarf that was a gift from my mom."

"Wow." Scout blinked. "That seems very out of character."

Lane slid a glass across the island toward her. "As was running off and hiding under a couch at the photoshoot we went to and being all squirrelly with you and getting herself tangled up in a net hammock at work."

"Wait, *what*?" Scout took a sip of the wine. "She got tangled in a hammock?"

"Almost guillotined her paws right off." He took a sip of his wine and went to check on the pasta, which appeared done. "I'm going to serve this up. Can you grab the bread out of the oven?"

"Sure." Scout went over to help.

"The oven mitts are—"

"Second cupboard on the left," she finished. "I remember."

Something flickered across his face, but he turned before she could decipher what it might be. Scout slipped the mitts on and retrieved a baguette split in half and smothered with butter and herbs. They worked together, getting the meal ready to eat and moving around one another as if they'd been choreographed.

She remembered where everything was, fetching the forks without him asking, and grabbing a jug of water from the fridge. A few minutes later, they were seated at the table across from one another and Scout was having a hard time figuring out whether she was existing in the present moment or whether the memories had finally sucked her back into the past.

"Cheers." Scout held her wine glass out to Lane's and they chimed when they touched. "To favors."

"And old friends."

Scout took a sip, willing the wine to work its magic and start loosening her up. After the talk with her grandparents, she felt tight as a spring, and then getting a call from Lane with him asking for her help…

Rattled didn't even *begin* to cover it.

"So, how can I help with Star?" she asked, spearing a mushroom with her fork and twirling to pick up some pasta.

When she popped it into her mouth, she had to stop herself from moaning. It was such a simple meal, but Lane had a knack for flavor and he could make even something basic like pasta with a red sauce taste exquisite.

"I feel like she's been acting up ever since you came to my apartment that first time and…it's making me wonder if perhaps she misses you. Or something." He chewed a mouthful of pasta and Scout held her tongue, because she wanted to hear everything Lane had to say. "I uh, had some advice that maybe she's feeling a sense of unfinished business between us."

"Advice from who?" she asked.

"It was a..." He looked like he was trying to think about how to word his answer. "A pet communication expert."

"And what the heck is that?" She laughed. It sounded like one of those job titles that said one thing and meant another. "Sounds like a psychic or something."

"Well, yeah."

Scout's hand froze as she reached for her wine. "Let me get this straight. You took your dog to a pet psychic, and that person told you there's unfinished business between us and that's why your dog is behaving badly?"

"There's a bit more to it than that, but yeah." He raked a hand through his dark hair and laughed. The warm lighting from the fixture overhead brought out the burnished tones in the brown strands and it made his eyes look even greener than usual. "Don't tell me I'm being ridiculous, because one of us at this table already thinks it."

"You're not being ridiculous. It's an unusual turn of events, because I never saw you as the type to turn to the otherworldly for guidance."

"I'm not. But I'm desperate." He stabbed at a mushroom. "And the next step is putting Star through some training, which would take up a lot of time. I'll do it, of course. I want her to be happy and she's clearly...not, at the moment."

"Do you really think my leaving had that much of an impact on her? I mean, I was only here a month." Even as she said the words, Scout knew it wasn't a meaningless amount of time. It was short, yes. But it had been intense.

That month had felt like years. It had felt like everything.

"After you left she was..." His eyes dropped for a moment.

"She was really sad. She used to cry at the door and get excited anytime there was a knock."

Oof.

Guilty tears immediately sprang to Scout's eyes, but she blinked them away. "I had no idea."

Nobody had ever been sad to see her go before, except Lizzie. And Lizzie had been too young to know any better.

"Why would you?" Lane asked. "I don't mean that as a snide way of pointing out that you left. It's a genuine statement. You would have had no way of knowing."

"I would if I'd picked up the phone," she admitted.

Lane had called her a lot, trying to reconcile. Begging her to come home. Like a coward, she'd sent an email telling him that she was fine and staying with a friend but that she wasn't coming back. She'd signed off saying that she loved him, but in her heart, she knew it wouldn't work between them.

He'd stopped calling after that.

"We don't have to hash that out," Lane said. "But I thought maybe if you spent some time with Star, then…I don't know. Maybe it might soothe whatever raw feelings she has about it."

Scout bit down on her lip. It seemed like a Band-Aid solution—because she wasn't going to be around forever. And then when she left, wouldn't that make it worse? But she couldn't think of a way that didn't sound hurtful to say those things.

Not to mention, she was starting to think that never seeing Lane and Star again might cause some raw feelings of her own.

"I know it seems stupid," he said. "And I know there's a chance it won't work, but if it does, then maybe you might want to see Star every so often, even after we…"

He couldn't say the word. Her already tender heart ached even harder.

"Anytime I can have a little ball of fluff keep me company,

I will absolutely take it." She smiled. "And why not try, right? If that's not the problem, then it shouldn't cause any harm."

"That's what I thought." His shoulders lowered a bit and he let out a breath. "Thanks."

"Thank you, Lane. For being such a gentleman about this whole thing." She looked at him across the table, wondering how the heck she got so lucky to be married to a man like him even if it was doomed to fail from the beginning. "You could have slammed the door in my face when I turned up that first time. I've never forgotten what a good person you are."

"You, too, Scout. You, too."

After dinner, Lane went to fetch Star from her "time-out." When he returned to the main room, he spotted Scout standing by the window, looking out at the glittering skyline. Her long blond hair hung in a sheet down her back, and she'd wrapped her arms around herself. She was dressed for battle tonight—black jeans, a gray turtleneck sweater, which showed off her curves without being too tight.

He wondered where she'd been before this.

For a moment he didn't move for fear of distracting her and breaking the quiet beauty of the scene before him. He remembered the first time she'd seen the view, the night they returned home from Vegas. They'd stopped by her cramped apartment, where she told her roommates she was moving out and then she packed up everything she owned—which filled little more than a suitcase—and didn't look back.

Back then, Lane had only just purchased this apartment with the proceeds of an app he'd sold to Microsoft. It had been a big moment for two reasons. One, because he was making a name for himself and the sale was getting a lot of media attention. Two, it was a show of commitment to Unison and to Rav, that he was throwing all his attention into the collaborative project.

But that night he hadn't cared about anything besides her.

He pushed the door open and hoisted her up, carrying her over the threshold. She giggled, telling him that it was such a silly tradition. But the sound died on her lips when he set her down and she was drawn to the view like a moth to flame. Her palms flattened against the glass, and her breath created a ring of fog as she exhaled.

"This is…" Her voice was thick. "I've never seen anything so beautiful."

Lane wheeled her suitcase into the room and closed the door, hanging back so he could watch her. The sight of her standing there could have been a piece of art. A painting. Her joy and surprise were enough to keep his heart warm forever.

"Neither have I, Scout," he said. "Neither have I."

Lane cleared his throat and Scout turned. For a moment it looked like there were tears in her eyes, but she blinked and they were gone. His imagination was working in overdrive, clearly.

Either that or you're projecting.

"Here's the little rascal," he said, placing Star down on the ground.

At first she trotted around, clearly happy to be given free-range privileges once more, but when she spotted Scout, she suddenly became still.

"Hi, Star."

Star looked over to Scout and he would swear the little dog's eyes narrowed. Then, like an evil spirit had invaded the animal's body, she started scraping at her collar like she couldn't stand it being on her. She growled and tried to pull it away from her body, using her back leg.

"Star, no!" Scout came over to intervene. "Don't do that."

She crouched down and reached out, but Star wasn't having

it. The dog snapped, catching the side of Scout's hand with one sharp tooth and causing her to yelp in surprise. The dog skittered back, equally shocked that she'd almost bitten someone.

Star might be a little feisty from time to time, but she'd *never* bitten someone.

Scout's cheeks turned red, and she stood suddenly, her eyes darting over to Lane. "Sorry, she… I must have startled her."

What the heck was going on?

"Star, go to your basket." Lane pointed to the wicker dog bed which was piled with cozy blankets the dog loved to burrow into. Star reverted back to her usual self and trotted over to him with her tongue lolling out of her mouth, her eyes bright and feather-duster tail wagging. "Go on."

The dog did as she was told and Lane looked over to Scout. "You're bleeding."

She looked down. Bright red blood had welled in the scrape where Star had nicked her, and there was a rivulet slowly making its way down her little finger. "Ah crap."

"Let me get my first aid kit."

Curling her hand inward to stop the blood dripping, Scout headed over to the kitchen and grabbed some paper towels from the roll Lane always kept in his prep area. Pressing one to her hand, she headed to the bathroom. She needed a moment.

Her face felt hot and she was sure she must look like a tomato. Of course she knew that going straight in to touch the little dog was going to elicit an aggressive reaction, especially when she was in the middle of throwing a tantrum. Scout couldn't blame Star for that. It was her own damn fault.

But now she looked incompetent. In front of Lane—Mr. Got His Shit Together—no less. Just wonderful.

She locked herself inside the bathroom for a moment. Yep, her suspicions were correct. Looking at herself in the mirror, she was indeed bright red in the cheeks. Her eyes were also misty and there was a deep frown marring her forehead.

Take a breath. You can handle a little embarrassment.

She filled her lungs slowly, then held her breath for three counts before releasing it. In the few sessions of therapy she'd ever attended, that was the thing that had stuck. The power of breath. She took another one in and repeated the same steps.

Why are you such a mess?

Her reflection held no answers. There were days where Scout felt like she couldn't even get the smallest things right. She was prone to making mistakes the way some people were prone to bumping into furniture or speaking before they thought. It felt like she lived her life with the universe constantly sticking an invisible foot in front of her, looking for any opportunity to trip her up.

Self-pity never helped anyone. So you will pull yourself together and go out there as a confident woman. Then you'll excuse yourself and go home.

She didn't need to be here. It was only her sense of obligation that had made her come. But clearly she wasn't going to be much help with Star's issues.

There was a knock on the door. "Are you okay?"

Gathering herself, and after checking her makeup in the mirror to make sure she wasn't smudged, she opened the door. "I'm fine."

To his credit, he appeared genuinely concerned. His beautiful green eyes were locked on to her in a way that felt deliciously familiar, and the empathy she'd always found so very attractive was scrawled across his face.

"How's the hand?" he asked. "Do we need to take you for a tetanus shot?"

We. Like he'd be there with her.

"It's just a nick. Star doesn't bite people."

"I think she looked as surprised as you did." He raked a hand through his hair. "I don't know what's going on with her lately. All the barking and misbehaving… It's not like her."

"You did say it started around the time I came to your place. Maybe I'm a bad influence on dogs as well as people." She meant for it to sound like a joke, but there was a little too much hurt beneath the surface, so her words sounded brittle.

"You're not a bad influence," he said, shaking his head. "Don't say that."

She looked down.

"Let's get a Band-Aid onto it," he said softly.

Heading back into the small bathroom, she removed the paper towel and tossed it into the tiny silver trash can in the corner. Then she ran the water over her hand, grimacing at the sting, and gently washed the blood away. It was a minor cut. One of those injuries that looked worse than they were because fingertips tended to bleed like a stuck pig. After her hand was cleaned up, she splashed some water onto her face and then dried herself off.

Lane came into the bathroom with a box of Band-Aids in his hand. It was hard not to be aware of how close they were. The apartment had two bathrooms and this was the smaller of the two, which meant that his shoulder brushed hers as they stood next to one another. She could smell him—the scent of fruity wine on his breath and the faint whiff of cologne on his skin and the hair product he used that smelled a little bit like fresh laundry. The air was charged with little electric sparks, a sizzle and pop of energy that Scout hadn't felt in a very long time.

"Ready?" he asked, tearing the packaging off a Band-Aid.

Yes. No… I don't know.

Scout nodded.

His gaze tracked over her face, as if he was trying to glean some information. She hoped to hell that he couldn't hear what she was thinking—the vicious voices in her head that she'd lived with since she was a child. Lane had always been too good at that, looking closely. Seeing things she didn't want him to see.

"Give me your hand." He reached for her.

She could have done it herself, easily. Scout had fixed up more than her share of injuries over the years when she had no one to care for her. But in that moment, she desperately wanted someone to care for her. She desperately wanted *him* to care for her.

This is dangerous. You know what's at stake.

The divorce. Custody of Lizzie. The fact that her heart might be only one more disappointment away from shattering irreparably.

But all sensible thought was drowned by the need roaring inside her. Unfulfilled desires and loneliness and nostalgia created a siren song in her mind. His eyes tracked over her face, like he was cataloguing the details of her. She did the same—admiring the proud thrust of his nose and rich multifaceted green of his eyes and the lines that hadn't been there before.

She wanted him. Wanted to taste him. Wanted to feel him. Wanted to see if it was as good as it used to be.

He was a drug and she was chasing the high of him.

He touched her wrist, turning her hand over so her palm faced up. Then he wrapped the Band-Aid around the tip of her finger with such care it was hard to believe he felt nothing. It was hard to believe they'd snuffed out the spark between them.

"Lane…" Her lips parted, then closed, then parted again.

What are you doing? *This marriage is over. It was never a real marriage to begin with.*

But nothing could stop the tidal wave of wanting. Nothing but Lane, himself.

His eyes bored into hers and he brought her hand up to his mouth, his lips brushing the sensitive skin of her palm.

"There. All better," he said. His voice was rough, husky. It sounded like it used to when he whispered to her in the middle of the night, reaching under the covers and finding her warm and ready.

"Thank you," she whispered.

They stood, staring one another down. Sizing one another up. The air was so thick between them, she wondered if he might need to swim the last steps toward her. Or, at the very least, slice through the space with a knife so there was room to move. Her body was wound tighter than a spring and in the quiet she could feel her heart thumping.

You shouldn't do this. He's going to break you.

Not physically, of course. Lane was a teddy bear. Well, a teddy bear with a six-pack and an ass that looked like the peach emoji…but a teddy bear nonetheless.

But he could break her emotionally. As it was, Scout's heart was barely held together with blind optimism, duct tape and Instagram motivational quotes. One bump and it might fall apart completely. One bump from the one and only man she'd ever dared to love…

Do you want your heart crushed into a billion itty-bitty pieces, huh? There's too much at stake. You'll never be good enough for him. It won't work.

But those thoughts had cycled in her head so many times they'd lost color and meaning. They'd become shapeless and soft. They didn't resonate the way they should anymore. It was like she'd become desensitized to the risk of him. To the inevitably painful conclusion they'd find together.

And she could no longer stay away.

16

"Scout." His hands twitched. He wanted to touch her. She could feel his need vibrating in the air around him and it was headier than any drug. "I shouldn't... But..."

But.

She felt that catch down to her very bones. That tug. That *want*.

No good could come of this, whispering and brushing touches and stolen glances. The familiarity of it gripped her with concrete hands. This was why she'd fallen for Lane in the first place—because he made her feel desired. Wanted. Worthy.

All things she desperately craved.

Lane reached out and brushed her hair back over her shoulders. It tumbled down her back, and the action—so simple and so tender—was like a plug being yanked from a wall. She was disconnected from logic. From fear.

Stepping forward, she closed the space between them and placed her hands on his chest. Soft fabric met her fingertips and underneath he was hard and warm.

Real.

He drove his hands into her hair roughly and a shudder rippled through her. Rough wasn't Lane's style—not usually. He was considered and meticulous and thorough. The action showed her how on edge he was and...

It was glorious.

In a heartbeat, his lips were on hers and he shoved her back against the bathroom counter. Something behind them rattled and tipped over. But neither of them stopped. Their kiss was wild and explosive—teeth scraping, hands tugging and mouths gasping.

Scout fisted her hands in his sweater, feeling the fabric strain under her iron grasp. But she had to hang on—to him, to this moment, to her sanity. His tongue slid into her mouth and one hand slid up her waist, smoothing over the contours of her body, until it connected with the swell of her breast. It didn't matter that she had a sweater on and that she couldn't feel him skin to skin. With Lane, every single touch mattered. Scout rocked against him, keeping her lips on his. His body was coiled and she could feel his excitement pressing against her stomach.

She wanted him. He wanted her. Chemistry had never been their issue.

Lane's other hand reached behind her, shoving aside whatever had fallen. Then he hoisted her up, nudging her knees apart so he could stand between her legs.

Yes. More. Now.

This was how she remembered the nights they shared in Vegas—hot, passionate, insatiable lust.

She yanked her sweater up and over her head, tossing it to the floor. Then his lips were on her, crawling down her neck and over her chest.

"Back clasp," she gasped, arching into his touch.

He reached behind her and unclipped her bra—no fumbling, no fuss. That too was tossed aside. He palmed her bare breast and Scout began to grow fuzzy. The deep haze of arousal was pulling her under and she had no will to resist. Her nipples beaded and sweet relief came when Lane brought his head down and sucked one of them into his mouth, bringing her straight to the edge of mind-numbing pleasure.

He *knew* what she needed. What she liked. Knew her body, her mind, her pleasure points. He knew her like no other man ever had.

She fisted her hands in his hair, pulling his head up so that his lips connected with hers. Then she wound her arms around his neck, hanging on for dear life. In that moment she no longer cared if this was her undoing. If she would be no more than rubble after he'd scorched her to the ground.

It didn't matter.

Only this mattered. The scent of faded aftershave on his skin. The fire of his touch. The delicious blurring of her mind as she gave in to him. All the memories of their weeks in Vegas roared back to life in color and sound, the good bits amplified and the darkness that followed blotted away until she wondered if it had ever happened.

"I want you, Scout." His voice was sandpaper in her ear and it rubbed her raw. "I've *been* wanting you since…"

"Me too," she whispered.

He pulled his head back and looked at her, his green eyes full of emotion—Lane hadn't often been like this when they were together. He'd always been…perfect. Together. But now he was a man wading through his feelings and it showed like storm clouds drifting across his face.

"Don't ask me anything, please." She closed her eyes for a moment, unable to see the flicker of pain because she felt it right in her soul. "Just touch me."

The noise he made shot through her like a flaming arrow. "Then, I'm taking you to bed. We're not…we're not going to have a quick fuck in my bathroom, okay?"

He grasped her chin, yanking her face up to his. Her eyes fluttered open.

"Okay?" he repeated.

"Yes." She nodded. "Take me to bed."

He grabbed her hips and pulled her forward, encouraging her to wrap her legs around him. And then he carried her to the bedroom, navigating the apartment using one hand while his other cupped her ass and he kissed her. His breath was warm against her cheek, and when he reached the bedroom, she was shocked by how familiar it felt to be here.

She belonged.

Stop it. That life you keep fantasizing about? It's gone.

Except that was a lie. It wasn't gone, because it had never existed in the first place. Scout was never going to be a permanent fixture in his life. Their marriage was never going to be anything more than a fleeting, wonderful and frustrating experience—harder to grab on to than a wisp of smoke.

He laid her down on the bed and she looked up at him. It was hard not to want Lane. He seemed to fit her so perfectly— he seemed to truly *see* her in a way other men didn't. In a way other *people* didn't.

He hooked his fingers into the waistband of her jeans, rubbing the backs of his fingers against her stomach. This was really happening. Now. He popped the button on her jeans and pulled the zipper down slowly, his breath catching. Under his gaze she'd always felt beautiful. Treasured.

Until she hadn't.

Stop thinking so much. Just…feel.

He pulled the denim down over her thighs and discarded them on the floor. For a moment he watched her, silently. Was he having the same kinds of feeling as she was? Did he want to stop? Did she?

No.

She hooked her fingers under the elasticized lace of her underwear and held his gaze as she slowly shimmied it down her thighs, lifting her hips to help things along. He stood there like a statue, drinking her in. She pulled one foot out and then let the fabric dangle over her ankle until she used her other foot to drop the underwear onto the floor by his feet.

It was a declaration of intent. She wasn't going to walk away now.

He sunk to his knees at the edge of the bed and then came forward, sliding his hands up over her legs. He kissed the inside of her knee and moved higher, widening her. She shivered when he brushed the top of her inner thigh, anticipation building in the quiet room.

"Lane," she gasped, reaching for him. But he moved his head out of her reach. An icy hand gripped her heart. "What's wrong?"

He shook his head. "You're so beautiful."

She closed her eyes. For some reason, the words felt…raw. "You don't need to do that."

"What?"

"Make me feel like…like it means something." She couldn't think like that, because it meant something last time, and it broke her.

Emotion flickered across his face, but then it dimmed. He retreated. And in place was only fire and smoke.

"Then let's concentrate on what feels good." He spread her thighs with his palms, holding her wide-open. "Tell me you want me here."

"I *do* want you here. I want…" Her thighs were practically trembling under his touch. "You, Lane. Just you."

The sparkling city lights caught on the gleaming strands of his hair as he kissed his way up her inner thigh. His tongue brushed tentatively against the sensitive skin of her sex and her head rolled back. He hesitated only a moment before feasting on her, using his tongue and his lips until she writhed against him.

"Yes." Her hips rocked against his mouth, one hand finding its way to his head as her fingers drove through his hair and pulled him to the exact spot she wanted.

Scout arched her back, her eyes clamping shut as she lost herself to sensation. He slipped one finger inside her, all the while drawing her closer to the edge of release with his mouth. The scratch of his stubble caused sparks to ignite inside her. One, two, three. Fireworks.

"Lane," she gasped, her fingers tightening in his hair. "Yes."

The intensity built, ripples of pleasure blurring together until her entire body hummed with sensation. Her orgasm hit hard and intense. She grabbed his pillow and held it over her mouth, muffling the cries that came from so deep inside her it was like she was no longer in control of her body.

As she hit release and sank back into the hazy glow of satisfaction, she dropped the pillow beside her. For a moment there was nothing. Sound and light and feeling were all blotted out by one single thought.

How did she get here?

She looked down into the dim light to see Lane resting his

cheek against her inner thigh. His green eyes were like fire. She was thrust back into the past—to that hotel room in Vegas.

Their first night.

Scout had considered herself experienced, but sex had always felt a little…performative. But not with him. Not even for a second. Lane had the kind of hands that could make every single doubt fly out of a woman's head. He was confident but not arrogant. Sure of himself without being overbearing. He was the Goldilocks of lovers.

He's not perfect.

It was all too easy to put the man on a pedestal, especially when he touched her like that.

His lips found the curve of her hip, his hand smoothing over her thighs and stomach as if he could use his touch to commit her to memory. Or *re*commit, as it were. Had he forgotten how she felt? How she tasted?

Or did he remember everything in frighteningly vivid detail, like she did?

There were bad ideas.

And then there was Scout Myers.

But that was the thing about her… Lane knew the freight train was coming straight toward him and he still stood right on the spot, bracing himself. How could he not? She lay on his bed—the bed he'd shared with her—pale blond hair fanned out on the pillow and hazel eyes hooded and sultry.

Her hand reached out to pull him closer, and for a second, he hesitated. Not once since Scout whirled back into his life like the tornado she was had he thought they would get to this point. Lane was a man of great responsibility and control.

Sleeping with his wife was the antithesis of that.

Why couldn't he resent her for leaving, at least enough that he could keep his head in control rather than his dick? Why didn't he know better? Why couldn't he put his head before his heart?

She propped herself up on her forearms. "You should get undressed now."

Her voice was smooth and smoky, like whiskey. It coiled around him and silenced doubt and logic.

Just one night…

"Do you dare me?" he asked.

Scout's lips lifted into a wicked grin and she nodded, so Lane rose off the bed and took a step back. He tore his sweater and T-shirt off, noting how her eyes were locked on to him.

"You really want to do this?"

She sucked in a breath. "I do."

I do.

Couldn't she have chosen literally any *other* affirmation?

The sound of his belt sliding through the loops cut through the quiet room, and soon it hit the floor along with his socks and jeans. He stood in his underwear for a moment before drawing the last item down over his hips, feeling his erection spring up against his stomach.

He hadn't felt this excited in… The last time she was in his bed.

He fished around in his bedside drawer for a condom. Finding one floating right at the back, he carefully tore the foil packet open and rolled the condom down on himself. Scout shuffled back to climb under the covers, holding the edge of the duvet up in invitation.

As he got into bed beside her, the scent of her fruity perfume mixing with a bare touch of sweat, it was like he was entering a time machine.

"Stop remembering," she whispered, touching his face. "This is *now*, okay? Not then. Not before."

He crushed his lips down to hers, driven by need and emotion and the desire he'd had for this woman ever since he set eyes on her. When she kissed him, he let everything in his head get wiped away.

They were adults. Sex didn't have to mean something. It certainly didn't have to lead to anything.

This was about satisfying a physical urge. He pulled Scout toward him, encouraging her to straddle him. She did, without hesitation.

"I always liked you on top," he said, running his palms up and down her thighs. Her hair trailed over her body and when she arched her back slightly, rubbing against him, she looked like a goddess.

"I like being on top, too," she responded with a wicked smile.

He rubbed at her entrance. Scout hummed and pressed her palms down onto his chest, letting all that glorious blond hair tumble forward. As she came farther down, touching her lips to his, it fell in a sheet around them, making it feel like they existed in their own private bubble.

"Ready?" she asked, tugging on his lower lip in a way that made him want to burst on the spot.

"So ready."

She reached down between her legs and guided him inside her. The sensation was all-encompassing and he pushed up, gasping at the shock of how tightly she enveloped him. Scout rocked back and forth, getting comfortable. Then, when she opened her eyes and nodded, he gripped her hips and thrust up to meet her. She didn't hold back.

She grabbed his hands and brought them around to her ass. "Hold me here."

He sunk his fingers into her flesh and she pressed her face into his neck, rolling her hips over and over and over. Lane let his head fall back against the pillow, losing himself to the rhythm. "That feels so good."

She pressed her mouth down to his, meeting him thrust for thrust. Orgasm welled inside him, and when she whispered his name right into his ear, the past blurring in the edges of his mind, he plunged himself deep. He wanted that moment back—that blissful ignorance, that happiness, that completeness.

Why did they have to go and mess it all up?

"Lane..." Her voice was raw. Emotional. "Come with me."

He couldn't resist. He could never resist. With one last thrust, he rocked up into her and tipped over the edge, crying her name over and over like it was the only word he knew.

Like she was all he knew.

17

Scout woke in the depths of the night to an inky bedroom and a warm, delicious man by her side. Lane's arm was thrown across her stomach as he lay facedown, his head turned away from her. His dark, red-tinted hair was delightfully rumpled, and the sheets were draped halfway across his ass in the most enticing manner.

Don't get attached.

Scout slipped out from under his arm and got out of the bed. Beneath her feet, the floorboards were cool and the city glittered in the large window. It made her feel like she was suspended in midair. Lane's breathing filled the room. He'd always been a heavy sleeper, working himself so hard that the only option was to collapse into bed at night. He looked like a god who'd fallen to earth and decided to stay awhile.

Speaking of staying awhile...you shouldn't.

She made her way back through the apartment, collecting her clothes and turning off the lights as she went, leaving only a single lamp to light her way. Their dishes sat in the sink from their meal, as they'd gotten distracted by Star almost taking a chunk out of Scout's finger and then with her and Lane falling into bed.

He hated to wake up to a mess.

Quietly as she could, she collected the dishes from the table and stacked them into the dishwasher and located the saver for the wine bottle. No sound came from the bedroom. For a moment she stood in the middle of his apartment, feeling déjà vu wash over her.

She'd left in the night once before, and it felt like a betrayal to do it again.

This is a one-night stand. You're under no obligation to stay.

As if woken by the noisy inner workings of Scout's brain, Star lifted her head sleepily from her bed. Scout raised a fingertip to her lips. "Shh."

But the little dog didn't listen. Instead, she padded over to Scout and sat. Her tail wasn't wagging, but there were no teeth bared, either. She blinked, dropping her head for a moment and then tilting her marshmallow face back up as if to say, *So uh, about last night...*

Scout crouched but didn't try to touch the dog. "I'm sorry I invaded your space, but you didn't need to snap at me."

Star hung her head and Scout got the distinct impression she felt guilty about it. The dog let out a sigh, and then, to Scout's shock, she raised one paw, asking to shake.

Scout had taught her that.

"You're asking for a truce, huh?" She reached for the dog's paw and shook it. "Okay, truce."

When the dog returned her paw to the ground, there was

a faint movement in her tail. Just a flicker. Then it was still, again.

"I really did miss you, you know." She chewed on the inside of her cheek. "I'd never had a dog growing up. Living here was the first time in a very long time that I didn't feel lonely anymore, and you were a big part of that."

Star tilted her head to one side and then the other. The action always made Scout laugh, because she was so darn adorable. Was it possible that Star was acting out because she was mad about Scout leaving and then coming back? Did dogs feel those kinds of emotions?

Or was she simply trying to assign human behavior to an animal?

Her eyes prickled with tears, but she blinked them away. "I wish…I wish things had turned out differently. I don't know exactly what that might have looked like, but in a perfect world, we'd still be happily married and my sister would live with us and I'd cuddle you every day."

The dog came forward and pressed her nose into Scout's hand. Gently and slowly, so as not to startle her, Scout ran a hand over Star's fluffy head. The fur was soft beneath her fingertips and the dog's eyes fluttered shut for a moment.

"I'm sorry I left."

That was the first time she'd admitted to being sorry that she'd chosen to leave, not sorry that she *had* to leave. Tonight had muddied the waters, like she'd smeared paint over the past and now couldn't see it clearly anymore. At the time, leaving had felt vital. Necessary.

Her marriage was the reason her grandparents had kept Lizzie away from her, and for what? For Lane to keep her a secret from the world? For her to feel like she was a shameful smudge on his perfect life?

Scout stood, wrapping her arms around herself.

But then tonight, Lane had shown how he could make her feel wanted and seen and cared for. He could make her feel like no other person had *ever* made her feel.

"You were tempted by that last time," she said to herself. "And it didn't work out. Why would things be different now?"

Shaking her head, she put on her coat and grabbed her bag before slipping out of his front door and into the night.

That weekend, Lane had planned to visit Beth and the kids and give them a hand around the house. She was always reluctant to ask for his help, given how busy his work was, and Lane had given up trying to convince her it was okay to reach out. Instead, he was taking the approach of turning up in jeans, work boots and a hoodie, after checking that they would be home.

It was good to be independent, but there was a fine line between standing on your own two feet and making life more difficult than it needed to be. Beth had danced back and forth on that line ever since her divorce, trying to find her way as a single mom and wanting to prove to everyone that she had life under control.

And she did. Lane wasn't sure there was a more capable mother and woman than his big sister. But families were supposed to help one another.

Lane bowed his head and jogged up the steps to his sister's front door, two brightly wrapped gifts in his hands. It was raining and the droplets were gathering in his hair and rolling down the back of his neck. Jabbing at the doorbell, he bounced up and down to keep warm while he waited for someone to answer it.

The door swung open and Beth stood there, hair secured in a red bandana and white paint smudges on her jeans. There was a wariness in her expression, like she was already bracing herself for a fight. Sure, sometimes they didn't see eye to eye, especially where their brother was concerned, but that didn't mean Lane wanted to let any cracks widen in their relationship.

"I come bearing gifts," he said, by way of making it clear he wasn't there to pick a fight. "A few treats for my favorite munchkins."

"You spoil them rotten," she said, shaking her head and stepping back to let him inside, her expression more open now.

He grinned. "That's what an uncle is supposed to do."

"You set a high bar for the rest of us uncles."

The voice made Lane freeze on the spot, his grip tightening on the brightly wrapped gifts so hard that he split the wrapping paper on one corner. Resentment crawled up his spine, like a creature of the night coiling around his throat and tightening.

His younger brother, Todd, stood in the archway that led to the kitchen, dressed in jeans and a checkered shirt. In the time he'd been gone, he'd changed a lot physically.

Once lean and lanky, he was now heavier, with thick, muscular arms and a slight belly. A tattoo wrapped around one forearm, peeking out of the edge of where his shirtsleeves were rolled up. He had a beard, too, which made him look older. There was a quiet reservation to him, a stark change from the rambunctious, cocky young man Lane remembered.

His jaw tightened. "I guess that depends on how high you usually set your bar."

"Lane," Beth scolded, but Todd held up his hand.

"He's got every right to be mad, sis."

Well, that was even more change than the tattoos and beard. One of Lane's major issues with his brother was that he never seemed to understand how his actions affected others. A willful lack of self-awareness, Lane had once called it.

"It's good to see you." Todd came closer but didn't attempt to reach out a hand or engage in any physical contact.

He clearly knew that wouldn't be well received. "It's been a while."

"Two years. Where have you been?" Lane honestly had no idea.

"Here and there."

"Cryptic."

"You really want to know?" Todd asked. "I got the impression that you were all too happy to see the back of me."

Lane clenched his jaw, almost like he was trying to grind his snarky response into a pulp. He didn't want to upset Beth. But he had no intention of playing games with Todd, either.

"Would you want to spend time with someone who stole from you?" Lane asked coolly. He might not have a temper, usually, but there was something about his brother's return, coupled with everything going on with Star and Scout, that made his emotions feel too close to the surface.

But he'd never let Todd see that. He didn't deserve Lane's honest reaction.

"I'm a different man now," Todd said, drawing his shoulders back. That action wasn't aggressive, more like he was centering himself.

"Words don't mean shit, Todd." *Especially not yours.*

"I know, but you'll see." His younger brother nodded. "I'm happy to show you."

With that, Todd walked over to Beth and gave her a kiss on the cheek. He murmured something about going out for a coffee and being back later for a movie night with the kids. When the front door closed behind Lane, the silence was deafening. He looked to his sister, but she held up a hand.

"I didn't know either of you were coming," she said, stalking toward the kitchen.

Lane put the gifts on the table by the door and followed

her. He'd check in on the kids shortly. "I'm not blaming you, Beth."

"I still don't understand why you can't talk this out with him." She kept her voice low, so it didn't carry up the stairs. Dante was likely having a nap, and he could hear light thumping that indicated Ariella was probably working on a dance routine. "You're being a stubborn ass about it."

"*I'm* being a stubborn ass?" His mouth popped open. "Don't you think that's a little hypocritical?"

"You think I'm stubborn," she scoffed. "Why? Because I want my family back? Because I want my brothers to stop hating one another? Because I want things to be like they used to be? Gee, if that makes me stubborn, then I'll wear the label proudly."

Lane rolled his eyes. Stubbornness, unfortunately, was a deeply embedded Halliday family trait, supported by strong genes on both sides. They were all as bad as each other.

"Why is he coming over? He hasn't…" Lane sighed. "He isn't asking for money, is he?"

Beth's eyes narrowed. "Wow."

"What? That's not a stupid question. All things considered, I think it's a very smart question." He walked over to the coffee machine and pushed the power button. Todd had given him space, and he wanted to have this conversation with Beth, once and for all. "I want to make sure you're not being taken advantage of."

Beth scrubbed a hand over her face. There were bags under her eyes and her clothes were hanging a little looser than they should. He also noticed the slight scent of cigarettes in the air.

"Are you smoking again?" he asked, sniffing.

"Okay, stop." Beth held her hands up. "One, you're not my parent. *I'm* the eldest child in this family, so don't act like you need to look after me. Two, no, Todd has not asked me for money. In fact, he's been coming around to help with the painting and he even did some repair work on the gutters this week."

"Todd, our brother who wouldn't even build his own Lego."

Despite being annoyed at him, the edges of Beth's eyes crinkled with amusement. "I know, right?"

For some reason, that made Lane deflate a little. He pulled his sister in for a hug. "I don't want to fight."

"I don't want to fight, either, Lane. I understand why you're angry at him. I *really* do." She hugged him back and then went to the cupboard to pull out two coffee mugs. "He did a terrible thing. You're one of the most generous, kindhearted people I know and he took advantage of you in a major way."

He sighed. "Thank you for saying that. Sometimes I feel like you and Mom and Dad think I should forget it."

"They only want the same thing I do—for us to be a family again. You and Todd were so close when you were little." She popped a pod into the coffee machine and stuck the mug underneath to catch the dark, aromatic liquid coming out. "Mom and Dad feel like they failed, somehow, because of what happened."

"Todd was an adult. He knew the difference between right and wrong, Beth. That's on him. Not on Mom and Dad."

"He really *has* changed." Beth repeated the process and made the second coffee, putting a splash of milk into Lane's mug and a much heartier glug into hers. "Ever since he came back here, he's been helping around the house. He took the kids to the park last week and watched them while I went to see a friend. He even made them macaroni and cheese for dinner, and got Dante all cleaned up after his meal."

They were all things Lane couldn't do because he was busy with work. He could only throw money at his sister's problems, offering to hire people instead of being able to do it himself.

Running a business comes with a lot of sacrifice. You know that. She knows it, too.

"He's growing up," she added. "Becoming the adult I knew he could be."

"It's about fucking time," Lane muttered. "But that doesn't undo what happened."

"Forgiveness doesn't require the past to change, Lane. Because that's impossible. By that logic, you'd never forgive any-*one* for any*thing*. And what kind of a lonely life would that create in the end?"

"But doesn't forgiveness open the door for people to hurt you again?" Hmm. He hadn't meant to voice that question aloud, but it seemed it had been swirling in his head for a while.

Seems timely, given who you caught sneaking out of your apartment early this morning.

Oh yeah, that.

He'd awoken in a strange dreamlike state, muscles slightly aching but a deep sense of satisfaction burrowed into his bones. He stretched, reaching for a warm body, but found only cool sheets.

Whispers were coming from the living room, so he'd walked to his bedroom doorway and looked out. He saw Scout, fully dressed, and it lanced his heart. She was leaving without saying goodbye. Again.

Wasn't that the issue with forgiveness? People were who they were. Time didn't turn a cat into a dog, nor a free spirit into a committed partner. People who left would always leave. People who stole would always steal.

It was an unsavory fact of humanity, but a fact nonetheless.

And the sweet moment she shared with Star where she apologized for going away?

It meant nothing. Her missing a dog wasn't the same as her regretting abandoning their marriage. If she had the chance to do everything over, he had no doubt she'd leave again.

"If you spend your whole life trying to prevent yourself from getting hurt, then you're focused on the wrong thing," Beth said, taking a sip of her coffee and motioning for him to follow her to the table. "Hell, I could take that approach and end up alone the rest of my life because I'm worried the next man is going to be like Jason. Or, I could realize that my ex-husband was a one-of-a-kind piece of shit, and move on with my life."

Lane snorted. "That's a very good way of putting it."

"I know it's not easy." Beth placed her hand on his arm. "Forgiveness is like opening a door and not being sure if there's a room behind it or a sheer drop off the side of a cliff."

"That's *exactly* what it feels like," Lane said.

"I might have made a lot of mistakes in my life, but I *did* learn a thing or to." She pulled her hand back and smiled.

"We all make mistakes." He wrapped his hands around the coffee mug and let the warmth seep into his skin. "Trust me."

But *was* marrying Scout a mistake? It felt like the only mistake he'd made was how he'd handled things after they got married. Like not introducing her to his family. Like making her feel as though she wasn't part of his life. Like thinking they could exist in a happy marital bubble away from the rest of the world.

"You, making mistakes?" Beth snorted. "Please. What did you possibly do that could be classified as a mistake? Put your T-shirt on inside out?"

"I was married."

The room went so silent Lane was sure he could hear his

own heart beating. Then Beth burst out laughing, slapping her hand on her thigh. "Oh my god, you had me going there. Jeez, baby bro. Married? You? That's hilarious."

But when he didn't return the laughter, Beth blinked. Then shook her head. Then opened her mouth and closed it like a goldfish. "You're serious?"

"Yep." He blew out a long breath.

The only people who knew about the marriage were his lawyer, Rav (and therefore presumably Sarah) and Todd. After overhearing a conversation between Rav and Lane, his brother had threatened to tell their parents about the marriage if Lane didn't give him money. Lane, naturally, told Todd to go fuck himself.

That's when Lane and Todd's relationship started going downhill. The theft of the credit card information wouldn't come until later, but Lane was sure the seeds were sowed that very day.

God, what a mess he'd made. Technology was so much easier than people.

"Holy crap, Lane." She blinked. "When the heck did you get married?"

"I went to Vegas five years ago and I met a woman. I fell head over heels and we got married in a chapel there." He raked a hand through his hair. "It only lasted a month after we got back to New York. That's what happens when you marry someone you barely know, right?"

"Why did you break up?" Beth put her elbows on the table and leaned forward.

"A myriad of reasons, most of them related to being young and foolish." He let out a humorless laugh. "I was so worried about what everyone would think of me turning up married to a stranger that I made her feel like she wasn't welcome in my life."

Beth winced. "Oof."

"It happened right before Rav and I went to get funding for Unison, and the investors were scrutinizing everything. I was terrified of them pulling the plug if they found out I'd gotten hitched to some random woman in Vegas. It doesn't exactly indicate a man responsible for running a company, does it?"

"It's easy to judge," Beth replied with a shrug. "By all rights, marrying your high school sweetheart and making two beautiful babies and buying a house in the 'burbs should make a good marriage. But instead it made my life a misery. There's no 'right way' to be married."

"You think it's possible to make such a life-altering decision on a whim?"

"I think every couple is different. As much as I know you love your rules and parameters and signposts, love doesn't work that way. You can't QA it."

He nodded. "That's a good point."

"Did you love her?"

"I really did." He looked down at his coffee. "But I made poor choices."

"Do you remember as a kid how you used to *agonize* over which ice cream flavor to get? It used to drive me nuts how much time you wasted looking at every single option, making sure that you got exactly what you wanted. Changing your mind at the last second, because you thought of something better." She laughed. "You don't make poor choices, Lane."

He set his cup down. "Clearly I did. Otherwise it would have worked out."

"I'm not saying things couldn't have turned out better. I'm saying, you don't make poor choices. So the decisions that you made at the time were the best ones you could make. Perhaps it wasn't the choice that was bad, but the timing."

His sister's words hit him in his chest so hard he was shocked he didn't topple backward in his chair. Maybe she was right.

Scout had never been the wrong woman for him. Of that, he was sure. Because no one else had ever come close to her. What he felt for Scout was special. Rare. And they didn't break up because of a lack of love or even compatibility. If anything, they were perfectly matched in how opposite they were. They balanced one another.

But the timing of their marriage was terrible. They were young, her especially. He was trying to build a reputation beyond his years and she was still deeply scarred by her childhood. They didn't have the life experience—or the communication skills—that would've enabled them to handle such a complicated thing as being married.

What if things had gone south because the timing was wrong? Not because *they* were wrong?

Last night, when he'd taken her to bed, it was the furthest thing from a booty call he could possibly have imagined. Having her in his arms was like being put back together. Like being made whole.

On some level, he knew that he still loved her. But they'd screwed it up so badly before, he wasn't sure that kind of damage could be undone. Forgiveness was hard.

And he had always been better at walking forward than looking back.

18

Scout flopped back into her desk chair at the end of a long Monday and let out a big sigh. It had been one of those days where she'd run from one task to the next, barely stopping long enough to stuff some M&M'S in her mouth for lunch. She was dog-tired, but the good kind of tired.

For the first time in her life, it felt rewarding to work hard. To know she was growing a business, and contributing and furthering her life. Just as she was about to log off, her mobile rang. It was her grandparents' house.

She snatched the vibrating device off her desk, panic seizing her throat. Why would they be calling her? Had something happened to Lizzie?

"Hello?"

"Scout? You sound like you've run a mile." It was her grandfather.

"It's a busy day at the office," she said. "Is Lizzie okay?"

"Yes, I think so."

She could practically see him scratching his head. "Oh, I assumed that's why you were calling."

He let out a breath. "Well, I can't blame you for that, can I? It's not like we have much other reason to talk nowadays."

Not since you basically denounced me as your granddaughter.

She didn't respond to the rhetorical question and waited as he cleared his throat. It was so damn awkward between them. There had been plenty of times where she'd wished that she could avoid dealing with them altogether, but that wasn't an option. Besides, was it better to have grandparents who barely tolerated you than no family at all?

She wasn't sure about that.

"I spoke with Bill and he's more than happy to represent you in the divorce proceedings," her grandfather said. "Your grandmother and I will cover the cost."

"Oh." Scout blinked. "You don't need to do that."

She wasn't even sure how much the lawyer would charge, though she suspected he would give her a fair price because of his long-standing relationship with her grandparents.

"It's fine. You said you were looking for a better place and we'd prefer that you save your money for that."

What alien had invaded planet earth and taken over her grandfather's body? He never wanted to help her. What could his motive be in all this? Was he worried about her marriage affecting Lizzie financially? That was a laugh, because if anyone was at risk in this situation, it was Lane. Not Scout. Certainly not Lizzie.

"Uh, okay. Thanks," she said, simply because she was unsure what else to say.

"We…" He paused and she could hear sounds of him moving about his office. Pacing, perhaps. The old floorboards squeaked and groaned in the background.

"Yes?"

A little tendril of hope unfurled in her heart, that he might apologize for how they'd treated her over the years.

"We're considering your request to have Lizzie come live with you," he said.

"Really?" Scout sat bolt upright in her chair, a grin spreading across her face. "Are you serious?"

"It's not a decision we can make in a rush and I am not promising anything. But Lizzie really wants to stay in New York, and as much as it would kill me not to hear her chatter every day, I want her to be happy."

The words should have made Scout happy enough to fly over the moon. But they stabbed her. They were a seam ripper to the stitches on her heart. They tore open a wound she truly thought she'd healed.

Why didn't they ever feel like that about me?

She couldn't speak. Tears made her throat thick with grief for the family life she'd never had. For the one she'd tried and failed to build with Lane.

"And it seems like you really *are* making an effort to turn your life around," he finished.

He was happy because Scout was conforming to his ideas of what a person should be—she was working an office job, divorcing her Vegas-whim husband, acting all polite when she dealt with him. It should have pleased her, because all she'd ever wanted was his love. His acceptance.

Instead, it made her feel dirty. He only showed kindness toward her when she played ball.

"Thank you," she said through gritted teeth.

"I'll send you an email with Bill's details. Let's get this divorce thing sorted out, and then we can talk about what to do with Lizzie, okay?"

Why did it feel like he was using the divorce as a test to see if she really *was* going to fall in line?

You're overreacting. He's offering to help and you're trying to twist it into something evil.

Maybe. Or maybe she knew her grandfather better than he thought she did.

"Sounds good," she replied.

"Call me after you've met with Bill. He knows to send the invoice to me." He cleared his throat. "Goodbye, Scout."

"Goodbye, Norman."

She ended the call and stared into space. The conversation had left her feeling icky, like her grandfather was trying to stake claim over a decision that should be hers.

"It *is* yours," she said to herself. "You were the one who agreed when Lane brought it up."

Then, why had sleeping with him felt so good? And not just because Lane knew his way around her body like a man traveling the road home. Not just because he was as generous in the bedroom as he was out in the world. Not just because the way he looked at her was like *finally* having someone see who she truly was inside.

You still love him.

She couldn't. It was too risky. Too complicated. And now, too forbidden.

Scout drummed her fingers on her desk. Knowing all those things and being a woman smart enough to know a mistake when she was walking into one, why did she reach for her phone? Why did she tap out a message and hit Send before she could back out of it?

SCOUT: Sorry I left without saying goodbye.

Three blinking dots appeared almost immediately.

LANE: Had an early start at work?

Hmm. He was giving her an out. Old Scout probably would have taken it, too, to save face and not allow herself to be vulnerable. But it was tiring keeping everything locked up tight. The call with her grandfather, while mostly good news, had drained her.

She didn't have any walls left right now.

SCOUT: Nope. It was the coward's way out and I took it.

LANE: I saw you leave.

SCOUT: You did?

LANE: Yeah. I heard you talking to Star and I was standing in the bedroom doorway. You didn't look back.

SCOUT: I wanted to look back.

...

SCOUT: Why didn't you say anything?

LANE: I'm never going to convince you to stay. That has to be your decision.

Her heart ached. Scratching an itch with Lane had done nothing but inflame her desire for him—body and soul. *Was* she trying to turn her life around? Was she a smarter, more together person than she used to be?

In that moment, she wasn't so sure. It felt like an act. Like a mask.

Underneath it all, she was the same old scarred Scout with a tender heart and a hot-mess head. That must have been the only reason why she typed what she did next.

SCOUT: Want to come to mine? I owe you a meal.

LANE: Be there at seven.

Scout went home via the grocery store to grab supplies for dinner. After making a batch of soup, she had a speedy shower, washing the day from her skin with a fancy soap she saved for special occasions.

"You'd shower for anyone that was coming over," she said to her reflection in the foggy bathroom mirror.

Of course she would. But the perfume she'd selected was one she'd worn back when they were together—he'd bought the bottle for her in Vegas, and after she'd left, it had been hiding in the bottom of her sock drawer.

For some reason, she'd never been able to throw it out.

Occasionally, when she was feeling particularly masochistic, she'd take it out and sniff the lid because it reminded her of those blissful days. Now it was like she wanted to re-create the past. She wanted to be the woman she was with him—hopeful, starting to heal and grow like a bud blossoming in early spring.

Not the scarred, defensive, lonely person she was now.

You really are lonely.

She had Isla, of course. But now that she was with Theo, Scout didn't want to impose by popping around all the time. So their girl time had slowed a bit. She didn't begrudge her friend—it wasn't Isla's fault that Scout was so isolated.

When you have Lizzie living with you, things will be different.

She changed into something subtly sexy, faded black jeans with a slash across one thigh and a cropped T-shirt that revealed a sliver of taut skin above her waistband. As she was brushing out her hair after drying it, her stomach fluttered. She felt giddy like a girl about to go on a first date. Just as she was walking out to the living room to give the place a final once-over, the intercom buzzed.

"Hello," she said, pressing a hand to her stomach to quiet the butterflies.

"It's me."

That fluttering excitement turned molten as desire unfurled in her stomach at the sound of his voice—so smooth, so confident. *It's me.* There was a familiarity in the way he said it, like him coming to her apartment could happen any day of the week. Like they were together again.

Like they hadn't screwed it all up.

"See you in a minute." She tapped the button to release the external lock.

Underneath the burning anticipation, a small echo of fear reverberated through her. She looked around her apartment. It was…basic. Like an IKEA showroom with half the stuff missing.

Cheap furniture. Scuffed walls. Ugly popcorn ceilings.

But she didn't have time to dwell on it because there was a knock at the front door. Dragging in a breath, she forced herself to let go of being ashamed. She was grateful that she had a roof over her head, even if it wasn't the prettiest or fanciest roof. And Lane didn't judge people about things like that.

Scout wrapped a hand around the knob and pulled the door open. "Hi. Come in."

A half smile tugged at the corner of his lips as he entered her apartment. "Thanks for inviting me for dinner."

"It's the least I could do." The words popped out before her brain could catch up with her heart.

Heart? Uh, yeah right. Try a little lower.

Lane looked like he'd been sketched right from her fantasies. The reddish tones in his brown hair were more pronounced than usual, thanks to the warm, amber glow of the setting sun filtering in through one window. He was wearing his uniform—dark jeans, a black sweater and sneakers. But over the top, he wore a leather jacket, and stubble lined his jaw, giving him a slight edge.

Lane 2.0.

She'd never thought it was possible for him to be even hotter than he was before.

"To repay me for dinner?" he asked, his eyes searching hers.

She had to stop herself from pressing a palm to her chest to see how fast her heart was beating. "Uh huh."

"What's on the menu?"

"Spiced pumpkin soup with crusty bread."

His eyes lit up. Lane loved anything with pumpkin. "You really do remember all my favorites."

It had been one of the only things she could cook from scratch when she was in her early twenties, because all you had to do was chop the ingredients however haphazardly you liked, boil them in stock and then blend it. Simple. These days she added more nuanced spices to her soup and finished it with a drizzle of cream, but it was still a totally basic, yet healthy, thing she could make.

"I sure do," she replied, noting the way his gaze lowered a touch before he yanked it back up, like he was trying not to check her out. "Can I get you a drink?"

"I'm fine."

The silence stretched on. It wasn't uncomfortable, but there was an air of tension. Like a wire pulled taut. They were in a weird no-man's land. Married but separated. Attracted but resisting it. Sleeping together but avoiding commitment.

You slept together one time. It's not a pattern...yet.

Did she want it to be?

Yes.

"God, you look good." The words came out of him like a sigh and Scout's chest warmed with the compliment. Then Lane shook his head. "Sorry, I—"

"I like hearing it." She took a step toward him. "And I'm glad you came."

Her whole body hummed with desire. Desire for his body. For his mind. For his heart.

That's not yours to desire.

Lane raked a hand through his hair. He looked like he wanted to say something but didn't know how to word it. Wasn't that the crux of their relationship?

So much water under the bridge. So many things unsaid. So much potential wasted.

Suddenly, anger cut through the thick fog of lust swirling in her head. It was like she'd tried to bury a demon and it had suddenly come back to life. She was angry at her mother for making her anticipate destruction. With her grandparents for making her feel worthless. With Lane for trying to keep her a secret.

But most of all, she was angry with herself.

God, how she was angry with herself. For not having the guts to tell Lane the whole story about her grandparents. For walking out that night instead of opening up to him. For letting ego and fear dictate her actions. For being so broken and fragile that one hard knock had been enough to shatter it all.

"Lane..." She shook her head.

Instead of being angry and wallowing in self-pity, why don't you do something about it?

Voicing her desires was hard, even when she wanted something bad, like how she wanted Lane now.

"I hope you didn't come here thinking it was just an invite to have dinner," she said, pulling her shoulders back and looking him straight in the eye. "Because I don't want to eat right now."

"Then what *do* you want?" The word was rough and gravelly and sexy.

"I want you to take me to bed."

He closed his eyes for a moment and she could sense the turmoil in him. Maybe he *had* simply come for a meal and conversation. Maybe he wanted to clear the air after their night together and hear her side of things. Maybe he wanted to tell her that he didn't want to see her ever again.

But looking at him now, he was a man at war with himself.

The good side won. He stepped forward and slid his hand into her hair, cupping the back of her head and bringing his lips down to hers. All the swirling thoughts turned to smoke. Nothing mattered except this moment. With him. Both his hands were in her hair, his lips coaxing hers open. He tasted of mint and smelled like all the good moments in her life.

"You feel so good," he growled.

She sighed as he kissed his way down her neck. He feasted on her skin, stubble scratching with each searing kiss. She kept her arms around his neck, hanging on for dear life, and gasped when he pushed one hand underneath her T-shirt, palming her breast. Not wanting to wait, she reached behind and popped the clasp so he could touch her skin to skin.

His palms were at her breasts, thumbs brushing her nipples while he kissed her. Scout melted into his touch, turning liquid and clamping her eyes shut, blotting out everything but the feel of him.

"I don't know how you do it," he said, his voice rough.

"What?" she panted.

"How you take me from a man who's got his life together and turn me into—" he nuzzled her "—this."

"What's this?"

"Can't you tell?" He looked up at her. "I'm ruined, Scout. Fucking ruined because of you."

She reached for the hem of her T-shirt and pulled it up over her head. Then she shrugged out of her bra. Her hair fell around her shoulders and she stared at him. Open. Vulnerable.

For some reason, she wanted him to see her without her protection. Without her walls.

"You ruined me too, you know." Emotion rushed up inside her. "You weren't the only one who walked away from this with scars."

"Scars? I felt like I lost an organ, Scout. I lost a chunk of me when you left."

They stood, staring at one another for a moment. Hurt simmered in the air. Like waves of heat, it distorted her view of things. How could she feel so angry and regretful and desperate and hopeful and wanton, all at the same time?

"I loved you like I had never loved *anything*." He shook his head and dropped his gaze to the floor. "That feeling doesn't go away overnight."

"Does it go away at all?" she asked. Because that moment brought into sharp focus just how much her feelings for Lane *hadn't* gone away. "Because it hasn't for me."

Those feelings had been hidden away. Stored. Left to rot.

But either by miracle or curse, they'd lived.

"It hasn't for me, either." He smoothed his hands down her arms. "No matter how much I wished it to."

"Then, don't stop," she said, pressing up on her toes and whispering into his ear. "If we're already ruined, what do we have to lose?"

19

What the hell was he doing?

You're supposed to be divorcing her.

He'd come here with the sole purpose of hand delivering the papers. The lawyers had drafted everything they needed, but he'd wanted to go over it in person. Face-to-face. Because he didn't want this to be a coldhearted exchange, and he didn't want to see Scout walk away with nothing. If he could set her up with some funds to find a new place and allow her to get custody of her sister, then he wanted to.

She deserved that much.

But the second she'd opened that door, it was like his reasoning evaporated into thin air and his logic went along with it. Never mind that she'd walked out on him in the middle of the night *twice* now. Why did she still have such a strong effect on him?

Because she still means something to you.

Hearing Scout say out loud that her feelings for him hadn't gone away... If he thought he was ruined before, well, that was like taking a meat cleaver to his heart. All this time, and they still wanted one another. They still felt something.

Their love was like a weed that wouldn't die.

"Touch me, Lane." Scout looked at him with her big, luminous hazel eyes and he got the sense that for the first time—maybe ever—she was letting him in. "I...I shouldn't have left that night."

Which night?

But that was too dangerous a question to ask. It was a can of worms.

"Scout, don't." He shook his head. What a mess he was making of this.

"No, I spent our whole marriage not speaking up. I blamed our breakup on you not wanting to include me in your life. But the truth was...there was more to say. I kept things from you." There were tears in her eyes but she wouldn't let them fall. "My grandparents..."

"Tell me."

"When they found out about me getting married...that's why they didn't let me have custody of Lizzie."

The reality socked him in the heart so hard he couldn't draw breath for a moment. "Because of me?"

"Because of *me*, Lane. Because they thought me getting married in Vegas was irresponsible and showed that I didn't have the ability to make sound judgments and decisions." Her hands balled by her sides. "I knew the day I went to tell them that they would flip out."

"But you told them anyway."

"Of course I did. You were my husband."

Even with so much to lose, she'd never once thought about hiding him. She was ready to tell the world she loved him, even with dire consequences on the line. And what had he done? He'd dithered about what people would think and whether his investors would pull funding and whether his family would be furious with him.

And she'd lost it all for him.

"I kept trying to convince them, after we split. I kept turning up at their house, pleading with them to let me have Lizzie." She dropped her head. "They ended up giving me money to stay away from her. I didn't want to take it, but they put it into my bank account because they had all my details. I never spent a penny of it until I invested it in Isla's business. But that's what they thought of me. That I was so bad they had to pay me to stay away."

"I wish you'd told me at the time," he said, feeling even more ashamed at how much stronger and surer of her decisions she'd been than he had back then. He knew Scout looked at him as a pillar of strength. The one who had it all together.

But under the surface, he'd been a scared young man. Someone too fixated on not making a mistake. The marriage to Scout had been the only impulsive thing Lane had ever done in his whole life. But it had felt so right he'd been fooled into thinking it *was* right.

"I could have helped," he said.

Shame splashed across her face like red paint and she brought her hair over her shoulders to cover herself up. "I was too embarrassed to tell you."

"Your grandparents are messed up. That is *not* your fault." He touched her cheek and she raised her eyes to him. "I would never have judged you for that. Never."

The vehemence in his voice shook him. Even now, he still felt these intense protective urges for her.

"It's hard to always be a 'bad decision' or a 'risk' in peoples' eyes," she said softly. "And then I was in yours as well, even though I hadn't done anything wrong, and...I couldn't take it."

As much as he hated that she'd left, it made more sense now that he had the full picture. "I wish you'd stayed."

"Me too," she whispered.

I wish I had been there for you.

He brushed the hair back over her shoulders, baring her. Then he brought his lips down to hers, unable to resist the pull. Her hands came to the hem of his T-shirt, yanking the fabric up and over his head.

Her fingertips brushed his stomach as she grasped for the fly of his jeans, yanking them over his hips, taking his underwear with them. He did the same to her. It was cathartic in a way—almost like they were shedding their baggage. Shedding the past. Stripping away the bullshit and the secrets and the lies until it was only them, in their rawest forms.

She took his hand and led him through the apartment. It was small, builder's beige and cookie-cutter. Anyone could have lived here. For some reason, it made him ache for her. Because she was so vibrant and full of life—it was like she wanted a place to disappear into, instead of thrive in.

Guilt stabbed him in the gut. A huge gray cloud loomed over them and Lane had no idea what he was going to do. He knew they needed to commence divorce proceedings. Feelings might still exist—but they weren't getting back together. The trust was broken between them. Not to mention her grandparents would use it as another reason for keeping Scout from Lizzie—proof that she couldn't make good decisions.

What if they tried and everything crumbled again? Disaster. But he followed her like a man entranced. All he wanted right now was to drown in this complicated, complex and wonderful woman. He wanted to fall asleep with her face pressed to his chest and his nose buried in her hair because she made him feel like life was an adventure.

Scout let go only long enough to draw the covers back and grab a condom from her nightstand before her hand returned to his—fingers encircling his wrist—as she silently asked him to follow.

You can still put a stop to this.

But he had no hope of that. His brain was outnumbered—the primal parts of him and the softer emotional parts and the part of him obsessed with the past, all ganging up in his head. She got into the bed and reclined back, looking up at him as a hopeful smile lanced his heart.

"You're thinking too much," she said. "Like always."

"Am I?"

"Uh-huh." She sucked on the inside of her cheek. "I don't want to pressure you…"

"You're not pressuring me. I'm just…" Shit. "This is hard."

Her eyes dropped cheekily and then darted back up to his face. "I can see that."

He shook his head, feeling a little embarrassed all of a sudden. Wouldn't most guys be happy to jump right into bed with someone they were attracted to instead of getting all tangled up?

"I'm not over you." He looked at the condom in his hands. "I can't pretend like this is some fun diversion from real life, Scout. You're not…"

"What?"

"You're not a fling." He raked a hand through his hair. "This *isn't* nothing to me."

Why was he still so attached? By all accounts, their relationship was a complete and utter failure. Yet he acted like losing her caused some great big cavity in his life that couldn't ever be filled by anyone else.

Nobody but her. She was irreplaceable.

You love her.

No, he didn't. He *had* loved her and he wasn't over that feeling, but it was a past pain. Not a present one.

"It's not nothing to me, either," she whispered. "*You're* not nothing to me. I know we messed everything up, but I still loved you, Lane. With all my heart. Nothing can erase that."

He felt something snap inside him—some last frayed thread of restraint. Of logic. He tore the foil packet open. Then he tossed it aside and rolled the rubber along his length, taking his time to draw out the anticipation. When they were protected, he came into the bed, lowering himself over her and settling between her legs.

She rolled her hips up against him, encouraging him to press harder between her legs, seeking out her most sensitive spot.

"I'm glad you came," she said softly. "I've missed you."

The words were like a sledgehammer to his solar plexus. How did she slay him like that? He couldn't deal with that right now. His brain had only so much space, and tonight, he wanted to fill it with good things. With how he *wanted* to act instead of always being tangled up in *should*. In rules.

So he did. He sunk down into her, his hands sliding under her body so he could hold her tight as he moved his hips against hers. She responded by wrapping her arms around his neck. Their lips brushed and it was sweet and tentative and apologetic, like they were acknowledging the past and the roles they played. Like they were atoning.

When it felt right, he pushed forward, burying himself inside her, and was rewarded with her sharp gasp so close to his ear that he felt it right down to his toes. He rocked back and forth in a way that drew him in as deep as possible. Each thrust gave him something to explore—the feel of her silky hair brushing his hands, the hot breath against his neck, the sound of her gasps. Each detail was more perfect than the last.

"I'm sorry," she whispered into his ear as her thighs started to shake around his hips. He smothered her words with a kiss, pushing into her harder and faster, chasing the wave of her pleasure.

"I'm sorry, too."

The second her soft little mews turned to gasping cries, he followed her over the edge.

Scout stirred, her eyes fluttering open. How long had it been? A minute? An hour? A month? Hell, it could have been forever. Lane's body was wrapped around hers, naked and warm, and the sheets and duvet kept them cocooned from the world.

You can't just get up and leave this time, can you?

Not that Scout wanted to leave right now. Being wrapped up in Lane's arms was heaven. She could feel his heart beating at her back. The steady thump lulled her into a state of bliss and contentment, and he nuzzled his face into her hair.

This was the most content she'd been in a very long time.

On her long, lonely nights she tried not to reflect on the past, because that was a recipe for blinking into the darkness for far too long. But occasionally, when she was one foot into dreamland, she'd sleepily reach for him, and the jolt of finding cold sheets on the other side of the bed would have her curling into a ball and trying to block the memories out.

"What are you thinking?" he asked.

"Nothing at all," she said with a happy sigh. "You turned me to mush."

A deep, satisfied "hmm" rumbled behind her. "Good. That's exactly what should happen."

Scout looked out through the window. Rain was pouring hard and it created rivulets across the glass, caused the light to shift and distort. She rolled over to face Lane. He looked utterly delicious. His green eyes were hooded and his hair was sticking out in all directions, a reminder that they'd been a little rough and ready in the best way possible.

Making love with Lane was always...perfect. He seemed to know what she needed at all times, reading her like a well-loved novel. When she felt fragile he was tender and sweet, and when she wanted to lose herself, he took charge and didn't hold back.

She reached up to touch his face. "Are you still hungry?"

"Famished," he admitted with a crooked smile.

"Good thing dinner just needs to be warmed up." She leaned over and kissed him without thinking. And it was soft and tender. Familiar.

Rattled, she got out of bed and tugged her clothes back on. But the apartment was cooler now, and she layered a fuzzy yellow sweater over the top. Leaving Lane behind, she went into the kitchen to heat up their food.

For some reason, *this* felt more intimate than sex. Because leaving in the dead of night had helped her avoid seeing him in that post pleasure glow, hair messy and features relaxed and body warm. That was the Lane who could undo all the promises she'd made to herself.

The scent of pumpkin mixed with smoked paprika and cayenne wafted into the air, mingling with the toasted bread and rich butter coming from the oven. Scout stirred the soup until it was warm and then ladled it into two bowls, drizzling a thin swirl of cream in the middle and placing a chunk of toasted and buttered bread on the side.

As she was taking it to the table, she caught Lane watching

her from the bedroom doorway. He was dressed now and still looking as delicious as ever.

"You taking up a hobby of watching me from doorways?" she asked.

"I can't seem to stop myself."

She flushed. "Wine? I've got a bottle of pinot grigio in the fridge. It's nothing fancy though—"

"It's fine, Scout. Whatever you have is perfect." He took a seat at the table and inhaled. "This smells *good*."

Her heart warmed under the praise as she poured them a small glass of wine each and brought it to the table. "Please, don't wait for me."

"Oh yeah, this is exactly what I want on a miserable rainy evening." Lane dug in and let out a satisfied *mmm* sound. "So, have you spoken with your grandparents about having Lizzie come live with you?"

Scout nodded. "They're considering it."

"That's great news."

"I'm trying not to get my hopes up, but I *was* looking on real estate sites on my lunch break today. Brooklyn is so expensive these days."

"I'm sure we can figure that out."

"We?" She blinked.

"In the divorce." He looked down. "It feels awkward bringing it up after…"

"I know." She reached for her wine and took a long, fortifying gulp. Truth be told, talking about the divorce felt wrong after what they'd just done. Dirty, even. "But we have to talk about it at some point. My grandparents set me up with their personal lawyer."

"Wanting to make sure you go through with it, eh?" Lane let out a dark chuckle. "That seems on-brand."

Clearly she wasn't the only one who suspected that might be

their motive. Was it help or control? The line between those two things seemed so faint.

"In any case, I want to help. Knowing that our marriage was the reason they kept Lizzie away from you last time…" Guilt streaked across his face. "I feel terrible."

"Lane, that is so *not* your fault." She shook her head.

"I want to help." He dunked his bread into the soup and bit off a chunk.

"What do you mean?"

"Well, in divorces they usually split up the assets and—"

"No." She shook her head. "I'm not taking any money that you earned, simply because we were married for a brief period of time. That's not fair."

"It wouldn't be fair if you stormed back into my life demanding a cut. But you didn't do that," he said. "The fact that you could try to take half of everything and you don't even want a cent is a clear indication of your character."

"I like to think I'm a good person, even if I'm a bit of a hot mess."

He cocked his head. "You say that like it's a bad thing."

She snorted. "When is being a hot mess ever a good thing?"

"When you're a perfectionist from birth and all you've ever known is crippling pressure to achieve," he joked. "What you call being a 'hot mess,' I call living boldly. When we met in Vegas, I thought you were the most honest, refreshing person I had ever met."

She blinked. "Really?"

"There was something so 'I don't give a shit what you think about me' in your essence. I'd never met anyone like that. My mother was always worried about how we were perceived because her two sisters married into money and we were the 'average Joes' who felt like we could never keep up."

"You quickly learn to stop worrying about that when everyone thinks you're a dud," she said.

"You're not a dud. You only think that because short-sighted people have been trying to fit you into a mold that doesn't suit you."

Wow. Lane was right. Her mother had wanted Scout to be independent beyond what was possible for her age, so she didn't have to take care of her. Her grandparents wanted her to be a young woman who wasn't scarred and broken, because that would make her more compliant. Her teachers had wanted her to be more academic than she was, because that would make their lives easier.

"Do you feel like a dud when you work with Isla?" he asked.

"No," she replied honestly. "I work very hard at Paws in the City."

"Because she lets you be who you are."

"That's true." She shook her head, feeling as though her world had been rocked a little. "She doesn't fuss if I'm a bit late because I stopped to help my neighbor or if she needs to show me things a few times because sometimes the instructions don't stick. And she lets me run with any ideas I have, instead of trying to control everything."

"She sounds like a great boss."

"She's an even better friend," Scout said. "I'm lucky to have her."

"I'm sure she'd say the same about you." Lane sipped his wine, and the pale gold liquid caught the low lighting. Outside, the rain continued to pound.

"How are things going with Star?" she asked, wanting to turn the spotlight away from herself. "I know my visit probably didn't help."

"You know what, she's actually been good. Today she was

like her old self." His face lit up. "I took her to work and she was happy. No chewing or biting or scratching."

"That must be a relief."

"Hopefully it sticks," he said. "I'm expecting it's part of the Jekyll-and-Hyde act. But we'll see."

"I'd be happy to dog sit whenever you need," she offered. "I know you're such a good dog dad, but seriously. If you ever need someone to come over and keep her company if you're at a work thing or whatever, please call me."

"And likewise, anytime you want to see her...you can come around." He nodded. "In fact, we have to close the office this weekend for some building-related, security-test thing. So I was planning to take her to Central Park for a bit, if the weather is nice. I'm meeting my sister and her kids there. You're welcome to join us."

"You want to introduce me to your family now, right as we're about to get divorced?" she asked with a laugh.

He didn't return the laugh. Instead, he was somber. "I should have done it the first time. Making you feel like I was ashamed of you is the second biggest regret I have in my entire life."

Scout toyed with the stem of her wine glass. "What's the biggest regret?"

"Not tearing this city down to find you after you left."

Why couldn't they have met now? Why couldn't they have been better equipped to handle things? The wasted potential of their relationship made Scout want to weep. But in trying her hardest to find some positive in what seemed like a cruel joke from the universe, at least they had come together now to apologize to one another.

Closure. She'd never had it before and it was bittersweet.

"Well, mine was leaving you in the cold by not communicating with you when we were married, so I guess that makes us even," she said, mustering a smile.

They may not be able to erase the mistakes of their past, but at least they could do things properly now—getting divorced on civil terms, respecting one another, being honest about their feelings. Being friends.

But in her heart of hearts, Scout knew those things would never feel like enough.

20

After the conversation with Lane, something shifted within Scout. She started to view herself differently. He was right! People *had* been trying to squish her into a mold her whole life. And making a person constantly feel like they were coming up short because they were forced to meet someone else's standards was wrong.

Not to mention ineffective.

Because if she had been allowed to be her zany, emotional self from a young age, then maybe she would have blossomed into someone who used those parts of herself to find success. But it wasn't too late. *She* could give herself the opportunity to be who she truly was and screw anyone who didn't like it.

Scout had some big ideas to help Paws in the City.

But first she had personal business to take care of. After checking the address on her phone, she glanced up at the tall silver office tower in front of her. Bill the lawyer worked in the financial district, and Scout had taken the morning off to meet with him.

She walked through the turnstile into the foyer of the building, the chunky heels on her boots clacking over the marble tile floor. People streamed in and out, most in business suits in varying shades of gray, charcoal and black. One guy wore navy.

"What a rebel," Scout muttered to herself as she headed to the elevator.

Her knee-high black boots, matching tights and tiny cow-print miniskirt got a few sideways glances. Sasha Frise had totally inspired her to do a rewatch of *The Nanny*, which had made her want to dig out some of her obnoxiously patterned miniskirts from the back of her closet. Who cares that she was going to see some super serious lawyer today?

She was going to be herself, and that meant expressing her personality through fashion.

It took three elevators before she was able to get a space, and she squeezed in with half a dozen corporate types. The mirrored finish of the doors reflected a distorted version of her—making the red sweater she'd chosen to go over the black-and-white skirt seem overbright and out of place.

When the elevator dinged on the seventh floor, she stepped out and marched toward the door marked William P. Billings, Esq. Wait, so his name was Bill Billings and he billed people for his time? Scout snorted.

She pressed the doorbell by the frosted glass door and a woman opened it up, welcomed her into the office and led her into a blandly decorated meeting room. Black leather chairs were gathered around a glass table, and there was a unit to one

side with a coffee machine and a bowl of individually packaged mints. In a tower across the road, worker bees scurried
and tapped at their computers.

"Scout?"

She whirled around to find a man in his sixties standing
in the doorway, holding a laptop. "Hello, uh, Mr. Billings."

"Please, Bill is fine. I've known your grandfather since we
were in high school, so you're practically family." He offered
a warm smile and motioned for her to sit. She was taken aback
by his approachable tone and warmth.

Not at all what she'd expected from either a lawyer or a
friend of her grandfather's.

"Well, I'm sure Norman would debate that," she said stiffly,
as she took a seat. "Given that he cut me out of his will and
all."

Bill raised an eyebrow. "You're Scout Hannah Myers, correct? Eldest granddaughter of Norman and Joyce?"

"Yes."

"Then, as far as I am aware, you're in the will. Unless your
grandfather has retained another lawyer without my knowledge." He chuckled.

Scout sat there, stunned. She'd had a *huge* fight with Norman after she'd gotten married, and he'd pulled the pin on
sharing custody of Lizzie with her. She'd accused him of being
a terrible grandfather, saying that he'd only ever seen her as a
burden and that he wouldn't know how to care for a child if
they came with a manual. Then she'd made an awful comment about his involvement in her mother's tragic, disastrous
life and he had lost it.

It was the only time he'd ever yelled at her, because usually he was too detached to get his blood pressure up quite
so high. Joyce was the yeller, not him. But that day, he'd told
her to get out of their house and never come back. That she

was no blood of his and that she would be removed from the will immediately.

They hadn't talked for almost a year. Even when she'd gone to visit Lizzie, she wouldn't make eye contact with him.

"Are you *sure*?" Scout asked. "Maybe he took me off and then put me back on."

Bill cocked his head slightly, looking confused. "It sounds like there has been some miscommunication with your grandfather. He's always been adamant that he wanted both his granddaughters to have an equal share of his estate. I can't get into particulars, of course, but if you have any questions, then you should speak with him directly."

Scout nodded. "Sure."

"Now, about the divorce. New York is an equitable distribution state, which means the courts will divide the marital property fairly. If it's possible to come to a fair and equitable agreement between yourself and your husband first, that's great. But if he won't—"

"I don't want anything from him," Scout said. "This is just about the paperwork."

Bill frowned. "But you're entitled to—"

"I don't care." She sat up straighter and drew her shoulders back, in case he was thinking about not taking her seriously. "My husband is a good man and we haven't lived together for a long time. I didn't bring anything to the relationship, financially, so I don't want to take anything from him now."

The older man looked at her, completely befuddled. Scout supposed this was probably the first time he'd had a client who wanted nothing from their spouse.

Former spouse.

She sucked in a breath. "I know it's unusual, but we were young and we weren't together for long. I still…"

Love him.

"I still respect him," she said, nodding. "This is an amicable split. I simply want to do whatever paperwork is required so that he can…"

So that he can, what? Find someone else to fall in love with and marry?

The very thought of it was like jabbing her heart with a white-hot poker.

"Do his own wills and, uh, other legal things," she finished weakly.

"I see." Bill bobbed his head. "But these laws are in place for a reason, to make sure no party is disadvantaged by the relationship."

"I understand. But if I came with nothing, then I will leave with nothing. I'm not going to rob a man blind simply because there's a law that allows me to do so."

As nice as the money would be, Scout would never feel comfortable taking it. It would be different if they were married for years and she'd contributed to their life together. But the fact was, one month of marriage didn't entitle her to anything, morally. What kind of an example would that set for Lizzie? That it was okay to take from people, regardless of whether you deserved it? That it was okay to abuse a rule for your own gain? That you had to rely on other people to get by in life?

She wanted to be a better role model than that. She *would* be a better role model than that.

Lane turned his face up to the sky, letting the sunshine settle on his skin and sucking in a big lungful of fresh air. Well, as fresh as one could get in the middle of America's most populated city. But it was the mildest day they'd had in months, and Lane was in Central Park to meet his sister and his niece and nephew. That was worth taking a moment to celebrate.

In fact, this entire week had felt like a departure from his normal life. First he'd left work earlier than usual to head to Scout's for dinner. Then he'd taken Friday off work to visit the old folks' home with Star—in her final outing as Sasha Frise's stunt double. And now he was skipping his usual "I'll just go in for a few hours" on the weekend to do what normal people did on a Sunday—relax and enjoy themselves.

He couldn't help but feel this was Scout's influence. Her zest for life had brought some balance to his, helping him to see there was more to existence than being chained to his desk. No matter how much he loved his job. No matter how much he believed in what he and Rav were creating. No matter how much his career would always mean to him.

It couldn't be everything.

"Uncle Lane!" Ariella spotted him and ran full steam ahead, her arms outstretched. He caught her in one arm, swung her around so that she squealed with delight. Star barked at his feet, tail wagging.

Beth laughed when he returned Ariella to the ground and Lane leaned down to the stroller to give Dante a tickle. The little boy giggle and squirmed. *This* was what he needed more of in his life. Family time. Sunshine. Fresh air.

Sex.

Yeah, so that had been a bonus, too.

"This is a real treat seeing you during the day," Beth said, as she adjusted the bow in Ariella's hair. "I was starting to worry you'd turned into a nocturnal creature."

"Are you saying I should get a tan?" he joked.

"You *are* a little pasty, bro." Beth laughed. "Now, you said a friend might be coming?"

"Yeah. She hasn't confirmed, so I'll give her a few minutes before we take off."

Friday at the old folks' home had done something to Lane.

Seeing the sweet people who lived there and the utter joy that Star had brought them had cracked something in his chest. When he was their age, what would he have to show for his life? An incredible career. An issue of *Forbes* magazine with his picture in it.

A fistful of regrets about all the relationships you've screwed up.

Not just Scout. Not even just Todd. But the tension between him and his parents over what had happened with his brother. Even Beth, whom he was closer to than anyone, was put in the middle. Would he be happy when he entered his eighties knowing that he'd held a grudge for so long? That he was more determined to be right than to move on with his life.

"What kind of a friend are we talking about?" Beth waggled her eyebrows. Ariella was crouched down, playing with Star and trying to get her to shake hands.

"Remember how I said I was married?"

She gasped. "You invited your wife?"

"Yeah. I...we're..."

"Are you getting back together?"

"No." Lane shook his head vehemently. "It's not like that. We're getting divorced, actually."

A wrinkle formed in Beth's forehead. "Okay, then why...?"

"We're...friends," he said. "We've been talking again and it's been nice. She's a good person and I enjoy her company."

"But you still want to get divorced?" Beth scratched her head.

"I know. It's a little weird."

"More than a little. But hey, who am I to judge?" She shrugged. "It's not like I've got the high ground when it comes to relationships."

Divorce had changed Beth. Like Lane, she'd spent a good portion of her life being obsessed with perfection—being the perfect wife, the perfect mother. It had made her judgmental of others at times. But now that she was on her own, hard as it was raising two kids by herself, she was more easygoing. More like the Beth he'd known when they were kids. She didn't sweat the small stuff or get hung up on chasing unattainable goals. And she'd learned to be more gracious about the decisions other people made.

Well, unless you counted her unrelenting desire to put the family back together.

"I feel like we're doing a relationship in reverse," Lane said, shaking his head. "We started with marriage and now we're learning to become friends."

"Life's funny like that. You think things are supposed to go one way and they turn out the opposite." Beth laughed.

Lane glanced at his watch. It was almost ten after the hour, so Scout probably wasn't coming. He didn't blame her. Why would she want to meet Beth and the kids now?

But just when he was about to suggest they get going with their walk, Ariella gasped.

"Oh. My. God." She pressed her hands to her chest in the most dramatic fashion. The kid really was a ham. "It's…her."

"Who?" Lane asked, frowning. Then he followed the line of Ariella's pointing finger to where Scout was walking toward them.

She wore ripped light blue jeans with a pair of hot-pink sneakers and, in the same eye-catching shade, a cropped sweater that revealed a fine sliver of skin at her belly. Her long blond hair was floating free around her shoulders, all the way down to her elbows, and she wore a slash of bright pink lipstick on her full lips. The whole outfit was colorful and upbeat, fashionable yet comfortable. A balance of things that were perfectly Scout.

"Barbie," Ariella breathed. "What is she doing in New York?"

"She lives here," Lane offered, but his niece snorted and rolled her eyes.

"Uh, no." Ariella looked at him like he was the child and she was the adult. "Everybody knows Barbie lives in Malibu."

Beside him, Beth snorted and covered her mouth with her hand. Lane chuckled. "Tell you what, Ari. How about I ask Barbie if she wants to hang out with us today?"

Ariella's eyes widened. "But…but…I would have worn a different dress if I knew I was going to meet her!"

"You look great." Lane winked. Then he stood and waved at Scout, who waved back, a big smile breaking over her face.

"Oh my god, she's coming this way." The little girl was practically vibrating with excited energy. "Stay cool, Ariella. Stay cool."

"Is she six or sixteen?" Lane asked his sister under his breath.

"I swear, she came out of the womb a teenager." Beth rolled her eyes affectionately.

Scout approached, her smile looking a little nervous but genuine. "Hi, Lane."

"You *know* her." Ariella's mouth hung open.

Lane leaned over to whisper to Scout. "She thinks you're Barbie. Play along?"

"You know I will." She winked and crouched to greet the little girl. "Hi there. I like your dress."

"Oh, this old thing?" Ariella grabbed the hem of the purple dress and twirled. "I have a better one at home that my mom sewed patches onto. I didn't know you were coming, because if I had known, then I would have worn that dress instead."

"I think you look fabulous."

"I think you look fabulous, too." Ariella beamed. "Can I hold your hand?"

"Of course you can, sweetie." Scout reached over to ruffle Star's head, and then when she stood, she held her hand out to the little girl. At the same time, Lane made an introduction to Beth and the fivesome set off on their walk.

Lane watched as Scout and Ariella chatted, holding hands. Scout was patient with her, playing along with the Barbie thing and answering all her questions. They'd talked once about having children together—in the post pleasure haze, tangled up in one another while the city blinked outside their window. They felt too young for kids then. But one day. In the future.

Scout would make an incredible mother.

"Wow." Beth looped one arm through his and pushed Dante's stroller with the other. "She's something else."

"Isn't she?"

He could tell Beth wanted to ask more, but she chose not to pry because she knew Lane hated to be interrogated. But it wasn't the questions his sister might ask that had his stomach tangled up in knots. It was the ones he had for himself.

Why can't we give things a second chance?

Do we really have to get divorced?

What if I never find someone like her ever again?

Those were the most dangerous questions of all.

21

An hour and a half later, Scout's heart was full of joy. Ariella was the cutest little munchkin and reminded her in so many ways of Lizzie at that age, and Beth had been friendly and interested to hear about Scout's work with Paws in the City. Despite thinking the whole thing would be awkward—*and* contemplating backing out half a dozen times before she arrived at Central Park—she'd had a great time.

"It was *so* nice to meet you," Beth said, leaning over to give her a kiss on the cheek. "And thank you for indulging my daughter."

"Oh my goodness, that's not a problem at all. She's a delight." Scout bent down to give Ariella a hug and to wave goodbye to Dante.

"Goodbye, Barbie." Ariella squeezed her. "Have a safe flight back to Malibu."

"Who knows, maybe Barbie might stay now that she knows how fun New York is." Beth winked.

Scout and Lane waved as Beth led the kids away, Dante already fast asleep in his stroller, and Ariella, always an Energizer Bunny, skipping alongside them. Lane glanced over at her. "Fancy a drink?"

"What about Star?"

"There's a place with outdoor seating nearby that allows dogs," Lane said. "It's nothing fancy, but the beer is cold."

"You're speaking my language."

Scout walked Star, who kept looking over her shoulder every few steps as though worried Scout might vanish into thin air. It was warm out and Central Park was packed with people desperate for sunshine after the long winter months. The bar was also full and they waited for a table, chatting with people who stopped to compliment Star. She was quite the attention-getter, wooing children and adults alike. Eventually they were led to a table.

"Here, you can give her a treat." Lane palmed Scout some hard pellet things that Star liked.

"You were such a good girl today," Scout crooned as she looped the lead around the base of one of the chairs to keep Star secure.

The little dog sat, looking up with her pink tongue lolling out of her mouth as if to say, *Yes, I was a very good girl. Treat please!*

"Shake." She held out her free hand and the dog raised her paw up. "Drop." Scout pointed to the ground and Star lowered immediately down. "Very good. You've earned this."

She held the treat out and Star vacuumed it up like she'd never been given a proper meal before. Scout laughed and

Star's tail wagged happily. She nudged Scout's hand, requesting more attention.

"I'm so glad she's back to normal," Lane said. "Well, mostly normal. She decided to rip up a pillowcase from the laundry basket this week. But that was on me for leaving the bedroom door open."

Scout smiled. Lane must be the only guy who earned as much as he did—which had to be millions with how big Unison had blown up—who still did his own laundry, cooking and shopping. There was something so humble and normal about Lane that Scout admired. Success and money hadn't changed the core of who he was as a person.

"It was really nice to meet your family," Scout said, as she looked over the basic menu. "They seem like wonderful people."

A funny look flickered over Lane's face.

"Oh I didn't mean it like..." She put the menu down. "That wasn't me taking a jab at the fact that I never met them before."

"I know. You're not a petty-jabs kind of person." He sighed. "My family life is kind of complicated right now."

"Really?" You would never have known, looking at it.

They paused the conversation as a server came past to take their orders and whisk their menus away. Underneath the table, Star nudged Scout's leg and she leaned down to show the little dog some love.

"My younger brother, Todd, found out about us not long after we got married. He threatened to tell our parents if I didn't give him money to pay off a debt."

Scout gasped. "You're kidding."

"I wish I was." Lane raked a hand through his hair. "I refused, of course, and it turned out he was bluffing. He never said a word. But it caused a crack in our relationship that only got worse with time."

"Why would…? Was that really something he could use to blackmail you?" Of all the bad things people did in the world, a spontaneous marriage hardly seemed blackmail worthy.

"No, of course not." Lane shook his head. "I was nervous about telling my family because I knew my parents would have been disappointed and skeptical. But there's absolutely no way I would have given him money to keep it a secret. One, it wasn't a secret I wanted to keep long-term. Two, that would only set a bad precedent."

It wasn't a secret I wanted to keep long-term.

The words swirled in her head. At the time it had felt like life and death, but now with more years on her side, she could see things from Lane's perspective. He had a loving family— despite the issues with his brother—and they would have been upset to have missed out on the wedding. They might even have been concerned about Scout's motives.

Someone who was close to their family *would* worry about disappointing them.

Whereas Scout didn't think twice about telling her grandparents, because she knew nothing would please them anyway. At the time, though, she hadn't expected them to pull the pin on her caring for Lizzie. Naively, she'd assumed her being married might even make her seem more mature, because her grandparents would probably trust a stranger more than they trusted her.

"Things escalated after you left. I tried to set him up with interviews and networking opportunities, but he didn't want to make the effort. We had a fight about it and I called him lazy and entitled." Lane shook his head. "He said I got lucky in the tech world and I didn't know how hard it was for most people to get ahead."

Their beers arrived at the table and Scout reached for hers, pausing to clink her glass against Lane's.

"It all came to a head when he took out a credit card in my name and racked up twenty grand in Vegas."

Scout's eyes widened. "Oh my gosh."

"I went there to confront him." Lane took a long gulp of his beer. "It was only knowing it would crush my parents that stopped me from pressing charges. He took off after that. Didn't see him for a few years and now he's back, trying to make amends with the family."

"With the family or with *you*?"

"He's starting with the soft targets." Lane made a face. "Beth thinks I should forgive him."

"Right."

"Would you forgive someone for doing that?" he asked. It sounded like he was genuinely interested in her opinion.

"That's a tough one. Family should never treat one another like that," she said. "Theft is wrong. You've got every reason *not* to forgive him. But...not forgiving someone means continuing to hold on to those bad feelings. It's tiring, trust me."

"You feel like that about your grandparents."

"Yeah." She nodded. "I don't know if I can forgive them, but I've been carrying that hurt around since I was seventeen and...it's getting heavy."

She'd never admitted that to anyone before. There were times when she wondered what it would be like to let it all go. To unburden herself. Continuing to be hurt sometimes felt like she was allowing them power over her, even now.

It kept her in the passenger seat. Kept her at their mercy.

How else can it be? While they have Lizzie, you will always be at their mercy.

"You're very wise," Lane commented.

"Me? Pssh. Please." She took a swig of her beer. The sun was warm on the top of her head and she shoved the sleeves of her sweater up to her elbows. "I'm not wise at all. I've simply made enough mistakes that I have plenty of data on this stuff."

"Can't you take a compliment? Ever?" He laughed.

"I take compliments." She frowned. "When I think they're accurate."

"You don't have a good view of yourself, Scout."

"What's that supposed to mean?" She wasn't insulted, merely curious to understand the void between how he saw her and how she saw herself.

"In your head, you're still that hurt young woman who had nowhere to go when her family rejected her."

"I *am* that person. I've grown up, but I'm still that same girl."

"Don't you see, Scout? You can go *anywhere*. All the hurt you took in your life and you…" He waved a hand at her. "You still help people. You still care about the world. You still try to do better and be better. Fuck. Could you imagine how incredible the world would be if more people were like you?"

"It would be chaos," she said.

"Life is chaos. And frankly, I think some of us need more chaos in our lives. I've spent less time at work this week than in a *long* time."

"Why?"

"Because I had something else to do."

She looked down. The answer made her heart ache. Because Lane deserved a fuller life than just his job. But he'd buried himself in it after their split. The same way she'd tried to bury herself in not caring.

Eventually you came to a crossroads—suffocate in a coffin of your own making, or break free.

"What I mean to say is that you've been a good influence on me," he said.

"I think that's the first time *anyone* has ever said that to me."
She laughed. "So thank you for that."

Lane drained his beer and put the glass down on the table.
Remnants of foam clung to the inside, amber dregs sitting in
the bottom. The sunlight glinted off his dark hair, bringing
out the reddish tones and putting warmth into his skin. A hint
of stubble—also red toned—dusted his strong jaw.

"Want another?" Scout asked, nodding toward his empty
glass. She wasn't in a rush to go home. The sunshine, the real
conversations, the company...it was too good to be over after
only one drink.

"I, uh, I have a few beers at my place if you want to join me
there." The hope in his green eyes made her tummy flutter.

Yes. Take me home.

But she trapped the words on her tongue. She could feel
herself slipping into a routine with him, letting her guard
down and telling herself it would be okay if she just ignored
all the warning bells.

That's what happened last time, when she came back from
Vegas with him. She ignored the warning bells when things
started going south, burying her head in the sand until it all
blew up in her face.

Scout took a fortifying gulp of her beer. "Since we're making an effort to learn from our mistakes by communicating
properly now, can I be vulnerable for a minute?"

"Of course."

"I really *do* want to come back to your place, but I know
that it won't be a beer and nothing more," she said. His gaze—
totally open and without any walls at all—lanced her through
the heart. "And while another night in your bed sounds better
than I can even put into words, after we get divorced, I don't
want to become your booty call. I don't want to become 'just
sex' to you. I couldn't stand it."

"You'd never be that to me. Ever," he said. "I don't want to be that to you, either."

"Once the paperwork is filed and we're officially split, that's...that's it. We can be friends, but I can't let myself be anything more."

"I agree." He swirled the remains of his drink around his glass. "When it's done, it's done. No muddying the waters."

"Exactly."

"But we're not done yet." His eyes met hers, found heat there. Found spark and flame and wanting. "We're still married and...I want a chance to say goodbye to what we had. What we *could* have had."

"A chance to say goodbye," she said. Actually, that sounded perfect.

An opportunity for her to finally put to rest the feelings she had for Lane. A moment to celebrate and mourn the only man she'd ever loved. Lane had been part of the weight on her shoulders, and doing this would allow her to forgive him and herself for it all going so wrong.

Closure.

"Actually," she said. "That sounds wonderful."

They walked back to his apartment, unhurried and relaxed, with Star trotting ahead. It felt strange, to know the end was coming officially and to feel so mixed about it. On one hand, he was relieved that their story had one more chapter left. A *proper* end to the marriage and not the overnight evaporation that he'd had previously.

But on the other hand...

Walking with Scout, holding her hand and feeling totally and utterly content, made him wonder what they were giving up. Couldn't they have a second chance at love? A do-over? They were both older and wiser, more complete humans.

They could handle *all* the things that had been thrown at them before.

But there was so much water under the bridge.

How did anyone come back from something like that?

They walked into his building while Scout chatted animatedly about her work and some of the plans she and Isla had for Paws in the City. If anyone were to look at them, it would be easy to assume they were like any other happy couple. As they got into the elevator, she caught him staring at her.

"What?" she asked, tilting her head, an amused smile on her lips. The expression was like a glimmer of sunshine on an otherwise gray and dismal day. "You're looking at me like I'm a Rubik's Cube you want to solve."

"I'm just thinking about what comes after this. Not…" He shook his head. "Not in my apartment, but the next phase of our lives."

"You were always the one trying to map out the next steps and figure out what the future held."

She was right. The month they'd been together, it was him trying to move them forward. He was the one who planned their milestones and set their goals. He'd wanted to grow old with her. To become gray and wise and withered with her.

In his mind, that would have been a blessing.

But if he was the map and compass, Scout was the willfully lost wanderer—seeking adventure rather than plans. At some points, he'd wondered if the truth of it was that they were simply incompatible.

In the end it had been moot. They didn't go the distance.

"I never told you how much I appreciated it," she said. Her hand drifted out toward him. "Nobody ever thought about a future with me before. Not my mom, not my grandparents. Not any man I ever dated. You were the only one who thought I was worth a future."

The words hit him like a sucker punch. "Of *course* you're worth a future."

"It's hard to believe that when the people who were supposed to love you made you feel like a piece of trash." Tears glimmered in her eyes. "I'm sorry I was too frightened to see what a wonderful gift you gave me."

His body was so tight, a musician could have used him as a guitar string. His jaw tensed. His shoulders bunched. His fingers curled. He was fighting the feeling, fighting his reaction.

"You shouldn't be thanking me," he said. "I should be thanking *you*, for making me see what I was doing to myself. Working myself into the ground, burying myself. Trying to act like there was nothing more to life."

"I guess we're even, then."

She slipped her arms around his neck and dragged his head down to hers, lips meeting his open and hot. She was rough and tender. Firm and soft. And she tasted oh-so-sweet but mixed with something salty. Tears. Hers. She curled her fists into his sweater and he slipped his palm down her back, cupping her ass. Touching her was like heaven.

"I'm sorry," she murmured against his lips. "I'm so sorry."

"I'm sorry, too."

The elevator dinged and he held her hand, leading her to his apartment. They went inside and he freed Star from her harness, but the second his hands were unoccupied, he was drawn to Scout like a magnet. He lifted her up, coaxing her legs around his waist, and she locked her feet behind his back, hanging on as if he were her last tether to earth. Their kisses were deep and searching, like they wanted to know every inch of each other again. They wanted to rediscover themselves and each other. Because this moment meant something. It was *real*.

Tomorrow would come and…

Tomorrow it's over.

Lane walked them through the apartment and into his bedroom without bumping into a single thing. But his eyes and lips and hands never left her. His fingers tangled in her glorious blond hair as he kissed her senseless. She returned fire by sucking on his neck, biting and scraping her teeth. He was harder than he'd ever been in his life.

Even more than his wedding night.

But there was an undercurrent of discontent beneath the inferno of lust. As easy as it was to tell himself that saying goodbye was a positive thing, the inevitability of the sun rising played in the back of his mind. Tomorrow *would* come and he *would* have to face the consequences of his actions. He would have to understand what goodbye meant in reality and not just in theory.

Tonight might mean something to them both, and there was a good chance he'd spend the rest of his life regretting that he didn't fight for more.

22

Lane sunk to his knees on the mattress, still holding her. His green gaze roamed over her face, his thick lashes lowering for a moment as he pressed his cheek harder against her palm. God, he was beautiful. He was gentle in a way she'd never experienced with other men and yet…

When he looked back up at her, she saw the fire in him. There was nothing weak about Lane. His passion burned, and the combination of those two things never failed to make her melt. His eyes flicked back and forth, as though he was searching for something.

"If we're doing this, you need to get out of your head," she said, reaching up and cupping his face. "I want you here, Lane, in the moment with me."

"I'm here," he said. "I promise."

She leaned in to kiss him once more, her lips desperately seeking his. The stubble on his jaw rasped against her skin, and his thumbs whisked away the moisture on her cheeks. Why was she crying? This was what she wanted...wasn't it?

A proper end. Something final to mark this moment in her life. It felt like reward and punishment rolled into one. Atonement and self-sabotage. It hurt so goddamn much she wanted to crumple into a ball. Was it possible that losing him would be even more painful the second time around?

What if you don't lose him?

"Hey, no more tears." He kissed her cheeks and then moved back down to her mouth.

"Sorry, I just..." She sucked in a breath. "It's a lot."

"I know."

He slipped his hands under her body so he could cradle her. For a moment they held one another, saying nothing. She let herself sink into the safety of his embrace, let herself be held. Cherished.

I love you.

She couldn't bring herself to say the words out loud, but she felt them sharp and clear in her mind. She did love Lane. Perhaps she'd never stopped. Perhaps she never *would*.

Lane gripped the hem of his sweater and pulled it up, taking his T-shirt along with it. Scout's heart fluttered as she watched the fabric peel away from his sculpted body. He popped the button on his jeans and pulled his zipper down. Her breathing quickened as his thumbs hooked under the waistband and he shoved it all down—jeans and underwear—and then his socks joined the pile of clothing and he stood before her.

"Now you," he said, his voice like gravel. "Don't rush. I want to savor it."

There was a lump in the back of her throat. It did something to her when he took charge like this. Made her feel like she was looking down on herself, floating on a cloud. Made her feel safe. Cared for.

Desire swam in the room, thickening the air. She started from the bottom, taking off her sneakers and socks and dropping them over the edge of the bed. Her jeans followed. She slowly removed her hot-pink sweater and when she reached behind herself to unclasp her bra, Lane came back to the bed.

"Let me help," he said.

She turned on her knees and felt his fingers brush her skin. Goose bumps rippled across her, and he trailed his fingertip down the length of her spine. His lips pressed against her shoulder and she trembled, biting her lip to stifle a moan.

How did he do so much with so little?

He unhooked the clasp and slipped the straps over her shoulders and arms, treating her gently. She turned and lay back down, drawing her underwear down her thighs and flicking them off the bed with her foot.

"You're magnificent," he said, kneeling at the edge of the bed.

"You're pretty darn special yourself, Lane."

He came forward and pressed one hand down on either side of her, leaning forward to kiss the spot between her breasts. Sensation overwhelmed her, short-circuiting her brain. Rendering her useless for everything except feeling.

"Let me grab a condom," he said, reaching into his drawer and taking care of their protection. Then, when he came back to her, his fingers danced across her skin, tracing circles on her hips and stomach, delving between her thighs.

One last time…

How could she have let her own insecurities ruin something so beautiful? How could she have thought it easier to leave than to talk? How could she possibly wake up tomorrow and go on living knowing what could have been?

He was the lottery of men…and she'd given him up.

"Can we pretend I never left?" She grabbed his face and brought it up so she could see him. Read him. He looked as ruined as she felt. "Let's pretend we didn't screw everything up."

He nodded. "I'd like that."

"I've missed you," she whispered.

"I've missed you, too." His lips were at her ear, each word causing him to brush against the delicate shell. "Now let me feel all of you."

He pushed inside her, sliding deep and sealing his mouth over hers. Scout's body felt like a firework going off. Feeling him skin on skin was…so familiar. So perfect. His green eyes were ablaze, a mix of lust and regret and resolution gleaming there.

While they were both acting on instinct, it all came rushing back—the nights they'd spent together. The feeling of his fingers digging into her hips, hot breath at her neck, the way she used to nip at his skin. Not hard, and not to do any damage. But sharp, little actions that left him with tiny red marks the morning after. She liked to mark him. Claim him.

Make him remember her when he looked in the mirror, so he wouldn't forget how much she loved him.

"That feels—" she gasped "—so incredible."

"Meet me there, Scout." He quickened his pace, wanting to feel her explode. "Meet me there one last time."

The way he held her was a salve to her soul. And the way he called her name as he found release would be permanently imprinted on her memory. With one last thrust, he seated himself deep inside her, and she tipped over the edge, clinging to him and knowing with certainty that she would *never* get over this man.

★ ★ ★

There was no sneaking away this time. But there would be no meal and wine, either. Instead, Scout lay in Lane's arms, her head resting on his chest as the gravity of her decision sat like rocks in her stomach. His fingertips danced along her arm, skipping across her freckles like they were stones creating a path over a river. She couldn't stop touching him, either. Her palm smoothed over his stomach and chest and back down again in long, languid strokes.

Neither of them said a word.

The silence was broken by a scraping at the bedroom door and Lane let out a chuckle. "That dog can't stand to be alone for five minutes."

"It was more than five minutes," Scout teased. "A solid six at least. Don't sell yourself short."

"Smartass." He captured her mouth, kissing her long and deep, only pulling away when the scraping started again, more insistent this time. "Do you mind if I let her in?"

"Of course. I'm happy to have some doggy snuggle time." Scout reached over the side of the bed and grabbed Lane's T-shirt before he could put it on. Then she wriggled into her underwear.

"A smartass *and* a thief," he said, looking at her indulgently.

He pulled on a pair of sweats and went to get the door. Star raced inside like a fuzzy white rocket and launched up and onto the bed.

"C'mere, girl." Scout held her arms out and the little dog bounded over, diving into the folds of the duvet and snuggling up against Scout's armpit. She stroked Star's head as Lane climbed back into bed, and the three of them curled up—a broken family.

There was a hush over the apartment, and soon Star was softly snoring. Sunlight filtered in through the windows and it glinted off the buildings around them. It was like being encased in a gold glass bubble and Scout knew the moment could fracture at any second. She closed her eyes, doing her best to preserve the memory.

For all the things that had gone wrong in her life and all the bad decisions she'd made, Lane wasn't one of them. Maybe she was supposed to marry him. Maybe his impact on her—though their time was short—was necessary.

"Do you think…?" His voice was soft. "Was there any chance we could have made it work?"

"I honestly don't know." She glanced over at him and Lane had a groove between his eyebrows. "We rushed into things without thinking about whether we had the skills to deal with a relationship of that magnitude."

"Do you regret marrying me?"

The question was raw. Lane had torn himself open by asking it and Scout would honor him with the truth. For the first time ever, she wasn't going to leave anything unsaid.

"No." She shook her head. "Maybe I should, but I don't."

"Even if it meant that your grandparents stopped Lizzie from coming to live with you?"

"I don't think I was ready to be a guardian back then. As much as I hated them for it at the time. Now…" She blew out a breath. "It hurts to admit it, but I think they did the right thing. They've given Lizzie a good life with a solid roof over her head and way more stability than I would have provided her."

"But you can give her those things now," he said.

"I can." She nodded. "If they were looking for me to prove myself, then I've done it. I'm working a stable job, I can afford something close to her school—even if it's on the small side—and I'm not raging against the world anymore. I'm tamer now."

"Don't get too tame, Scout." He reached out to tuck a

strand of hair behind her ears. "Don't lose who you are to appease them."

She swallowed. "People need to change."

"People need to *grow*."

"That's the same thing."

He shook his head. "No, it's not. Because growing is improving on what is already good. Because you *are* good, Scout. You don't need to be like anybody else. You don't need to tick some artificial, adult checklist to prove to them that you're not like your mother."

Oof.

"You know how to stick a girl right in the feels," she said, hoping he didn't hear the slight shake in her voice.

Her whole life she'd worried about turning out like her mother—selfish and self-absorbed. Only concerned with her own needs and desires. But it had made her so sensitive to any kind of rejection that she lived her life anticipating the moment that she would be alone for good. She never expected anyone to stay. To love her.

"Can I ask you something?" he said.

"There's no point holding back now."

"Do you think your grandparents would keep Lizzie from you again if we didn't get divorced now?"

"Yes." The answer came almost subconsciously.

She hadn't actively thought about it, but she knew the correct answer. In many ways, divorcing Lane felt like a test. Had she *really* cleaned up her act and stopped making silly decisions? Was she *really* responsible enough to do the difficult thing instead of sticking her head in the sand?

If her grandparents found out that she'd been sleeping with her husband and falling back in love with him at the same time the end of their marriage was being legally documented, well, there was only one conclusion they could come to: Scout *was* just like her mother, a woman who couldn't seem to stay away from trouble and kept going back for one more hit.

Lane bobbed his head. "That's what I thought."

"Why did you want to know that?"

"Because I'm sitting here wondering why we're not giving this another try."

"Don't." She closed her eyes. "Walking away again already feels like hell."

"No point holding back now," he said, echoing her words. "But I understand why you need to go. I would never want to stand between you and your sister, Scout. I know how much you love her and it would kill me if I thought I'd ruined things a second time."

"She's all I have," Scout whispered.

"That's not true." He cupped her face and turned her toward him. "Your life can't be lived for one person or one thing."

"Says you."

"Exactly, says me. I *know* what a mistake that is now. I don't want you to fall into the same trap." The passion in his voice struck her right in the heart. "You have great friendships. You have a job you love. You make an impact on strangers in the street. You are so much more than you think you are. You'll find someone else to love."

"I don't think I will. Not like this."

A somber mood settled over them and Lane's eyes grew shiny. He looked away before she could figure out if they were tears or a trick of the light. "I don't think I will, either."

"We'll always be the ones who got away." She looked down at the dog sleeping against her side, and she stroked the space between her eyes. In her sleep, Star sighed contentedly. "But I don't regret it."

"Me, either."

Lane pushed up from his bed and walked over to a tall set of drawers. He opened a small one at the top, reaching in and pulling something out. It was a small, dark box. He carried it over to the bed. There was no denying what it was—the box her wedding rings had come in.

"You still have it." She shook her head as he opened it, revealing the simple yet beautiful matching set.

Since they hadn't been engaged prior to getting married, he'd bought her two rings at once from an upscale jeweler in Las Vegas. She'd felt like a princess that day, because she'd never been able to afford anything more than costume pieces herself. But these rings were authentic white gold with real gemstones. There was a plain band and one that was crested with a diamond and two smaller stones in a pale pink. Lane had said he liked the design, because it reminded him of how two people could come together to create something that was bigger than either of them alone.

"They were your rings. It didn't feel right to get rid them." He shut the box and handed it to her. "I still want you to have them."

She closed her hand around the box, emotions swirling like a tornado inside her. Lane leaned over to kiss her one more time.

This was goodbye. She could feel it in his kiss—the cacophony of emotions. It was like looking into a kaleidoscope of the memories they'd made together. There was no going back now. Everything had been laid on the table.

It was over.

23

TWO WEEKS LATER...

"You may now kiss the bride."

Scout dabbed at her eye with a tissue as she watched her best friend get married. Theo leaned in and grasped Isla's face with both hands, bringing his lips down to hers. The small group of people inside the private room at an exclusive restaurant cheered. Next to the bride, Dani jabbed one fist into the air and let out a loud wolf whistle that made everyone laugh.

A waiter in a black-and-white uniform seemed to appear out of the woodwork, getting glasses of champagne into everyone's hands. Scout hadn't been to many weddings in her time, but this was probably the smallest—aside from her own, of course. In fact, at a quick count there were fewer than fifteen people in the room, including the bride and groom. The event had been organized swiftly and there was no lengthy ceremony, no official bridal party and no bouquets or boutonnieres. There wasn't even an aisle, let alone seats for the bride's and groom's sides. Theo and Dani had walked Isla into the room, one at each side of her like the tight unit they were, while a piece of soft classical music played.

They'd each read a short pledge to one another, exchanged rings, and after the official stuff was done, they were married. Scout already knew there would be no speeches or cake cutting and since there wasn't a bouquet to toss, that was out, too. Just champagne flowing, amazing food and great conversation. It was like a dinner party with fancier dresses, and despite feeling a little emotional about the whole wedding thing, Scout was thrilled to watch her best friend get married.

She'd never seen Isla look so happy. She kissed Theo once more, and people started to mingle, congratulating the happy couple. There was a woman with short hair and glasses who was fussing over Isla and making Dani laugh. There was an older Italian man chatting with Theo—a longtime friend of Theo's grandmother, who'd passed away in the last year.

The couple practically glowed with happiness.

"That was so lovely," August said with a sigh. She stood next to Scout in a gorgeous green dress that set off her red hair perfectly. She kept tugging at the neckline, however. "But I swear, they make these dresses for people without boobs. I'm really wishing I'd just duct-taped it to myself so I wouldn't be living in fear of one of the girls popping out unexpectedly."

A few feet away, a flash went off. "That would make for quite an action shot."

"I'm glad there's no press here. Could you imagine the

headlines? Chubby redhead traumatizes wedding party with her misbehaving melons."

Scout was midway through taking a sip of her champagne and snorted. "Not while I'm drinking!"

"It won't be a nip slip, it'll be a bazooka bust-out!" August giggled. "A mammary misadventure."

"A cha-cha calamity," Scout chimed in.

"A sweater-stretchers scandal."

"Sweater stretchers?" Scout laughed so hard, a tear escaped her eyes. "I've never heard that term before, it's perfect."

Isla looked over, grinning but confused as to what the women were giggling about. But before she could venture over, the photographer guided her and Theo to a huge window so they could take some photos.

"Thanks for the laugh. I needed that." Scout used her free hand to dab at the tears in her eyes without smudging her mascara. Then she stashed her tissue away in a cleverly concealed pocket in her dress.

"How are you holding up?" August asked, her face filled with concern. Even though they hadn't been friends for too long, she was one of the most empathetic people Scout had ever come across. The kind of person who *genuinely* cared when they asked how you were doing.

"Great. Good." Scout twisted the ring on her right hand. She'd been wearing her wedding ring all week, but on the "non marriage" hand, and she hadn't figured out if it was comforting or self-punishment. "Fine."

"Hmm, downgraded from great to fine in only three words." August gently knocked Scout with her elbow. "What's the real answer?"

"Miserable," she admitted.

After leaving Lane's house, Scout had called Isla and August, and both women had dropped their plans to turn up at her apartment with wine and ice cream. She couldn't be more grateful to have friends like them and she'd spilled her guts about the whole thing, crying her eyes out until they were puffy and red while her friends topped her glass up and took turns hugging her.

"I know there's no point dwelling," she added with a sigh. "And I am truly happy for Isla. But it's reminding me a lot of my own wedding day."

"You have to feel the feelings," August replied encouragingly. "If you bottle it all up, it'll come out at some point, and you don't get to choose when that happens."

"True." She sipped her drink. "I have to remind myself of that. I definitely grew up in an environment where emotions were treated like a disease."

"Girl, same." August let out a dark, humorless laugh. "Emotions may as well have been cooties to my parents."

"I know Lane is destined to be the one who got away, but there's part of me that can't let it go." She sighed. "How do I jump forward to the place where I'm okay with it?"

"If you figure that out, let me know." August frowned. "I've been trying for *years* and I still haven't quite worked it out."

"Really?"

August was generous with a lot of things—her knowledge, her time, her money. But it had taken her a while to open up about her personal life. All Scout knew was that her relationship with her parents was a little rocky and they didn't support her chosen career path. That was it.

So news of a "one who got away" was new.

"It's a long story," August said.

"What's the TLDR version?"

"I had a massive crush on a guy my whole life, and then when he tried to make a move, I freaked out because I'm an idiot. That night he met the woman of his dreams and married her a few months later." August sighed. "She died, and now he thinks love is dangerous and sharing a milkshake is too much commitment for him."

"Oh August." Scout touched her arm. "I'm so sorry."

"That's life." She shrugged, but Scout could tell she was also feeling a little emotionally rattled by the wedding. "I had my chance and I blew it. Now he's not the kind of guy I could ever be with."

"And you still haven't made peace with it, huh?" she said, and August shook her head. "That doesn't bode well for me."

"What's life without a little emotional turmoil, right?" August laughed but it sounded hollow.

"Would you change things if you could do it over?" Scout asked. They'd drifted to one of the windows looking out over the city, and Manhattan sparkled before them like a city of diamonds and glass.

"I know I'm supposed to say that regrets are pointless and life leads you where you need to be, and yada yada yada…" August fiddled with her earring self-consciously. "But I would kill to go back to that night and change things."

Scout nodded. "Me too."

"But we can't change the past, can we? We can only learn from the stupid things we do and make a promise that we won't repeat our mistakes." August linked her arm through Scout's. "And then we call our friends when we need to have a cry."

Scout leaned her head on August's and the two women stood there, lost in their own thoughts and memories.

August was right. She *couldn't* change the past.

She'd made herself a lonely bed for one, and now she had to lie in it.

Lane approached his parents' front door, a brightly wrapped gift in his hands. It was one of those evenings where a fine mist of rain had made the ground glossy and slick, and he was careful with the last step because it was slanted. Jabbing at the doorbell, he bounced up and down to keep warm while he waited for someone to come.

A second later, the door swung open. "Lane, my boy!"

"Hey, Ma."

His mother, Brenda, was a vivacious woman with a big smile and bigger hair. She staunchly refused to accept that the 80s were over and single-handedly kept hairspray companies in business. The higher the hair, the closer to God, she always said.

"You look like a million bucks." He gave her a squeeze and then handed her present over before planting a kiss on her cheek. "Happy birthday."

"Rav and Sarah are already here. I really like her."

Lane walked into the house, rolling his eyes once he knew his mother wouldn't be able to see. "Yeah, Ma. I know."

"I'm just saying."

He raised an eyebrow. "You're always 'just saying.'"

"I want you to be happy," she said, patting his arm.

"That's a lie. You want me to find a woman who will give you lots of grandbabies."

"Babies will make you happy." She grinned, completely unrepentant. "Speaking of which, where's Star?"

Star.

"We went for a big walk this afternoon and I decided to let her stay home and rest."

While the statement was true, there was something he was leaving out. Star was officially driving him nuts again. This time she wasn't chewing or snapping or destroying his house. She was crying by the front door.

Just like the last time Scout left.

It was a daily reminder of what he'd lost. Star would sit at the door and cry, and then when she'd given up on that, she would mope around the house like someone had stolen her lunch. Nothing cheered her up. Not shiny new toys, not going for long walks, not snuggling on the couch. She wanted Scout.

The one thing he couldn't give her.

They were a pair of sad sacks right now. But Lane had promised himself that for his mother's birthday he would be on his best behavior. That meant (a) leaving his personal troubles—and his dog—at home and (b) being civil to his brother.

I'm not sure which one is going to be more difficult.

He followed his mother into the open-plan kitchen and living area. Beth was pouring drinks at the island, and Rav and Sarah were chatting with her. Lane's father was seated on his favorite chair, bouncing Dante on his knee, while Todd sat cross-legged on the ground as Ariella read one of her books to him. Lane did the rounds, saying hello to everyone and kissing his niece and nephew.

"It's been ages." Sarah came over and pressed a glass of wine into his palm. "It's so good to see you."

Sarah looked like a pixie—she was petite, with cropped blond hair, blue eyes and tons of freckles. With Rav's brown skin, inky black hair and long, lanky frame, they were polar opposites in appearance, but they were the most in-love couple he knew.

"Thanks for coming," he said to them. "It means a lot."

"Of course." She smiled, glancing over at his mother, who was heading into the kitchen after putting her present on the sideboard, along with a few others, and laughing while Rav said something to her. "We're always happy to see your family. Plus I'd literally cross the world for her cooking. You're lucky to have such a great family."

He couldn't help but let his gaze flick over to Todd, who caught him looking. Lane swallowed. Was this how it would be the rest of his life? For a brief second, he'd thought about not coming tonight to avoid dealing with Todd. But that idea had been dismissed as quickly as it came, because he'd never do that to his mother.

Out of the corner of his eye, he saw his brother get up as Ariella skipped over to her grandmother to beg for some chocolate. Todd approached him and Sarah.

"Mind if we have a word?" he asked. "In private."

"I'll leave you to it." Sarah smiled and went to help in the kitchen.

Lane hesitated. What could his brother possibly say that would make any difference at all?

You thought that when Scout turned up on your doorstep and look what happened. You forgave each other. You got closure.

Still, it wasn't like they'd gotten a happy ending.

"Please," Todd said, looking him right in the eye.

"Fine." Lane motioned for him to go ahead into the small room that operated as the family's office. It was cramped, and papers littered the desk, like usual. "What do you want to say?"

"Look, I know you probably hoped that I'd disappear off the face of the earth and never come back." Todd let out a breath. "But being away these past couple of years…it made me see that I took this family for granted."

Lane folded his arms across his chest, as if trying to crush the snarky response that wanted to bubble up inside him.

"Especially you." He lowered his eyes to the floor and Lane sensed genuine remorse in his brother's voice. "I felt like people compared us from the moment I was born and nothing I did would ever make me live up to you. I let it create resentment inside me. I felt inferior, and instead of working on myself, I let that feeling fester until I thought you were the source of my problems."

"I never did anything but try to help you," Lane said

through gritted teeth. "Ever since we were kids, I was your biggest supporter."

"I know. I *worshipped* you when we were kids, but as I got older, I…" He raked a hand through his hair, and for a second, it was like looking in a mirror. "I let it mess me up. Taking the money from you like that. Shit. It wasn't even about the money. I wanted people to notice that I was doing something."

"You wanted them to notice you were…" He stopped short of calling his brother a thief, because he knew it would only inflame things. "Doing something unethical?"

"I was out of my mind. I was drinking a lot…too much. *Way* too much." He pulled out his wallet and produced a blue chip. "But I'm six months sober now."

Lane didn't even know that his brother had struggled with drinking, let alone alcoholism. The knowledge shocked him to his core.

"Congratulations, man. Good for you."

"Don't feel bad for not knowing," he said, as if reading Lane's mind. "I hid it well. People don't tend to question a young guy who hits the drink, because they just think he's partying. It doesn't excuse what I did. Not by a long shot. But, I'm trying really hard to put my life back together. I've got a job as an apprentice now, at a tattoo shop. I met the guy in my AA meetings, and he's showing me the ropes and teaching me how to run a business. So long as I stay sober, I can keep working with him."

Lane was stunned speechless. It was like talking to a stranger—none of his brother's old cockiness and sense of entitlement was there. He wasn't dodging eye contact or talking like he had somewhere else to be.

"They won't let me tattoo anyone yet. But I'll get there." Todd nodded, as if reassuring himself. "They really like my designs, so I've drawn up some cool things for a dude who works there. One was a snake wrapped around a Harley."

"You always were a great artist," Lane said. His brother had filled notebook after notebook with sketches as a kid. "Good for you."

"I uh, I drew up a payment plan to get the money back to you." Todd still had his wallet in his hand and he pulled out a piece of paper that had been folded half a dozen times. On it were some crude calculations in pen. "It's gonna take a while, because the apprenticeship doesn't pay much. But I'm doing odd jobs on the side and once I get my own station and can start taking clients, it'll speed up."

"We can talk about it—"

"I *will* pay you back. It might take ten years, but I'll do it." There was a serious intensity about his brother that Lane hadn't seen before. He looked like a man who'd figured out which direction he wanted to take and was striding along that path. "I won't go to my grave knowing I robbed my own brother and didn't make things right."

"I appreciate that."

"Do you think you can forgive me?" Todd asked. "I don't expect it, because I know I screwed you over. But being away from the family made me realize what I'd sacrificed because I was more interested in feeling sorry for myself than making my life what I wanted it to be."

The words lanced him.

Had Lane been doing *exactly* that, ever since Scout left? Only instead of being dependent on any substances, Lane had become dependent on work. It was an easier addiction to hide, because he'd always been driven and ambitious. It was an acceptable thing to do. Noble, in some people's eyes.

But in the end, Lane hadn't made his life what he wanted it to be, either. His best friend and business partner had to practically drag him out of his office to socialize. He had to bring his dog to work because he avoided being in his home as much as possible. He eschewed new friendships and relationships because he was convinced people would hurt him.

What kind of a life was that?

He might not be able to have Scout back in his life, but Lane *could* have his brother. It wasn't too late to forgive. It wasn't too late to accept Todd's apology and his plan to fix things. It wasn't too late to pull his head out of the sand and stop acting like a wounded animal.

"I'm glad you've turned your life around," Lane said. "And I appreciate you offering to make things right. It means a lot."

"You have my word, Lane. I'm not the same guy I was back then."

"I'm glad to have my brother back."

Tears glimmered in Todd's eyes and he stepped forward, embracing Lane in a big bear hug and releasing him a moment later.

"I'm glad to be back," Todd said gruffly. "And I swear, Beth didn't put me up to this. If anything, she told me not to rush into trying to win you over."

"Really?" Lane glanced out the door to where his sister was eavesdropping a few feet away. She offered him a sheepish smile.

"I guess she felt bad for meddling, but I told her it was my job to patch things up. And that asking for forgiveness doesn't mean I'm entitled to it." Todd nodded. "My sponsor told me that."

"Sounds like a wise human."

"He is."

The two men stood awkwardly in silence for a moment, before Lane muttered something about needing to get back to the family. Forgiveness would come slowly—a hurt that big wasn't erased with one conversation—but even being open to the possibility of reconciliation showed that Lane had shifted his beliefs.

If someone had asked him a few months ago whether he would be ready to forgive his wife for leaving and his brother for cheating him, the answer would have been no. But his time with Scout had shown him that every story had two sides—good people could make bad decisions when put under pressure—and that everybody deserved a second chance.

Most of all, Lane could now forgive himself for all the mistakes he'd made in his marriage and for not being the best version of himself back then. It wouldn't bring Scout back. That ship had sailed. But Lane could still have a relationship with his brother. He could still put himself out into the world and make new friends. He could still *live*.

Maybe he could even find love one day. Because Scout had shown him that love was something he didn't even know he was missing.

24

After the wedding, Isla and Theo took off for a few days to some exclusive resort in Hawaii. They weren't going to have a traditional honeymoon because Isla didn't want to leave her sister alone for that long. Instead, they'd planned a longer vacation to Italy in the summer when Dani was finished up with school.

For this short period, however, the Paws in the City office would remain open and Scout was in charge. It was both thrilling and terrifying. She'd never been in charge of anything...well, ever. Hadn't even led a group project in school. Not once.

She plopped down at her desk and sucked in a breath as she looked around the tiny, quiet office. Isla had moved all her meetings to after she was due back, so Scout wouldn't have to juggle too many things. But Scout had one goal for the three days her boss was away.

Secure a hot new client.

Specifically, a hot new client who would bring some buzz to the agency. Up until this point, all their clients had been animals of varying degrees of fame. But what if Scout could find a famous *person* with an adorable pet who would attract lots of attention? She had a bold idea and a target.

Wes Evans, Broadway wunderkind, and his Australian professional-ballerina wife, Remi Evans, had a cute-as-pie husky pup. Now, when she'd seen Wes at the charity photoshoot, he'd made it clear he wasn't into social media. After doing some digging, Scout had found out it had something to do with an infamous dating app that no longer existed. Remi, however, had a large following on Instagram and Tik-Tok, where she choreographed clever ballet routines to modern music.

The videos where she danced with her puppy, Lamington, were the most popular ones. She'd even trained the smart little dog to do tricks which she timed with the music.

It was unconventional to sign a human to an animal social media agency, granted. But who said she couldn't sign a duet? Human and animal as a package deal. Remi would surely be looking to raise her profile as a dancer and help bring more attention to her husband's show—in which she had the starring role—and Star could use Lamington's cute face and adorable antics to grow the Paws in the City business.

It sounded like a match made in heaven.

Isla had said they needed a client, whether new or old, to break out in the industry, and Lamington could be that client. In fact, Scout had a totally out-of-the-box idea for a charity event which involved a special one-time version of Wes's modern ballet *Out of Bounds*...but with dogs.

Was it a wild idea? Yes. Would it likely take a ton of convincing? Absolutely. Was it impossible to make a ballet with dogs? No idea.

But could it get a *huge* amount of attention both for the ballet and for the agency if they could pull it off? Scout was sure of it.

What you call being a "hot mess," I call living boldly.

She let Lane's words settle in her head, giving her confidence. If she wanted to help Isla build something amazing with Paws in the City, they would need to be bold. She would need to stop letting her fear of rejection hold her back from chasing after what she wanted. She would need to stop worrying about being a "hot mess" and start believing in herself.

She looked at the blank email in front of her, with only the To field completed. She'd gotten Remi's email through August, who knew their dog groomer.

"You can do this. Just put it out into the world and see what comes back."

With her fingers hovering over the keyboard, she made the decision to stop fearing the future. Remi might say no. She might not respond at all. And Scout couldn't pin all her hopes on one idea.

"If this doesn't work, you'll come up with another idea. And then another. And another."

She wouldn't stop until she'd figured out a way forward.

After typing the email she read it at least five times for spelling mistakes and then she moved her mouse over the Send button, hesitating before squeezing her eyes shut and clicking. Was it a sad fact that she'd never put any of her ideas out into the world before? Yes. But she would be making up for that now.

She stared at her computer screen. Nothing happened.

"People don't respond to emails in three seconds, silly." She shook her head and got up from her desk.

But to her shock, a few minutes later her computer pinged and a new email flashed up in her inbox. It was from Remi Evans. Holding her breath, she clicked open the email.

Hi Scout,

Thank you so much for reaching out. Wes brought home a goodie bag with information about your agency recently and I thought it was such a clever idea.

And the idea of a puppy version of *Out of Bounds* is genius! I would love to talk more about the opportunity for a charity collaboration. I'm off on Thursday. Shall we meet up then?

Remi

The email included her phone number, and for a moment Scout could only stare. Then she let out an excited squeal and pumped her fist into the air. She couldn't wait until Isla was back so she could tell her all about it.

In fact, she should probably prepare some material to take to the meeting. Scout headed into Isla's office to grab a client welcome pack just in case the meeting went well. As she went to grab one from a box sitting on the floor, she noticed a manila folder on Isla's desk with a hot-pink sticky note on top that said "Scout Review," written in blue ink.

She shouldn't have looked. It was wrong and a breach of privacy.

But Scout had never been the kid who could avoid shaking a gift to see what was inside before she was officially allowed to open it. Biting down on her lip, she flipped the folder open. Inside were some handwritten notes—because Isla was analog like that. She liked to write everything down by hand because it helped her think better. *And* she was the kind of person who was organized enough not to lose her notes.

Promotion to account manager, date effective…May? June?

To do:
Speak to recruiter for admin position.
Draft job descriptions.
Figure out where the heck we're going to fit an extra person in this tiny space. Rotating WFH schedule? Desk share?
Talk to Scout about pay schedule for new role. $10k performance bonus.

A $10,000 bonus.

It wasn't lost on Scout that this was the exact amount of money that she'd given Isla as an investment in Paws in the City when Isla decided she wanted to strike out on her own. It was also the exact amount of money that Scout's grandparents had paid her so she would stop asking for custody of Lizzie several years ago. The money had sat untouched in her bank account until she'd drawn up a check for Isla, because Scout refused to use a cent of it herself no matter how dire things were. Dipping into the "stay away" bribe would have felt like rock bottom.

But giving the money to Isla so they could lease their office had felt like she was finally doing something good with her life. Now Isla wanted to give it back, but she was framing it as a "bonus" so Scout wouldn't feel like the money was tainted anymore. Not to mention the fact that Isla had been working on giving her a promotion anyway, even without her finding the next big thing.

Isla trusted her.

Her eyes welled, but she blinked and looked up at the ceiling, wondering how she got so lucky to have a friend like Isla. Nobody else had ever given her a chance in life the way Isla had. Now this.

That money would pay for the first month's rent in a new place, new furniture to make sure Lizzie was comfortable, *and* there would be enough left over for a little safety net. Now all that was left to do was to finalize her divorce with Lane and get her grandparents to give a formal okay for Lizzie to come live with her.

It was all coming together.

By the following day Scout's good mood had dimmed significantly. It was time to meet with Lane and the lawyers to go over the divorce paperwork. Bill had indicated it should be a quick meeting since there weren't any assets to split up, but there were some things they had to confirm. Lane had wanted them all to be in a room together to make sure everyone was on the same page.

After that, the paperwork would be filed and a court date would be set. Then she would be legally single and free to move on with her life.

It should have felt like freedom. Instead, it felt like an abyss.

Scout looked at herself in the reflection of the silver elevator doors. That morning, she'd dressed without thinking in all black, with a shift dress, opaque tights, cardigan and pumps all matching. It looked like a funeral outfit.

The doors opened on level thirteen—a jab from the universe that was not lost on her—and she stepped out into the building's hallway. Scout, for once in her life, was early. Instead of entering the lawyer's office, she leaned against the wall outside to gather herself.

Her stomach churned. She'd barely eaten all day at the Paws

in the City office, subsisting on coffee and a few bites of a sandwich that had tasted like sawdust in her mouth.

Everything about this felt wrong.

The second elevator dinged and the doors slid open and out walked Lane. He was dressed in a black suit—something she'd only ever seen on their wedding day—and a white shirt with a black tie and shoes. He caught her eyes across the hall-way, looked at her outfit, looked down at himself and burst out laughing. For a moment the sound lifted all the weight off Scout's shoulders and she found herself laughing, too, at the absurdity of it all.

"We've certainly dressed for a somber occasion, haven't we?" His green eyes twinkled. Even on the most miserable of days, his amusement made her feel like everything would be okay, even when she knew it wouldn't.

He came over to her and leaned forward, brushing his lips against her cheek. His cologne was fresh and woodsy, and she desperately wanted to curl her hands into the lapels of his jacket.

"In all honestly, I don't know whether to laugh or cry," she said, clutching her hands tighter around the handle of her purse to stop herself reaching out for him. "Neither one feels quite right."

"We're doing the right thing." It sounded a hell of a lot like he was trying to convince himself. "Your priority is your sis-ter. Family has to come first."

She raised an eyebrow in silent question.

"I'm making amends with Todd," he said. "It'll be slow, because part of me still doesn't trust him and he needs to earn that back with his actions. But I'm not keeping the door closed, if you know what I mean."

"Good for you, Lane. That shows what kind of a person you are."

"A wise woman told me that not forgiving someone means continuing to hold on to bad feelings." He smiled. "I needed to hear that. Because I could see how in ten years it might have twisted me even more. I don't want to become a person who hangs on to grudges for a lifetime. That's not...that's not who I am. That's not who I want to be."

"I'm proud of you."

"Thanks."

They stood in silence for a heartbeat, and the door to the lawyer's office swung open. A woman Scout recognized as Bill's assistant poked her head out.

"Hi, Scout," she said. "And you must be Mr. Halliday. We're ready for you both whenever you want to come on in."

Scout tried to muster a smile. "Thank you."

The door closed again and Scout looked at Lane.

"I'm going take another minute out here, if that's okay," she said, her voice cracking.

If she walked into the meeting room and immediately burst into tears in front of everyone, she wasn't sure she'd ever get over the humiliation. Lane nodded and left her standing there, disappearing into the office. Muted voices came from inside.

Closing her eyes for a moment, she slumped back against the wall. "What am I doing?"

"I thought you'd be inside by now."

The voice made her eyes fly open. Her grandfather stood in the hallway, one of the elevators closing behind him.

"What are you doing here?"

Norman was wearing navy slacks and a sports coat, a scarf tied loosely around his neck. His large frame was stooped slightly as he walked toward her, his limp looking more pronounced than usual. The cold tended to stiffen his muscles.

"Bill told me you were submitting the papers today," he said. "I figured you might want some family support."

"That's why you're here?" she asked, the stress eroding her verbal filter. "To support me? Not to make sure I go through with it?"

Her grandfather frowned. "Why would I need to make sure you went through with it?"

Scout looked up at the ceiling for a moment. "Because you think I made a stupid mistake marrying a man I barely knew."

"Yes, I believe marriage is a serious commitment," he said. "And I don't think anyone that young should be getting married, especially not to someone they don't know. But you ended the relationship, so clearly you feel it was a mistake, too."

"I don't, though." She swallowed. The need to cry clogged the back of her throat. "I don't think it was a mistake."

"Then, why did you call things off?"

"Because..." So many reasons, some of them right and some of them wrong. "I *was* too young to handle being married. But that doesn't mean the man I chose was a mistake, because he wasn't. He's a good man and he would have made a great husband if I'd just..."

"What?"

"...let him in." She looked up at her grandfather, sadness and anger and frustration all mixing together into one fire-fueled knot. "But I couldn't do that, because I was scared that if I let him see the real me, then he wouldn't love me anymore. Because why would he love me when my own family doesn't?"

Her grandfather winced. "I have never said that I don't love you."

"Yeah, but you showed it." She pushed off the wall. "You kicked me out of the house when I was still a child. You made me feel like I only deserved to be part of the family if I fell into line and turned myself into everything you wanted. Like I had to *earn* my place as your grandchild."

"That is *not* true."

She caught the spark of emotion in his words. She'd hit a nerve. "Then, why did you do it, huh? Why did you put me out on my ass when I was still a teenager?"

"When I told you to get out of the house, I didn't mean forever." He tossed his hands in the air. "You needed a break from us and we needed a break from you. I knew you were staying at Isla's house, and I called her mom every other day to check on how you were doing."

Scout blinked in surprise. She'd always assumed that they had no idea where she'd gone. It had happened right after the school year ended, and she'd found work stacking shelves in a grocery store.

"We were expecting you to come back after a few days because you'd learned your lesson. I had no idea that you'd take off for good." He let out a breath. "And before you ask why I didn't come looking for you, I did. I came to Isla's house and spoke with her mom, who told us that you said you never wanted to see us again. As far as you were concerned, we might as well be dead."

She *had* said that, on her eighteenth birthday as she'd blown the candles out on a cheap cake feeling totally and utterly alone. Her teenage anger had been a bonfire out of control.

"I was a kid and I was hurt. What did you expect?"

"It was like looking at a reincarnation of your mother. History repeating itself. I heard the same words from her when she walked out of our home after we found drugs in her schoolbag."

"So you gave up on me?" Tears pricked her eyes and her lip quivered. "You just wrote me off because I reminded you of her."

"We were trying to protect Lizzie. She was young and impressionable and we knew we could raise her in a way that would put her on the straight and narrow."

"And I was a threat to that."

"At the time, yes. You were." He shook his head. "You were drinking and smoking and hanging out with all the wrong people. Isla, aside, of course. But you were starting to run with a bad crowd and I couldn't blame you. The environment that you'd grown up in...it was inevitable."

The words were like a blade across her heart. They'd sacrificed her stability and well-being to save her little sister from being influenced. They'd committed the cardinal sin of choosing one child over another.

"Do you have any idea how much it messed me up?" She looked at him, imploring the older man to see her as the person she was instead of who she'd been. "I couldn't commit to anything—not a job, not any new friendships, not a man who actually loved me—because I believed I'd end up getting rejected just for being me. I was so scared of being left behind that I made it my inevitability."

He didn't say anything.

"That month I spent with Lane was the only time I've been truly happy and loved in my entire life." She jabbed her finger at him. "And you made me feel like an idiot for doing it, for seeking out someone who made me feel good, just because I didn't do it in a way that you deemed acceptable. Then you punished me by keeping my own sister from me because I refused to fall in line."

"That wasn't punishment, Scout. We were doing what was best for Lizzie, and you didn't have a steady job. You didn't have any plans for the future. You were living with a stranger." He ticked the items off on his fingers. "There was no way I could put her into that situation, not to mention that you had no idea the kind of responsibility it takes to care for a child under ten. You had no experience, either."

She looked at the ground. He was right, of course. If she took her own emotions out of the equation, she could see that it would have been hugely irresponsible for him to allow Lizzie to come and live with her. The only reason they'd even been considering sharing custody before that was because Scout had promised to move close to them so they could be on call should anything happen.

"I know you think everything we do is about punishing you, but it isn't. I'm not going to claim we were the best parents, because clearly we weren't," he said passionately. "Your mother was a handful from the beginning, and we were woefully unequipped to raise her. And yes, maybe I should have dragged you home. But I'd tried that with her and it backfired completely. At some point, I figured I had to let you decide for yourself."

"And the money you gave me? You wanted me to stop asking to have Lizzie come live with me. You paid me to stay away."

"I did *not* pay you to stay away. I put that money in your account because I felt guilty that our relationship was so broken and I didn't know what else I could do for you." He looked as emotionally exhausted as she felt. "You really thought we paid you to stay away?"

It had felt like it at the time. They'd argued again, and Joyce had told her that if she kept asking about having Lizzie come and stay with her that they'd stop taking her calls. For a while, they'd limited how often they would let her see Lizzie. So she'd taken the threat seriously.

But was it possible it was the heat of the moment? Perhaps. Still, why would she assume the money was meant to help when it felt like they'd given up on her? When they'd picked one child over the other.

"Why *wouldn't* I think that? I've spent this whole time believing that you thought I was a failure and a bad person. But I'm not." She drew her shoulders back, reaching deep inside for the confidence blossoming inside her. Confidence that was watered by Isla's friendship and August's wisdom and Lane's love. Confidence that she wanted to nurture and grow. "I'm flawed, yes. And I'm messy and tardy and I can make rash decisions. But I'm good where it counts, in here."

She tapped her chest.

"I'm trying every day to be better than I was before and to learn from all the mistakes I've made. But I can tell you now, marrying Lane was not one of them." She looked to the frosted glass door as shadows moved inside. They were probably wondering what the hell had happened to her. "My only mistake was running away when things got hard."

"Then, why are you here?" her grandfather asked. He looked thoroughly confused.

"Because I thought you would keep Lizzie from me again if I didn't go through with this. It felt like a test to see if I was finally the kind of granddaughter you wanted me to be—the one who did what she was told and followed the rules." A tear dropped onto her cheek and she whisked it away. "But I'm not that person. I hate rules and I need freedom and flexibility to be happy. I…"

She couldn't remain under his thumb anymore.

As much as she desperately wanted to keep Lizzie in New York, at some point Scout had to live for herself. She had to start building the life she wanted without influence from her grandparents. Without squeezing herself into a box for them. Because what example would she set for her sister if she was miserable without Lane? If she turned away from love just to make someone else happy? To prove herself?

Would she want Lizzie to emulate that? Hell no.

"I love Lane," Scout said. "It might not make sense to you, but that doesn't change how I feel. I love him and I don't want to divorce him."

25

"I love him and I don't want to divorce him."

The reception area of the lawyer's office went deadly quiet. Lane had come out of the meeting room, along with Scout's lawyer, to see what was holding her up. Her words echoed through the intimate, tidy office space and the woman sitting behind the front desk widened her eyes.

"Uh…" Mr. Billings glanced at Lane, his mouth hanging open in surprise.

"Let me go talk to her," Lane said.

He paused at the door after the voices outside had gone quiet. He wasn't certain who Scout was talking to—or arguing with, as her tone suggested—but he could certainly guess. Sucking in a breath, he pushed the door open and found Scout standing with an older gentleman.

Both of them whipped their heads around to look at him and Scout's eyes widened in horror. He had no idea what to do. This whole situation…well, it felt like he was trying to pilot a rocket to the moon.

You love her. That's all you need to know.

So he walked over to Scout and grabbed her hand, squeezing. If nothing else, he would stand by her side and show her that she wasn't alone. That he was on her team. That he was here for her, no matter what.

Everything else could be worked out.

"Exactly how much of that did you hear?" Scout asked, looking up at him.

"Just the important bit," he replied.

"Wonderful." She sighed. "Just freaking perfect. Today is going swimmingly."

He couldn't help but grin like a child with Christmas presents laid out in front of him, because even though the mood was dark…Scout loved him. She didn't want to end their marriage.

More importantly, she was finally standing up for herself.

"Stop smiling. This is terrible," she said, but a smile of her own twitched on her lips. "I'm making a fool of myself."

"No, you're not. You're standing your ground and fighting," he said, looking into those mesmerizing hazel eyes. "So now I get to be proud of you."

"Lane…" Scout said, gesturing to the man standing with her. "This is Norman. My grandfather."

He'd been an ogre in Lane's mind, even after Scout left. But now, seeing the man in front of him, he was only a human. Flawed, like everyone was. But human.

"Your granddaughter is an incredible woman," Lane said. "Despite all the hurdles she's faced in life, she still has a thirst to better herself and those around her. She is impossibly kind and generous and loving, despite years of not receiving those things herself. She is as resilient as a person can be, and yet she's still tender. She cares about her little sister more than anything in the world and I care about Scout enough that I would sign those divorce papers if it meant her keeping Lizzie close. We would both make a huge sacrifice for that young girl.

"Now, if you still have reservations about whether she would be cared for in our home, then I don't know what further proof we could provide. Because we were both willing to walk away from the best thing that had happened to either one of us, for Lizzie's sake."

Norman Myers looked from Scout to Lane and back again, his gaze dipping to where they held hands, clinging to one another like they were magnetically attached. On some level, that's what it felt like. Because so many things had tried to pull them apart, but they kept coming back to one another. They kept hanging on instead of giving in.

"Our home?" Scout asked, looking up at him with hope dancing in her eyes.

"Wherever that might be—Brooklyn, Manhattan... California." He swallowed. "Wherever you need to be, I'll be there with you."

"There's no need for you to follow us," Norman said, holding up a hand. "It's clear we all need to sit down and have a serious conversation, Lizzie included. Because this is her life and she deserves a say. But if she really wants to stay in New York, then...then we should talk about how we can make it work. I don't want to rip her away from you, Scout. I have never wanted that. But I understand how, in my desire not to make the same mistakes a third time, I have given Lizzie many things I have not given you. And you have blossomed, in spite of it."

"Thank you," she said, her voice watery.

"Come by the house when you can," he said. "And I will leave you to decide what you're doing here today. It is not my place to interfere."

Norman turned and made his way to the elevator, which opened before he got there. Someone inside held the door as two people exited. A second later, the elevator doors closed, and Lane and Scout were left alone in the hallway outside the lawyer's office.

"They're *absolutely* listening in to this conversation," Lane said, glancing at the frosted door.

"I don't care." Scout turned to him and grasped his other hand. "Thank you for sticking up for me."

"I should have done it a long time ago. I'm sorry I ever made you feel unworthy, Scout. I regret not shouting it from the top of the Empire State Building with all my heart."

"And I regret assuming you would be like the rest of my family," she said. "Yes, you could have made me feel more included when we got back to New York, but I packed my bags after a single strike. Everybody makes mistakes—I know that more than anyone—and I didn't give you a chance to fix things. I didn't give you the benefit of the doubt, even for a second."

"Do you think we can do better a second time around?" he asked, leaning his head down to touch his forehead against hers.

"Oh, no question. *Infinitely* better." She smiled and it made her whole face sparkle. "I think we'll smash it out of the park second time around."

"A home run."

"Not just a home run. A grand slam."

"Hey, you made a proper baseball reference," he teased. "Good for you."

"I'm learning."

"You certainly are."

He stared into the eyes of the woman he loved, feeling like his life was expanding in all the right ways. There was no way he was going back to how things were, with long days of nothing but staring at a computer screen.

This woman had taught him what it meant to live fully, and he was never going to forget it.

"I guess we'd better make it official," Lane said. "I wish I'd kept your ring so that I could do this properly, but it's the thought that counts, right?"

He lowered himself down on one knee. But as he opened his mouth to declare his love and his intent to stand by her side for a second time, Scout surprised him by reaching for a slender gold necklace. As she dragged it up, he caught sight of two dainty rings dangling from the chain, which had been hidden away inside her dress.

"You've been wearing them," he said.

"Even though we were supposed to end things today, my brain wouldn't accept that we were over. I've worn them every day since you gave them back." She unlatched the clasp of the necklace and slid the rings off, handing them to Lane before securing the chain back around her neck. "And I want to wear them every single day going forward."

Lane reached for her hand. "Then, will you marry me again, Scout? Let's do it properly this time. Let's talk when we make mistakes and be vulnerable even though it's scary. Let's make our second chance forever."

"Yes." Scout nodded, a wide smile on her face and tears in her eyes as Lane slipped the rings back onto her finger, where they belonged. "I love you so much, Lane."

"I love you, too, my darling wife."

As he stood and pulled Scout into him, he caught sight of the lawyer's office door being held open, the two lawyers standing next to one another and looking thoroughly befuddled. They probably hadn't seen a proposal in the middle of a divorce meeting before.

But Lane was thrilled to be the first.

He clasped Scout's face with both hands and brought his lips down to hers, kissing her long and hard and so thoroughly it was a certified miracle that he didn't push his wife against the wall and have his way with her right there in the hallway.

But there would be plenty of time for that.

Plenty of time, like forever.

ONE MONTH LATER...

Lane turned his car into Scout's grandparents' tree-lined street. The entire drive to Brooklyn he'd noticed that Scout had been unusually quiet. Today was a big day. The *biggest* day.

Lizzie was moving in with them.

Scout's grandparents were heading to California in the next month, and Lizzie would be moving into the apartment with Scout and Lane. That was only a temporary situation, however, because they were currently looking to buy a house in Brooklyn, close to Lizzie's school. Norman had offered for them to live in the family home while they were on the other side of the country, but Scout had refused. Too many bad memories there. Too many things she still had to untangle in her heart.

So they would find a new place, a blank slate, and they would make new memories.

"Are you okay?" he asked as he killed the engine. "You're quiet as a mouse."

"I can't believe this is really happening." She turned to Lane. "This is what I've wanted for so long and..."

"It's not too good to be true," he said, placing his hand on her thigh and squeezing. "I promise."

Scout laid her hand over his and her rings sparkled. He

would never get over the rush of happiness he felt whenever he saw her wearing them again.

"You knew I was thinking that, huh?" she said, smiling sheepishly.

"Yep. But that's okay. It's my job to remind you that everything will work out and I'm more than happy to do it." He leaned over and kissed her. "Come on, let's not keep them waiting."

Outside the air was mild and the scent of orange blossoms filled the air, floating from one of the neighbors' backyards. Lane retrieved Star from the back seat and he laughed when she licked his hands.

"Who's in a good mood today?" Scout crooned, bending down to scratch her head. "Such a sweet, happy girl."

Star's tail wagged so vigorously, it shook her whole body, and she looked up loving as if to say, *It's me! I'm the sweet, happy girl.*

And she was. Star was fully back to her old self—no more crying at the front door, no more chewing furniture. Scout had taken to waking up early to fetch Star from her doggy bed so they could snuggle for a while before the day started. Now that Lizzie was going to be living with them, Star would be showered with more attention than ever.

And *boy* would she love it.

The trio walked up to the front door, Lane and Scout hand in hand, and when they rang the bell, there was a clatter inside. Lizzie flung the door open, her cheeks pink from excitement. She looked *so* much like Scout it was like seeing a time-reversed version of her. Lizzie's long blond hair was pulled back into a ponytail and her thousand-watt smile could light an entire city.

"You brought Star!" She bent down to cuddle the dog, and

Star's tail was a white blur behind her. The two had gotten along famously in the last month.

"You're already packed." Scout leaned in and gave Lizzie a hug, pressing a kiss onto the top of her head. There was a small pile of boxes in the entryway, all marked in great detail with black marker and hearts over the *i*'s. Two pink suitcases were there, too, busting at the seams. "Look how organized you are."

"Hi, Lane." Lizzie waved shyly. They were still getting to know one another, and he didn't want to rush the young girl into giving hugs until she was ready, so he held out his hand for a high-five, and she cracked her palm across his.

"You didn't tell me I needed to rent a truck," he teased, and she blushed. "It's a good thing we're going to be moving into a bigger place. In fact, we looked at a place this morning that had walk-in closets in the bedrooms."

"Really?" Lizzie's face lit up. "Even in mine?"

"Yep." Lane nodded. "And it's a ten-minute walk from your school."

They'd made an offer on the spot. It wasn't a done deal, but Lane was feeling confident about it.

"What color is the bedroom?" she asked, eyes narrowing as though she were already mentally decorating the place.

"White."

She wrinkled her nose. "Boring."

"You can paint it any color you want," he said. Scout slipped her arm around his waist and rested her head on his shoulder. "When we move in, we'll have a redecorating party."

"Oh my gosh, that's perfect. Because I was watching this channel on YouTube that's all DIYs and I have *so* many ideas. Do you think we could hang fairy lights from the ceiling? Oh, and a big mirror so I can take photos of my outfits for Insta.

I could even film TikToks! Maybe I could have a bigger bed, too. Because single beds look like little-kid beds. Oh and..."

The teenager's ideas rushed out of her like water cascading over the edge of a waterfall. Her energy was infectious, and Lane found himself trading ideas with her for other parts of the house, including everything they needed for a super comfy theater and video game room in the basement. Turns out Lizzie loved first-person shooter games, and they'd already spent some time playing Halo together.

For the first time in as long as he could remember, work was the furthest thing from Lane's mind and yet he was more excited about the future than ever.

Scout left Lizzie and Lane talking about their plans for the new house and went to find her grandparents. Joyce and Norman were in the kitchen, making sandwiches. She stood in the doorway quietly, watching them.

They were both so gray now, but when Norman teased Joyce, she smiled and it brought a youth and vibrancy to her face. For all their faults, they were truly in love. Scout hoped that one day she and Lane would be like that.

You don't have to hope. You know it.

And she did.

"Oh Scout." Joyce looked up. It wasn't necessarily the warmest greeting, but the chill had certainly left her grandmother's tone of late.

After the divorce meeting that never went ahead, Scout and Lane had gone to see them, and all four adults had talked. The heart-to-heart was cathartic in a lot of ways. It was also infuriating in others. Complicated, most of all.

But they had taken a step toward healing, and even if it felt like there were miles to go, at least they were heading in the right direction.

"Stay and have something to eat," Joyce said. "I have a feeling Lizzie is going to have you both working hard setting up her new room."

Scout laughed. "I think you might be right."

"You take care of our girl, okay?" Joyce said, her eyes misty.

At one point, such a comment might have made Scout snap, taking it as a slight or focusing on how they seemed to care more about her little sister than they did about her. Now Scout tried to take the words at face value, leaving her own feelings to one side. It was funny how much easier that became when Scout felt loved by other people.

The past month with Lane had been the best of her life and they'd celebrated passing the one-month milestone a second time, by cracking a bottle of champagne and christening the new couch, which was thankfully a million times better than that ugly hunk of black leather he'd had before.

Laughter floated in from the other part of the house as Lane told a joke and Lizzie's giggles were almost ear-piercingly loud. Scout couldn't help but smile.

"You chose well," Norman said quietly from the other side of the kitchen, where he was filling up the kettle to make a pot of tea.

"Yeah," Scout said, looking toward where the two people she loved most in the world were goofing around, "I really did."

The family ate lunch together and Lizzie dominated the conversation, acting like the glue keeping them all together. Norman shared some details about the house they were going to rent near the university, and Lane chatted with him about the property market in Brooklyn. Quietly, Scout sat back in her chair and watched as Joyce fussed over Lizzie's chipped nail polish, her face soft with love.

It might not be a conventional family. It might not even

be the kind of family that most people wanted for themselves. But she was grateful for her place at the table and for the fact that everyone was trying to make up for the past. Norman had given her access to Lizzie's college fund information and Joyce had given her a box of old things that had belonged to Scout's mother. In return, Scout was doing her best to keep them involved and updated about their plans so they didn't feel like they were going to be cut off from Lizzie.

She'd even invited them to come and stay at Thanksgiving, once they were settled into the new place.

Star pottered around the table, eagerly hoping that someone would drop half a sandwich. No such luck. But Joyce did throw a little ham down there when she thought no one was looking, which made Scout smile.

Under the table, Lane reached for her hand and toyed with the ring on her finger. Most of all, she was grateful that life had afforded her a second chance with the man who'd helped her see that forgiveness had the power to heal.

Instead of hiding behind her scars, she wore them proudly. She was building the kind of life she'd always dreamed of— one filled with laughter, love, paws and the promise of good things to come.

Now, more than ever, she embraced a little messiness in life because it was a sign she was being who she was. A hot mess with big dreams and the love of her life by her side.

26

6 MONTHS LATER...

"I think I'm going to puke." Scout pressed a hand to her stomach and closed her eyes, hoping it might encourage her stomach to stop churning. "Why am I so nervous?"

"Wedding-day jitters are *real*." Isla laid a hand on her arm. "Don't drink any champagne. Trust me."

Scout tried to laugh at the memory of Isla's infamous "viral incident" where she accidentally broadcast a young starlet puking all over her Met Gala ballgown after she'd downed a glass of champagne. It was hard to look at the career-ending event as a bad thing anymore, not when it had opened the doors to so many incredible opportunities. Paws in the City was thriving, and Isla was a rising star in the business world. And Scout was not only along for the ride, but she had a hand in the company's success, too.

Everything was going well. Sasha Frise was back to her fluffy, non-pink self and *Out of Bounds X Paws in the City* had launched to *huge* buzz. What could be better than a Broadway dance show with dogs? Nothing, if the media had anything to say about it. And Scout had signed her first three solo clients in the last six months. To say she was smashing her goals was an understatement.

Today, however, had nothing to do with business. Scout and Lane had decided that if they were going to do marriage properly this time, then they had to correct one of their biggest mistakes: existing in a bubble. They'd worked hard to build the important relationships. Lane and Lizzie were getting along great, Scout had totally won over Lane's parents and siblings, and Lane and Todd were working on healing their hurts.

Today they were having a celebration of marriage by standing up in front of their family and friends to declare their love for one another. Like a wedding, but without any of the legal stuff.

"You'll be fine. This is a wonderful thing." Isla rubbed her arm, her brows creased. She looked like a million bucks in a shimmering light blue dress that was split up to one thigh and had delicate double straps and a draped cowl neckline. "Do you want me to get you a glass of water?"

Scout nodded, feeling more than a little pathetic. "Yes, please."

Despite working hard to slay her doubt demons—*and* being surrounded by supportive, loving people like Isla and Lane and Lizzie—there were some days where the Imposter Syndrome came flooding back. But she was better at believing in herself now. Better at believing she had the ability to succeed. Better at believing she didn't need to change for anyone.

She breathed slow and deep and tried to focus on something *other* than her nerves. Lane was sipping Scotch by the window. Since they were already married, it didn't seem necessary to do the whole you-can't-see-the-bride-in-her-dress-before-the-ceremony thing.

Lizzie and Dani were giggling over a video playing on a tablet. The teens looked older than their years, with their hair styled and makeup done. Lizzie wore a soft pink dress that flared out over her legs and stopped at the knee. She'd picked it herself and requested a tiara to go along with it. Since Lizzie had moved into Scout and Lane's new place in Brooklyn, Scout had tried to make sure life felt like a dream, filled with all the things she could ever have wanted.

Her grandparents were settled in California now and Lizzie Skyped with them every weekend, without fail. They hadn't been able to make it out for the wedding, because of her grandfather's work, but they were planning a visit for Thanksgiving, and Scout surprisingly found herself looking forward to it. She had nothing to be ashamed of these days and no need to impress, which took the pressure off. Knowing Lizzie would be over the moon to see Norman and Joyce was good enough for her.

August was also in the room, talking with Theo and Lane. Her bright red hair looked incredible against her dark green dress, and she had both men in peals of laughter at a story she was telling.

Theo's living room had the most incredible view of the city, and Scout was so grateful he and Isla had volunteered to host the "before party" for the "not a wedding."

But even the magnificent view wasn't enough to steal the spotlight from her husband. Lane caught her eye and winked.

His easy smile warmed her heart. She loved that everyone got along so well—it made for some fun evenings out, even though August complained about being a fifth wheel, which was so *not* true.

"How did I get so lucky?" Scout whispered to herself.

Even the dogs got along. Lane had brought Star over for a play date with Camilla, so they both had company while everyone was at the ceremony, which was taking place at an exclusive restaurant nearby. The two dogs had gone wild for a short time, and now they were both playing with Camilla's extensive collection of toys.

These people—and animals—were family.

The diamond on her ring finger sparkled, refracted rainbow light glittering in representation of the love she and Lane had nurtured. The love that had surprised them, so swift and so quick it had taken their minds years to catch up to their hearts.

"Here you go." Isla pressed a glass of water into her hand as the doorbell chimed. "Oh, that must be the limo driver!"

As Isla hurried over to the door, her stiletto heels clicking across the tile and her dress swishing around her legs, Scout sipped her water. The moment of cool relief was short-lived, however, because her stomach immediately lurched and it was no longer churning.

Oh yeah, she was *really* about to regret that sushi she'd had for lunch.

Setting the glass of water down on the coffee table, she headed swiftly toward the bathroom. Bracing her hand on the doorframe, she almost stumbled into the spacious room and closed the door behind her, flicking the lock.

Lowering herself to her knees in front of the toilet, she lifted the lid up. Everything she'd eaten that day came rushing up and she had no choice but to let it happen.

After a few minutes of heaving, she sat back and flushed

the toilet. Then she tried to clean herself up. She must have been even *more* nervous than she realized. Not surprising, since Scout had felt like a chronic failure most of her life. It was easy to stay in that space, never trying. Never having to face disappointment because you didn't put yourself out in the world.

But now she *was* trying. She was doing and thriving and that meant she had more to lose than ever before.

For some reason, the thought didn't settle badly in her gut. She was proud of herself for getting to this place. It was a sign that she wasn't the woman she used to be. That shouldn't make her nervous enough to puke.

Maybe it wasn't…

Holy shit.

She tried to count the days back to her last period. Seven weeks. She was usually regular as clockwork, but work had been so busy she hadn't stopped to think about why she might be late. She and Lane hadn't exactly been "trying" for a baby. It was more of a let's-see-what-happens type deal—no pressure, no expectations.

"Scout?" Isla's worried voice sounded on the other side of the door. "Are you okay? You poor thing. I understand how nerve-racking this day can be, and especially after all you've been through…"

Scout got to her feet and unlocked the door, sliding it back a few inches. Isla was doing her usual mother-hen thing, and being full of empathy. "I don't think it's nerves."

For a minute Isla didn't register what was going on. Her brows knitted together and she shook her head, but when Scout's meaning finally dawned on her, she gasped. "Really?"

"I don't know for sure. But…" She bit down on her lip, excitement bubbling in her veins. "I think I might be pregnant."

"Oh my god!" She clamped a hand over mouth. "You think?"

"I'm late, and yes, I'm nervous about tonight. But I'm not normally *this* pukey." She shook her head, trying and failing to tamp down her excitement.

Don't get ahead of yourself, girl. Maybe it was bad sushi.

But she knew in her gut that it wasn't.

"If you want to confirm, I have a few tests stashed in the back of the cupboard." Isla pointed to the door at the far end of the bathroom vanity and Scout raised an eyebrow. "Theo and I have been thinking we might try. Not right now, of course. I want to wait until Dani's started her junior year and has gotten settled in at the new school first. But you know me, always prepared."

"You sure?" The need to know was like an itch under her skin. Scout had never been good with waiting.

"Go for it."

Scout closed the door and found one of the tests. It felt surreal to try and pee on a stick while wearing a wedding dress that cost more than she'd ever spent on a single item of clothing—but Lane had insisted on treating her.

You deserve to have a dress that shines as much as you do, he'd said.

When she was finished, she stood and paced back and forth across the bathroom as she waited for the test to confirm her suspicions. Was she about to become a mother? For years she'd assumed that having a child wouldn't be something she'd ever experience. It seemed like a life event for people who had goals and plans and who had their shit together.

You do have your shit together.

This past year had really shown Scout how wonderful life could be. She'd moved in with Lane and their marriage was more blissful than ever. She was a good dog mama and a good employee. She loved her work. Loved her friendships. Loved waking up in the morning with a sense of purpose.

Scout knew in her heart that she'd proven everyone wrong. That, in many ways, she'd proven *herself* wrong. She had the ability to make a positive impact on the people around her. And maybe she would have the opportunity to make a positive impact on their child.

Sucking in a breath, she looked down at the white plastic stick in her hands. Twin blue lines stared back at her and the air fled Scout's lungs.

She was pregnant.

Lane's heart was so full he was sure it was going to burst. Getting "married" to Scout all over again had been more than he could ever have hoped for. And doing it without any secrets, without any fears, made it the happiest day of his life.

Scout had been in fine form, glowing like the radiant woman she was, winning everyone over with her funny stories and beaming smile. To say his mother was smitten with her new daughter-in-law was an understatement.

But now it was time for them to leave everyone behind for the evening. They'd booked a fancy hotel room, and Isla and Theo had very kindly offered to have Lizzie and Star for a sleepover so the "newlyweds" could have a night free of responsibility.

As they rode up in the gold, mirrored elevator toward the top floor of the hotel, Lane glanced at Scout.

"You're quiet," he said, reaching for her hand. Seeing the ring back on her finger meant the world to him and it sparkled under the warm lighting.

She glanced at him with a smile. As much as he loved her fresh-faced without any makeup, he also loved this glammed-up version of her. Sultry dark shadow ringed her eyes, bringing out the gold-and-green tones in her hazel irises. Her blond hair was swept up, revealing dangling earrings and a chain around her neck that was so fine it almost looked like a sprinkle of glitter rather than metal. Her white dress was sleek and modern, and it showed off her body to perfection.

He loved all versions of her—the professional version, the playful version, the sultry version, the vulnerable version. There wasn't a single facet of Scout that didn't captivate him.

"Actually, there's something I need to tell you." She twisted her wedding ring around her finger.

"Okay." He tried to ignore the knot forming in his stomach. In the past, he and Scout hadn't been the best communicators. They'd both shied away from conflict, and it had almost torn them apart for good. But he had faith that whatever was in front of them, they would tackle it as a team. "Tell me."

"Well, you know I wasn't feeling well earlier…"

He nodded. Scout had barely eaten or drunk a thing the whole night—sticking to plain items and water so as not to encourage her stomach to act up. It seemed a shame to miss out on those things on such a special night. Normally she loved a glass of wine or champagne when they were out, so he knew she must have been feeling really under the weather not to…

His eyes widened. No way.

"Yeah." Her eyes sparkled, as if she knew exactly what he was thinking. "I'm pregnant."

For a moment Lane didn't move. Didn't react. They'd talked about having a baby in very academic terms. Some day in the future. One day when. At some point.

"Oh my god." He shook his head as if trying to make sure he hadn't fallen asleep and started dreaming. "Really? You know for sure?"

"I took a test at Isla and Theo's place and I was so shocked, I didn't know what to say. I thought maybe I should wait for a special moment and my head's been spinning this whole time." She pressed her palms to her cheeks. "I didn't want to say anything with everyone around, and I swore Isla to secrecy. But then I realized I don't know if I'm supposed to do something special to tell you or... I have no idea how this works."

"Oh Scout." He reached for her and pulled her to his chest. "I'm over the moon."

"You are?" She looked up at him, her hazel eyes filled with tears. "Even though I'm going to stumble through this totally clueless?"

The fear and hope in her voice lanced him.

"*We'll* stumble through it together, okay? I don't know how to be a dad any more than you know how to be a mom. But we know how to love, don't we? We know how to be supportive and listen and believe in someone other than ourselves. That's what a child needs, more than anything else."

She nodded, and it looked like a weight had been lifted from her shoulders. Excitement filtered into her expression—tears replaced by a natural twinkle in her eyes, frown smoothed out, lips curving upward. "You're going to be a great dad, Lane."

"And you're going to be a phenomenal mother." He leaned in and brushed his lips against hers. "I'm so happy."

"Me too," she whispered. "I'm scared but also happy."

"That means we're doing the right thing. Scared but happy is the place where we step out of our comfort zone in the direction we want to go. There's no one else I'd rather have a family with than you, Scout. I love you so much."

She crushed her lips to his, squeezing her arms tight around his neck as she kissed him long and deep. Having this incredible, brave and kindhearted woman in his arms was the best feeling in the world, and knowing they were going to have a baby...

His life had never felt more complete.

The elevator dinged and they pulled away from one another. Scout's cheeks were flushed and her lips were a little puffy. She looked vibrant and delectable and gloriously present. No more walls. No more holding back.

"I love you, too." She grabbed his hand and squeezed. "I can't be more thankful that we found our way back to one another. I owe Star lots and lots of doggy treats for helping us get there."

He chuckled. "Just promise me one thing, okay?"

"What's that?"

"That we won't let anyone else choose the name for our kid. I can't handle another Twinkle Stardust situation."

Scout threw her head back and laughed so heartily, tears gathered in her eyes once more. She held his hand as they walked out of the elevator as if officially stepping into their new life, unafraid to draw on one another when they needed a boost of strength. Their love felt more rock-solid than ever.

And Lane knew, without a shadow of a doubt, that a wonderful life lay ahead.

★ ★ ★ ★ ★

Acknowledgments

First, I must say a huge thank-you to each and every reader who has ever taken a chance on my stories. Your enthusiasm, comments and emails mean the world to me. Knowing my characters make a connection with you is the best feeling ever!

As always, thank you to my incredible husband, Justin. In the time I wrote this book, we were dealing with so much. Your love and support are what got me through it all, even when it felt like life was determined to shake us around.

Thank you to my dear friends and writing confidants Taryn and Becca, whose friendship is the kind we can only hope for in life. I'm so glad to have you within my Relator circle. Thank you to all the people in my personal life who ask how the writing is going, knowing they could get literally any response. To my parents, my sister, my in-laws, Albie, Luke,

Jill, Russ, Kate, Shiloh, KG, Myrna, Madura, Jeanette and Tammy. You're all amazing.

Huge thank-you to my incredible editor, Dana Grimaldi, for being so enthusiastic and supportive. Ours is the kind of working relationship I'd always hoped for as an author and I'm so thrilled we got to work on this series together. And to the rest of the amazing team at Harlequin, thank you for being as excited about this series as I am! It's a dream come true to write for HQN.

And, as always, thank you to my coffee machine for greeting me every morning and being a key contributor to getting my brain working enough to write. You're the real MVP.